D0898816

UNWED

Switched Series
Book II

Veezie Harrington is like the beautiful mansion at Nine Gables. A coat of paint covers the outside, but the inside is a harbor for shameful little secrets.

KAY CHANDLER
A multi-award-winning author

This novel is a work of fiction. Characters, places or incidents are the product of the author's imagination and/or used fictitiously.

Cover Design by Chase Chandler

For

My precious grandchildren. Chandler, Tucker, David, Micah, Judah, Grace, Faith, Josiah, Hope, Gideon, Mercy, Joy, Jubilee, Boaz, Malachi, Titus, Sam, Seth, Jack, Allie, Camille and Shepherd.

My quiver is full

PROLOGUE
Flat Creek, Alabama

March 10, 1938

Dear Ducky,

I said when the time was right I'd tell you how a hick like me wound up at a swanky place like Nine Gables. Trust me, it ain't all pretty, but you've been a real friend, girlie, and it seems only right that you should know the truth.

The whole cockeyed scheme was concocted the day I was born, when my mama (who I never had the pleasure or displeasure of meeting) paid a midwife to secretly switch me with the newborn daughter of a penniless couple. A quack claimed I had the markings of a lunatic and being as how the wealthy Ophelia Harrington had her dignity to uphold, she couldn't bear for her highfalutin friends to know she had a young'un who weren't just right.

So soon as I'm born, the midwife snatches me up and whisks

me away from that big fine house in Flat Creek, known as Nine Gables. And then she dumps me off at a rundown shanty in Goose Hollow, Alabama, tricking Sally and Monroe O'Steen, who never had a lick o' learning, into thinking I'm the daughter of their loins. God told Jacob kings would come out of his loins, and I reckon Ophelia Harrington felt she was due a Princess, and it wouldn't be me, since I was doomed to be loony.

So, I grow up with the O'Steens—a family poor as meatless gravy. Twenty-two miles down the road, the O'Steens little loin child, answering to the name Harper Harrington, is being petted and pampered by George and Beulah, the family servants— enjoying what should've been mine from the beginning. She learned quick enough how to be a real lady, whilst I was busy learning how to scrap for food to keep the lining of my stomach from sticking together.

Then Ophelia Harrington died. And what happened next shocked everybody, including me and Harper. Ophelia wrote a letter on her death bed, saying she found out the quack was the real loony and that her own flesh and blood (that would be yours truly) wasn't the lame-brain he made me out to be. Confessing she never bonded with the young'un she raised, (that would be Harper), Ophelia made a will and left everything to me—Nine Gables, rich farmland stretching two counties, the Harrington dough—the works.

A letter was attached to the will: *"May God forgive me for denying my own flesh and blood. I feel no sympathy for Harper, the child I reared, for she's enjoyed a life of plenty, which her biological parents couldn't have provided. Now, it's time to provide for my own."*

Don't that beat all? So, with little money and nowhere to go, Harper set out to live in the rundown shanty where I'd been living. Now, there ain't nothing in Goose Hollow to brag about, except a good-looking doctor. Everybody for miles around is crazy about Dr. Flint McCall, and it didn't take Harper long to find out why. Six weeks after she moved there, they got hitched, and folks who knew her before the will, claim she's happier now than she ever was.

And me? Well, I moved into the big house, Nine Gables, and oh my soul, what happened eight months later, haunts me still. May 7, 1937 will be a day I'll never forget.

I reckon by now you're thinking I oughta be real grateful to Ophelia for setting things straight in the end—giving me my just reward so as I could live happily ever after.

But nothing ain't never sliced so thin that it ain't got two sides.

Love,

Veezie

Chapter One

May 07, 1937

A shrill cry, sounding more like a bat screeching than a newborn baby, caused Veezie Harrington's arched back to fall flat onto the plump feather mattress. Sweat drenched the satin pillowcase beneath her head.

The doctor blew out a heavy breath, as if he'd been the one doing all the work.

She reached down and rubbed her belly. Every inch of her body ached from twelve long hours of pain, but it was over. *Over? Was she loco?* It'd never be over. The real pain had just begun.

Beulah, the Harrington maid, stood next to a dry sink beside the fancy-carved poster bed. Her calloused brown hands wrung a wet rag over a porcelain bowl. When she turned, her mouth flew open and an eerie-sounding groan tumbled out.

Veezie's throat tightened as she focused on Beulah's pinched face. She dared not ask questions for fear her curiosity might suggest the idiotic notion she was changing her mind about the fate of the child. A thousand times a thousand she wished to renege, but for the sake of her baby, she had to stick to the original plan. Boy? Or girl? Did it matter? She didn't want to know. Didn't want to see it. It'd be easier that way.

The soaked cloth in the maid's hands fell to the floor when she slapped her hand up to her head rag, allowing water to trail from her wrist to her elbow. Her lip quivered. "Oh my stars, doc, po' little creature ain't no bigger'n a wharf rat. I ain't never seen no baby what had—"

He cut her off. "I've delivered a lot of babies, Beulah, and without a doubt, she's the most beautiful newborn I've ever seen. You have a little girl, Veezie. Look at her."

She jerked her head in the opposite direction. "No. Take her away." She'd known Flint McCall since the first day he arrived to practice medicine in the Goose Hollow community, about twenty miles from Flat Creek. She supposed she knew him better than most folks and the raspy sound in his voice told her something peculiar was going on. Why didn't he let Beulah finish her sentence? *What's wrong with my baby?*

"Look at her, Veezie." His voice quaked. "She's perfect. Like a flawless diamond. Take her in your arms and hold her."

When Flint made an attempt to lower the tiny creature, Veezie clinched her eyes shut. Why was he taunting her this way? Didn't he know how she ached inside? How she longed to keep her baby?

Well, she wouldn't give in. She couldn't. "Leave me be, Flint."

"Veezie, I'm not asking. I'm telling you to turn around and hold out your arms. Now! Your baby needs you."

Her hands knotted into tight fists at the roughness in his voice. She opened her eyes and glaring into his troubled-looking face, she whimpered, "*My* baby? *Mine*? I ain't got no baby. Take her home to your wife, Flint. That was the plan. Remember?"

Beulah wiped Veezie's sweaty brow with a cold, damp cloth and pushed a wisp of hair back of her ear. "There, there, sugar. You just got the blues settin' in. Why don't you do like the doc says?"

Veezie's throat couldn't have ached more if she'd swallowed a bullfrog. If Flint only knew how she longed to hold her baby in her arms and to count all the little fingers and toes. But how could he understand? He was a man. The tears she'd shed since that first kick inside her belly could fill a gallon drum. She dared not look for fear she'd never be able to go through with her plan.

Flint's brow furrowed. "Veezie, I'm sorry I couldn't administer the ether, but it would've been too risky for the baby. You went through a lengthy, painful delivery. You're hurting and you're tired. I get it. But this is not about you and your feelings at this point. The baby's tiny and there's a frightening chance she won't make it. You can have all the poor-pitiful-me parties you want after today, but at the moment you have a responsibility to this little girl you brought into the world." His voice trembled. "She may not make it, even if you hold her . . . but I'm pretty sure she won't if you don't."

The tiny bundle cuddled against his broad chest could've fit in a cigar box. If she took one look at her baby's face, she'd never be able to let her go. *Don't you worry, baby girl. He ain't gonna let you die. He's a doctor. Besides, he wants you for his own.*

Flint leaned over the bed. "Veezie, you're going to hold this baby if I have to tie your arms around her, so you might as well reach for her now."

She glared at the way his throbbing temples pumped in and out when he gritted his teeth. The cold eyes and unfamiliar gruffness in Flint's voice reminded her of the scene from the picture show, *Dr. Jekyll and Mr. Hyde* when Jekyll claimed all human beings are made up of both good and evil. With Flint's sleeves rolled up to his elbows, his shirt tail hanging out and his trousers crumpled, there seemed to be two people living inside one body. There was nothing about the rumpled, hateful-talking doctor that hinted of the neat, gentle friend she knew as Flint McCall.

With a toss of his head, he slung a shank of brown hair away from his bloodshot eyes. "You idiotic, bull-headed woman," he bellowed. "I won't allow you to lie here and let this precious baby die, simply because you're feeling sorry for yourself. Get over it, Veezie."

Beulah crossed her arms over her plump bosom. "Begging yo' pardon, doc, but that kinda talk ain't getting us nowhere. There's a heap o' truth in the ol' sayin', 'honey draws more flies than vinegar.' Reckon we ought to send for the preacher? I 'spect

Brother Shep Jackson over at Flat Creek Fellowship Church can pray a body into doing most anything. Seems to have a knack for it. Understands troubles, he does." She shook her head gently. "God bless him, he's had his share. Want George to hitch up the wagon and go fetch him?"

Veezie burst into sobs. "A *preacher*? You crazy? Y'all might as well announce it in the newspaper that Veezie Harrington gave birth to a little—" She bit her lip. Couldn't say it. "No! I don't want nobody to know. Nobody, ya hear?" She pulled the covers over her face and rubbed the soft satin comforter between her fingers, comparing it to the moth-eaten woolen army blanket she'd slept under for twenty-one years. Yet, she'd gladly give up all the silks and satins and go back to the way it was, if only. . . But there was no going back. "I'm tired and sleepy." Her chin quivered. "Get that squalling young'un outta here, Flint."

"I'll be happy to when she's stable. I'm gonna try to save her but I can't do it alone."

He jerked the sheet back. Veezie bit the inside of her mouth. The warmth of her baby's skin against her bare chest caused her body to go into tremors as she struggled to keep from crying. She didn't fight Flint when he picked up her arms and gently crossed them over the infant. Hot tears seeped from the corners of her tightly closed eyes. *You'll always be on your mama's heart, sweet thing, but I gotta let you go. People talk...*

The Reverend Shepherd Jackson tucked a 4x6 picture of his late wife under his pillow, as he'd done every night for almost two years. Silly, he supposed. Yet, he continued the nightly ritual because the bed seemed less empty, somehow.

Nothing could take the place of his sweet Jenny's warm body next to his—the fresh smell of Palmolive shampoo in her hair and the faint scent of Jasmine toilette water behind her ear. As crazy as it seemed, he slept better with the photo under his head. He considered asking the church to allow him to move out of the parsonage, where he and Jenny shared their last days together. The house was too large and empty without her and there was a small deserted farmhouse a couple of miles down the road that he'd be willing to rent. He shrugged. The notion was preposterous. To suggest such an idea would send Cora Dobbs and Eunice Watts into a telephone frenzy. Anytime a motion was made to change church procedure, the two women busied themselves by calling disgruntled members who hadn't attended services in several years to come cast a negative vote.

It was only eight-thirty, but Shep yearned to fall asleep and shut out the pain. Minutes after settling into bed, a point he failed to include in his sermon notes came to mind. He sat up, switched on the lamp beside the bed and picked up his journal. He wrote: *We serve a great God who cares for the poor, sets at liberty the bruised, heals the brokenhearted and sets the captives free.*

Shep could preach it because he believed every word to be truth. He'd prayed for countless hurting people and seen God set captives free and heal the brokenhearted. Consumed in his grief, he prayed, "What about me, Father? I pray for everyone else, but my heart is bruised and broken, too. Who's going to pray for *me*, Lord?" After turning out the light, he eased his hand under the pillow and touched Jenny's picture.

Rain pelting the tin roof usually helped him fall asleep, but tonight it'd take more than a heavy rain to quiet his restless spirit. Some days were worse than others. Today ranked at the bottom on the bad-day scale. It never took much to trigger the memories. Sometimes, the smell of a rose, Jenny's favorite flower. Or the words to a song that she used to sing. Other times, out of nowhere the painful longing to see her—to hold her once more—would leap on him like a tick on a hound dog's ear. An itch he couldn't scratch.

Chapter Two

A warm wetness washed across both sides of Veezie's face, down her neck, soaking the fine linens beneath her shoulders, but she dared not lift a hand to wipe the tears.

Her tense arms remained crossed around the baby's tiny body. Strange, she didn't want to hold her, and now she didn't want to turn her loose. Yet, the thought of holding on caused her heart to race. *Does she have my golden hair? Or is it red, like his?* She'd made such a mess of her life. Giving up her baby was the only decent thing she'd ever done.

Beulah took the corner of the sheet and dabbed at Veezie's damp cheeks. "Shh! It's gonna be all right, sweet pea. Ol' Beulah's right here beside you. We gonna get through this, ya hear? Lawsy, child, if I knowed who got you into this fix, I'd wring his sorry ol' neck."

Beulah's gentle round face twisted as she pleaded, "Sugar, I do wish you'd look down and take a peek at 'er. Doc's right. She's cute as a June bug and to tell the gospel truth, she ain't much bigger. I've birthed a passel of babies myself, but I ain't never in all my born days seen a baby this tiny draw a breath. She must be a real fighter. Strong-willed, like her mama." Beulah picked up the small flannel blanket, which Flint had tossed aside. "Doc, don't you reckon I oughta swaddle her?"

"Not yet, Beulah. I want her skin to stay snug against Veezie's, but keep the cotton sheet on top of her and fold a quilt to place on top of the comforter. These next few hours are crucial. I want her to feel Veezie's heartbeat until I can get her stabilized. I've called Harper and she's on her way with the bassinet."

Veezie would've screamed if she hadn't been afraid of frightening the baby. It wasn't supposed to be like this. According to the plan, as soon as she had the baby, Flint was to immediately take it home to his wife, Harper, without anyone knowing the identity of the little foundling. She hadn't counted on feeling her little girl's body next to hers—and now Flint had sent for a bassinet, as if he planned to leave her. Well, he couldn't. She wouldn't allow it. Was he trying to make her change her mind? Had Harper changed hers? Maybe they decided they didn't want a baby. Well, he'd have to find a good home for her. Didn't he realize the awful names folks would call her little girl if they knew she had no daddy?

"Flint, you ain't leaving that young'un here. Harper promised to raise her. Y'all ain't got no right to go back on your word."

"Veezie, Harper and I are eager to get her home. But I can't take a chance on transporting her too soon. Harper will stay at Nine Gables for a few days, and working together, our little diamond may have a chance. But it's gonna be an uphill battle. As soon as Harper gets here with the bassinet, I'll fashion an oxygen tent around it and tuck some heated bricks in with the baby. But your job at the moment is to help sustain her life by keeping her snug, near your heart."

The lines on Beulah's forehead creased like a freshly furrowed field. With her head bowed, she lifted her voice in a song—an old Spiritual called *Hand Me Down My Silver Trumpet*: "If religion was sumpin' money could buy, all the rich would live and de poor would die . . . " She stopped. "Doc, I feel about as useless as a polecat at a picnic. Ain't there something I can do to help?"

"Are the bottles and nipples sterilized?"

"Yessir. I done took care o' that and I sent George to Mr. Will's store to buy a few cans of Carnation milk to fix a formula. He oughta be back by now. But bless yo' heart, you look plumb tuckered out. Why don't you run on down to the kitchen, doc, and eat a bite. It's all laid out on the table and coffee's in the pot. I'll stay up here and look after our patients."

"Thanks, Beulah. It's been a long night for all of us." He pulled a syringe from his black bag and held it up as he filled it with liquid from a small brown bottle.

Beulah's eyes widened. "What's that for?"

"It's called Ergometrine. It'll slow the bleeding to keep her from hemorrhaging."

"Aw pshaw, doc. Ain't no need for needles. I been saving spider webs, and I reckon I've saved enough to do some good. Spider webs stops all kinds of bleeding. Want I should get 'em? Just smear the webs on a rag and lay it on 'er—"

Flint didn't attempt an argument. Beulah was too steeped in old wives' tales for him to ever convince her that spider webs were incapable of stopping blood flow.

Veezie's fingernails dug into her palms when he pulled a corner of the sheet back and injected the stinging medication into her right thigh.

Flint leaned over the bed and in a gentle voice, whispered, "Hold on, angel." Veezie didn't need to open her eyes to realize he was talking to the baby and not to her. He said, "Beulah, I'll go downstairs for that coffee, now. I'll be back in a couple of minutes and we'll see if we can get a little sugar water down her. But for now, let her rest against Veezie's breast."

"Yessir, doc."

The underneath sides of Veezie's closed eyelids burned. Beulah sat nearby, singing a woeful-sounding song while rocking back and forth in an annoying creaky rocker. Moments later, the singing stopped at the exact same time the creaking ceased. Veezie stiffened when she felt the covers peeling back and a rough, calloused hand tugging at her unwilling arms, lifting them and planting them by her side. A whiff of air cooled her sweaty, bare skin as the baby was lifted from her body.

Then the sound of an unforgettable piercing scream rang in

her ears. She didn't have to ask why Beulah was wailing, or why Flint's feet pounded up the stairs. Her muscles tightened when she heard him rush into the room.

Beulah wept, "Oh sweet Jesus, help us, she's gone. She's gone! Po' little thing's done up and died on us."

Veezie jerked the sheet up to her chin and opened her eyes. She wanted to ask Flint to let her look at her little girl—but what right did she have to ask, now? Now that she'd let the sweet little thing die. She bit the inside of her cheek until she tasted blood. Was God punishing her for being bad? But why would he take it out on the baby? *Tweren't her fault. I shoulda died, instead.*

The doctor lifted the small bundle from the maid's arms and openly wept.

Beulah sniffed. "Doc, you want I should lay the little angel out for ya?"

Then, as if a cyclone swooped down and swept away all the pain, Veezie's mind and body went numb. She tried to gather her scrambled thoughts, yet nothing made sense. She glared at Beulah. "Why are you crying? And wh . . . what are you doing here, Flint? I ain't sick." With the satin comforter clutched between her fingers, she glanced around. "This ain't my room. Where am I?" When she jerked up in bed, peculiar sharp pains shot through her body. Slowly, she slid back down and groaned. "What am I doing here? Why am I in somebody else's bed?"

Her focus shifted upward to the tulip-shaped globes on the crystal chandelier, then like a butterfly, her gaze fluttered down to the fancy carved mahogany bed posts, flitted over to the huge armoire and finally landed on the floral wallpaper that stretched from the twelve-foot ceilings to the polished oak floors. "This is all mighty pretty, but I reckon I need to go home."

Beulah pressed her hand on Veezie's brow. "You *is* home, sugar. You lie still, now."

Flint sailed out of the room, holding the bundle, and slammed the door behind him. Veezie's brows squished together. "What's his problem?" A thin smile formed on her lips as she pointed out the window. "Look! Ain't that a mockingbird in the willow tree? I believe it is. Yep, it's a mockingbird, all right." She murmured, "I wish I was a mockingbird."

Beulah craned her neck and stared out the window. She shook her head. "I don't see no bird, sweet pea." She dabbed the corner of her eyes. "You try and get some rest, sugar. Ol' Beulah needs to go help the doc take care of sump'n."

Chapter Three

A week later . . .

Shep Jackson sat on the couch in the parsonage living room, sipping coffee from a saucer and reading *Beside Still Waters,* by Charles Spurgeon. The illustrious author always seemed to inspire him and tonight Shep needed all the inspiration he could muster.

He glanced up at the short chain hanging from the light socket and with a smile, recalled how cute Jenny had looked trying to reach it. On tip-toes with her fingers barely touching the brass pull, she'd stretch her five-foot two-inch frame and swat the chain back and forth before ever getting a grasp. The sweet memory turned bitter. He'd promised her he'd lengthen it to make it easier to reach. Why did he procrastinate? He shrugged dismissively. It didn't matter now. Nothing much seemed to matter anymore. Startled by the phone, he leapt to answer it. No doubt, someone calling to say the sickly Widow Barnes had passed away.

"Brother Jackson, this is Harper. I hope I didn't disturb you."

"No, Harper, what a nice surprise. How are the newlyweds?" He'd become quite proficient at putting forth a gleeful front to hide his pain.

She giggled. "Swell, thank you. I meant to call you sooner, but I stay busy. I never realized how much work was involved in keeping house, but I wouldn't trade back for anything."

"You certainly sound like you're coping." Maybe she was. Or maybe, like him, she'd learned how to mask the ache churning inside.

"Coping?" She snickered. "I'll admit I was overwhelmed in the beginning, but I can't imagine my life without Flint and the kids. I'm extremely happy, Brother Jackson. You may not be aware, but Flint and I are raising my three young siblings, Jim, Lucas and Callie. Of course, I didn't even know they existed until I moved to Goose Hollow." A pause followed. "Preacher, you said if there was ever anything you could do for me, that I should call."

"And I meant it. Just ask."

"Have you met Veezie, the girl who moved into Nine Gables? Ophelia's biological daughter?"

With nothing but lame excuses to offer, he said, "I'm sorry to say I haven't, Harper. I've been meaning to go by and invite her to church but according to several members who've tried, she doesn't cotton to visitors. From what I hear, she's a rather unconventional character. They say she's instructed the maid to shoo off any callers." Shep flinched, disgusted that in his shame for being negligent, he stooped to repeating hear-say. If he lived another day, he'd make it a point to visit. "So tell me what you know about her."

"I don't feel it my place to divulge a confidence, Brother Jackson, so please don't ask me to explain how or what I know, but suffice it to say that the poor girl is in the depths of despair. Veezie isn't well, and I'm terribly worried about her."

Such compassion, yet he expected no less from Harper.

"Preacher," Her voice grew somber. "Veezie's hurting deeply. I wish I could share the details with you, but I can't. Would you please pray for her?"

"Consider it done, Harper." It was too late tonight, but he'd make a point to go by and visit with her tomorrow after church.

Sunday afternoon, Veezie fluffed her pillow, then eased back down and stared out the window, rubbing her forehead. Perhaps if she rubbed hard enough, she could block out the memory of her baby's haunting cries. She liked it better when she couldn't remember.

From her bed, she could see across the road. Old man Bentley, a tenant farmer, was plowing the field with a mule, getting ready to plant. The pecan trees along the fence row were budding. A blue jay flew back and forth, building a nest in the magnolia tree. Why did everything have to remind her of new life? Her gaze fixated on the raised window. What would it be like to jump from the second-story? Would the fall kill her immediately? What if she didn't die, but was maimed for life? If she was going to do it, she needed to do it soon, before Beulah returned from church. Beulah meant well, but she hovered over Veezie like a chicken hawk watching a hen house.

George had already picked up her dinner tray, so he wouldn't be checking on her again for at least thirty minutes. What right did Beulah have to insist the caretaker stay home from church to keep an eye on her? His job was to care for the grounds—not to become her shadow. She slid out of bed and hobbled over to the raised window, grunting with every step. The muscles in her stomach couldn't have hurt worse if someone had clamped a tightened vice on her insides. Beulah called it "afterbirth pains." But the real afterbirth pains were in her heart.

Just as she unlatched the screen and looked down, a brown Ford Woody Station Wagon pulled up in the yard. Veezie groaned at the sound of the doorbell. She eased out of her room, and standing in the upstairs hallway, peeked down in time to see George hobble toward the front door. She stepped back and cupped an ear, though the old caretaker's voice was quite loud.

"Why Brother Jackson, I ain't seen you in a coon's age. I reckon the last time was when Miz Ophelia died. Had you on my mind, though. Beulah and me was just talking about you, last night. Won't you come on in?"

Veezie threw up her arms. *A preacher? Why in Sam Hill wouldn't he be in church on Sunday?* She glanced at her watch and rolled her eyes. A quarter past one.

"Thank you, George. It's good to see you. How have you been?"

He didn't sound like a preacher. Or at least not like Brother Charlie from Goose Hollow, the only preacher she'd ever known. But then Brother Charlie was in his eighties, and his voice had a sort of holy, vibrating sound. Especially when he got wound up, preaching about fire and brimstone. No, this man had a smooth-sounding voice, like a much younger man. Though she'd never considered it before, she supposed not all preachers were old.

"I'm tolerable, preacher. Just toler'ble. This ol' rheumatism slows me down, but I manage. Here, let me take your hat. Beulah ain't come home from church, yet. Them folks at St. John's don't let out quick as you folks over at yo' church. Sump'n I can help you with, preacher?"

"I came to see about Miss Veezie Harrington. I had a call from Harper last night, saying Miss Harrington is ill. Harper seemed right worried and asked me to keep her in my prayers. I thought while I was out visiting this afternoon, I'd stop by and get acquainted."

Veezie could've chewed a ten-penny nail in half. Harper made a solemn promise not to tell anyone about her condition. *I should've gone ahead and jumped.* A sharp pain shot through her lower abdomen, bringing tears to her eyes.

George stammered. "I don't know, preacher. She ain't up to seein' folks. Ya might better wait for Beulah to get back. Miz Veezie . . . well, she ain't at herself. Po' little creature's been through a heap of changes. The move, ya understand. But I know in time she'll be just fine. I'll tell her you come by. I sho' will."

"Good job, George," Veezie muttered. "Hand him his hat and shove him out the door." She bristled when the preacher didn't appear to get the message.

He said, "Well, George, she's blessed to have you and Beulah watching out for her. But if you don't mind, I'd appreciate an opportunity to meet her and have a short prayer. I won't stay long, I promise. Harper was rather vague, but I gather Miss Harrington's problem has to do with a depressed state of mind?"

"Yessir, I reckon that's it, preacher. Miz Harper told you right. Miz Veezie's all down in the dumps, not knowing which end is up. But I'm sure she'll be at herself 'fore long. Moving from one life to another is bound to be unsettlin' for her."

The sound of boots on the marble antechamber floor sent her shuffling back to her room, each step more painful than the last. *Horsefeathers! I think he's coming up. I oughta fire George.*

Veezie moaned as she crawled into bed. The door! It was ajar. Why didn't she close it? Yet, surely, he wouldn't be such a dope and enter without an invitation. She curled up under the covers, closed her eyes tightly and waited. If she pretended to be asleep, perhaps he'd go away.

From the gossip circulating around town, Shep expected to walk in the room and find a homely-looking woman—but the figure lying in bed was anything but homely.

Delicate curls the color of fine corn silk framed her lovely face. The peculiar sound of her erratic breathing concerned him at first, but a smile sneaked across his face when her nose twitched. Looking like a disgruntled angel, she lay with her eyes clinched so tightly that her brow creased and her nose crinkled under the strain. Poor thing seemed to be putting forth such an enormous effort to convince him she was asleep that perhaps he should be gallant and leave. He wasn't quite sure why he didn't.

Veezie didn't hear the man leave, but no doubt he did or else he'd be in her room by now. Her shoulders relaxed. She turned her head toward the door and opened her eyes.

He stood in the open doorway, leaning against the door jam and grinning as if he'd won a prize.

"Hello, Miss Harrington. I tried to tiptoe up the stairs, so I wouldn't disturb you if you happened to be asleep. I'm pleased to see you're awake."

She jerked the sheet over her face. *He tricked me.* "Go away."

"I won't come closer if you don't want me too. I heard you weren't feeling well and I wanted to stop by and have a word of prayer with you."

Veezie didn't respond, yet it didn't stop him. As he promised George, he prayed and left. Though she wanted to be angry at George, or Beulah, or Harper, or the preacher . . . or the whole lot of them, she couldn't deny it sounded good hearing someone talk to God in her behalf, even though it *was* too late. The words to his prayer rolled around in her head. *"Guard her heart, dear Lord."* Sounded good, but what's the point in guarding something that's already been through the thrasher and left in a million broken pieces?

When Beulah returned from church, she clomped up to Veezie's room. She plumped the pillows and pulled the satin comforter back, folding it at the foot of the bed. "George tells me you didn't eat nothin' for dinner. Now, that jest won't do, sugar. You can't stop eating."

"You can't tell me what to do," Veezie shot back. "I can do anything I want."

"Well, ain't you in a foul mood? Who put them sandspurs in yo' britches?"

"Didn't George tell you?" She snubbed and wiped her nose on the back of her hand. "Harper sent the preacher up here, knowing I didn't want nobody finding out about me. And George let him come all the way up to my room."

"Shug, George done and told me what happened and it couldn't be helped. Harper didn't tell the preacher yo' troubles. She only asked him to pray for you. Seems to me you can use all the prayers you can get. Besides, Brother Jackson ain't one to judge, even if he did know the whole truth, which he don't." Beulah's eyes twinkled. "But, glory be, he sho' is a good-looking horse."

Veezie's brow furrowed. "Who?"

"Who is we talking about? The preacher, of course. Handsome as all git out, ain't he?"

"I dunno know. Didn't see him."

"Whatcha mean? You done and said—"

"I said he come up here, but I didn't say I *looked* at him." She pointed toward the door. "He stood way over yonder and I just got a glimpse." Her lip puckered. "Didn't wanna see him."

Beulah snickered. "Well, if I was forty years younger and a white woman, I'll tell you the truth, I'd be sitting on the front pew o' his church every Sunday morning, just to look at him." Her body shook when she chuckled. "I hear tell every white woman in Flat Creek got religion when Brother Shep Jackson moved to town. Yes'm, he sho' is mighty . . ."

Veezie's eyes widened. She shot straight up in bed and slipped her finger to her lips. "Shh! Listen."

"Oh, Lawsy, what's wrong, sugarfoot?"

"Don't you hear her? My baby's crying, Beulah. Go get her. I want to hold her."

"What you talking about, sugar?" The old woman's smile faded and giant tears drew a shiny path down her dark brown face. "Has you forgot? Honey, yo' baby done and died."

"Hush old woman," she screamed. "It ain't so. Why you wanna lie to me? Where'd you put my baby?" Veezie pressed hard against her temples but the spinning in her head wouldn't stop. Then, as if someone pulled a plug and let the air out of her, she slumped and fell back on the mattress.

Beulah grabbed the limp body in her arms and held tightly, crying, "Don't leave me, child. Everything's gonna be all right.

You'll see. Stay with me, sweetpea. With the Good Lord's help, we gonna see this through." Beulah rocked back and forth, wailing, "Oh, sweet Jesus, forgive her, for she know not what she do."

But she knew. She knew exactly what she was doing when she allowed that no-good scoundrel Jack, to have his way with her. And if God is everywhere and knows everything, the way Beulah claimed, then all the praying in the world wouldn't amount to a pocket full o' hickory nuts.

She was bad. She knew it. And what's more, God knew it.

Chapter Four

Shep stepped behind the pulpit Sunday evening and opened his Bible to preach, when the meddlesome Eunice Dobbs stood and frantically waved a handkerchief high in the air.

"Excuse me, Reverend."

He groaned, inwardly. The woman reminded him of Gravel Gertie in the funny papers, with her frizzy white hair and a scowl that would make a bulldog turn tail and run.

He gave a nod. "Mrs. Dobbs?"

"Preacher, I'm sorry to interrupt, but before you begin, I have a special prayer request." She thrust her hand to her heart and then went through the motions of putting on a well-worn sanctimonious mask. Her brows drooped and with downcast eyes, she thrust the handkerchief to her face and dabbed at invisible tears. Her voice quaked with precision, as she began. "Church, my heart is breaking over something that Sister Cora shared with me, earlier. She said her Aunt Ludy told her that a neighbor's husband overheard a woman at the Washateria telling about something dreadful that's taking place right under the nose of this church."

Shep tugged on the collar of his shirt, a habit of his, when something made him nervous. And Eunice Dobbs and Cora Watts had a way of making him extremely nervous.

Eunice pushed her wire-rimmed spectacles down on her long nose and looked out over the crowd. "Folks, we need to lift up Dottie Weems tonight, God bless her. They say she caught Fred over at Lorene's house again, and it's no secret that the last tow-headed young'un Lorene gave birth to, looks exactly like . . ."

Shep leaped from the podium to the second pew and before the gossipy woman could finish her sentence, his hand rested on her shoulder. "That's enough information, sister. Thank you for that prayer request. I think we now understand how and for whom we need to pray." As the organist played *Send the Light*, Shep stepped back up to the pulpit.

The sermon he'd labored over all week, no longer seemed to excite him. His delivery fell flat. Maybe it was time to move his ministry elsewhere. Had he used up his effectiveness? Shep loved the people at Flat Creek Fellowship, but with the two busy-bodies and their hen-pecked husbands in the church, he spent more time trying to straighten out their messes than he did preaching the gospel.

After church, Shep went home to an empty house. Gracie would soon be home from college and maybe he wouldn't have so much time to brood. Like her mother, she could fill a room with sunshine just by walking through the door.

He opened the ice box and chipped off a little ice to go in his sweet tea, then sliced a tomato and made a sandwich for supper. Eating at the kitchen table intensified the loneliness, so he usually took his meals to the living room or on the porch if the weather was nice. But tonight he had a reason for sitting at the table. He took one bite from his sandwich and then reached for the notepad lying with his Bible. He wrote: *Dear fellow church members, after much prayer and supplication, I feel it in the best interest of the church for me to turn in my resignation. I pray that each one of you will keep—*

He wadded the paper and started over but after the third attempt he realized he wrote out of his frustration and not because God was finished with him in Flat Creek. He'd read several explanations concerning what the apostle Paul referred to when he spoke of the thorn in his flesh. For the first time in his ministry, Shep was confident he had the answer: Paul had a Eunice Watts in his life. God must have created two of them.

He took a swig of tea and tried to get his mind off his own giant thorn. His thoughts turned to the young woman at Nine Gables. What would cause a beautiful girl with so much to live for, to withdraw from life and choose to spend her days lying in bed, shut off from the rest of the world? She didn't appear to be sick. Her cheeks had a healthy glow, her eyes looked bright and she had enough energy to be feisty. The image in his head brought forth a smile.

###

If only that nosey, stubborn preacher hadn't driven up yesterday at that precise time, Veezie's pain would now be over. No more haunting cries in the middle of the night. No more aching lumps in her throat. No more tears. She'd be free from the agonizing guilt and shame. She could've jumped yesterday. Now, she wasn't so sure. She lay in bed glaring out the window. Wishing.

Just as the sun sank beneath the pecan orchard across the road, Beulah barged in and plunked a white wicker tray on the bed in front of Veezie. "Brung you some supper, sugar."

Veezie pushed the tray forward, sloshing the glass of sweet iced tea sitting in the wicker well. "Take it back down. Told you earlier, I ain't hungry. Now get this outta my way before I dump it on the floor."

Beulah promptly moved the tray from off the bed and plunked it down on the bedside table. She reached over and picked up a plate and fork from off the tray, and sank the fork into a mound of chicken salad.

Veezie lifted her shoulders. "I hope you plan to eat that yo'self, ol' woman,' cause I ain't got no plans to eat it."

Postured like a prison guard, legs apart, shoulders back and a scowl on her face, it wasn't hard to see that Beulah was no pushover. "I fixed you something special, girlie, and I want you to eat it. Sit up and try ol' Beulah's chicken salad. Yo' mama used to serve my salad to her bridge partners and oh, my goodness, how them snooty ladies did let on."

Veezie stiffened. She wouldn't give in. She couldn't. If she did, she'd never be able to control the stubborn ol' woman.

Beulah's brow knitted together. "Now, sit up, I said."

Veezie clamped her mouth shut and ground her teeth together. Didn't the old goat know who she was talking to? These confounded servants were getting a little too high and mighty and it was time they learned their place. Now was as good a time as any to start teaching them a lesson. "You no-account woman, you can't boss me around. You the *maid.*"

Beulah leaned forward with a big clump of salad on the end of a fork and poked it toward Veezie's mouth. "Open yo' mouth or I'll open it for you. I ain't about to let you lie up here and die on me."

Veezie covered her mouth with her hand. "I don't care if I die. Go away." But the old woman didn't budge. Weren't servants supposed to do as they were told? Veezie's shoulders slumped. "I declare, you the beatenest maid I ever seen."

Beulah's frown faded and her eyes lit up when she chuckled. "And how many would that be, shug? You seen a lot o' maids in yo' time, have you?"

"Well, maybe I ain't seen a lot, but I hear tell what they supposed to be like, and you ain't it." Veezie's eyes crossed as she looked down at the fork Beulah held under her nose. It wasn't the chicken salad loaded down with apples and celery that caused her to change her mind, but it was the smell of freshly baked dewberry cobbler, topped with whipped cream, sitting nearby. She removed her hand and shrugged. "I reckon I'll eat just a tad. But not 'cause I'm scared o' you, 'cause I ain't. You may not have a job after today, no how. I'm thinking about hiring me somebody to take yo'—"

Beulah poked the fork in her mouth and kept cramming it down until Veezie swallowed the last bite of salad, ate four soda crackers and finished off the dewberry cobbler. The old woman stood, and with a wry smile, announced that beginning the next day, Veezie would be expected to come downstairs for breakfast. According to Beulah, everyone knew a woman was supposed to stay in bed for nine days after birthing a baby, but Veezie's nine days were up, and there'd be no more trays hauled upstairs.

Fussy ol' cuss.

Tuesday morning Veezie awoke to bright bands of light. She sat up, stretched and glanced about the room. The white organdy curtains were tied back, shades were up and sunrays beamed through the windows. Beulah had been in the room, but there was no breakfast tray.

Veezie threw the covers back and slung her feet off the side of the bed. "Cantankerous woman. I'll learn her who's boss around here." She reached above her head and jerked on the thick cord to ring the servant's bell.

Fifteen minutes later, she yanked again. For nine days Beulah forced her to eat breakfast when she wasn't hungry, and now on the tenth day when she was starving, she couldn't get anyone to respond to her calls. She'd give Beulah the what-for if the good-for-nothing maid ever decided to check on her. But what could she say that she hadn't said already? No need threatening to fire the bull-headed black woman. Beulah was no moron. She was smart enough to know Veezie couldn't do without her, in spite of all the ranting and raving about letting her go. The mouth-watering scent of smoked sausage wafted up from the kitchen.

Grumbling, she jerked off her nightgown, slipped into her unmentionables and pulled on a pair of silk stockings. She could think of only one advantage to being poor. She never had to worry about so many foundation garments, which Beulah insisted were a must for all well-dressed young ladies. After clipping the stockings to her garter, Veezie looked at the waist clincher and cringed. No way would she be able to pull the hook and eyes close enough to meet.

She plopped down at the vanity and took out a loosely crocheted snood. According to Beulah, all the stylish ladies wore them. But after several attempts to gather her long hair into the mesh contraption, Veezie tossed it aside. What was so special about a hair covering that resembled a small crab net, anyhow? With a few hairpins, she pulled her long blonde locks up and twisted a bun at the nape of her neck.

Dressed in a maroon gored skirt and a white blouse with tatting around the collar, Veezie turned sideways and gazed at her new figure in the mirror. A little curvier—a mite distressing, being she hadn't lacked for generous curves since the age of thirteen—

but not too bad, considering what she'd been through. She trudged down the long staircase and ambled into the kitchen. Now that she was up, it was good to be out of bed, though she wasn't ready to admit it.

Beulah lifted her arms in the air and let out a whoop. "Well, thank you, sweet Jesus," she shouted. "Oh, sugar, I been praying and a hopin' you'd come down them stairs."

The look of delight on Beulah's face made Veezie forget the nasty things she'd planned to say. Her lip curled into a smile. She could've told Beulah it wasn't the prayers as much as the smell of sausage frying that lured her out of bed. But she didn't. She held her head back, closed her eyes and inhaled. "I'm starving."

Beulah's gold tooth sparkled. "Well, hallelujah! That's what I been waiting to hear. Honey child, today is yo' startin' point. Yes'm that's what it is, all right. Yo' startin' point. Yesterday's gone and they ain't gonna be no more yesterdays."

Veezie swallowed hard. Was it possible? Could she really start over with a clean slate?

Beulah grabbed a bar of lye soap from the window ledge above the sink and lathered up to her elbows, then dried off on the tail of her apron. "Hold yo' taters, shug, and ol' Beulah will have you a breakfast fit for a queen, in no time flat." Her eyes twinkled. "I think I might know somethin' you'll like. George picked me a peck of dewberries yesterday. When Miz Harper lived here, she sho' did love my dewberry flapjacks. What about you, hon? Could I stir you up a batch?"

No doubt about it, the old woman could be as ornery as a three-legged mule at times; but no one had ever seemed to give a flip whether Veezie lived or died until she came to Nine Gables last fall and met Beulah and George. "I reckon I could eat a couple o' flapjacks with some of that sausage." She dropped her head and mumbled, "If it ain't too much trouble."

As round as she was tall, Beulah's whole body shook when she laughed. "Trouble? Ain't no trouble at all." She poured batter on the griddle. Then with a sparkle in her eyes, her gaze traveled slowly from the top of Veezie's upswept hairdo, all the way down to the navy and white spectator pumps. "You look nice, sugar. Real nice. Where ya going, all decked out?"

"I ain't going nowhere. Just been thinking this morning about what you said one night up in my room. And I reckon you're right. You thought I weren't listening but I heard you."

"I seem to recollect saying a heap o' things, honey child. Maybe more'n I ought."

"You said it ain't no need to brood no longer. Whether I like it or not, life goes on and I might as well start trying to live it. But now that I'm down here, what do I do next, Beulah? How can I live with myself, knowing I let my baby die?"

Beulah flipped the pancakes and shook her head. "You promised you wouldn't say that no more. I told you a hun'erd times you didn't kill that baby. That young'un was too frail and nothin' you coulda done would've saved her. Po' little creature was bluer than them hi-drangies growing on the south side of the house."

"But Flint said—"

"He didn't mean it, sugar. He spoke out of his own pain. Him and Miz Harper, well, they was counting on raising that baby and he was hurt, same as you was. You both had your own way o' dealin' with the pain. But doc didn't blame you. None of us did."

Beulah was wrong. Harper blamed her. Why wouldn't she? "She hates me. I know she does."

Beulah's eyes widened. "Oh, honey, you don't know Miz Harper the way I do or you'd know better. She ain't one to hold a grudge, more 'specially when a body ain't to blame. You had nothin' to do with her losing Nine Gables. You didn't know about the will no sooner 'n she did. Besides, I got a feeling Miz Harper is happier than she's ever been. Now, you go sit down at the dining table while I take up these flapjacks."

"I hope you're right, Beulah. But I can't help wondering how I'd feel if I was in her shoes." The irony made her snicker. She glanced down at her feet. What was she thinking? She *was* in Harper's shoes.

Veezie plopped down at the long table, properly set with Blue Willow dinnerware on a freshly starched white tablecloth. She picked up her linen napkin and stuck it in her lap. In the center of the table was a beautiful bouquet of gardenias that Beulah said George picked from the garden. Veezie sniffed the air to get a whiff of the sweet-smelling flowers. What a perfect setting. She had everything she could possibly want—except the one thing she wanted most of all. Veezie wanted to be loved. Really loved. In the daylight.

After three plate-sized dewberry flapjacks drowned in George's thick cane syrup and three sausage links, Veezie pushed back from the table. "Beulah, why don't folks like me?"

Beulah plunked her hands on her hips. "Well, land sakes, where did *that* come from?"

"Oh, Beulah, it's a fact and you know it. Folks think I'm too dumb to catch on when they poke fun at me. But I ain't as stupid as they think. I don't fit in nowhere. All my life, I wished I was somebody else. When I found out I *was* somebody else, I thought it'd change everything. I could be Harper and she'd be me. I'd finally get some respect. But nothing ain't changed. People still snicker when I talk and treat me like I'm lower'n a cockroach."

"Sugarfoot, ain't you never heard it's the empty wagons what make the most noise? Don't pay no attention to what folks say."

"I can't help it. It hurts me. Hurts me bad. What's wrong with me, Beulah?"

"Shug, you gotta learn to love the skin you in if you want other folks to admire ya. And it's plain to see you don't like the woman living inside yo' pretty little skin."

"Why should I? She ain't worth squat."

Beulah walked over and wrapped Veezie in her arms. "That's a lie of the devil, sugar. You're precious in the sight o' the Lord."

But was it so wrong to want to be precious in the sight of folks on earth? Was it? "Nobody never gave a flip about me." She bit her trembling lip. "And then one night I was walking down the road, chasing lightenin' bugs and I heard music coming out of the Silver Slipper. I walked inside and right off I discovered that without even trying, I was popular with the men folk. So I kept going back. Just wanted to feel special. That's all."

Beulah's brow furrowed. "Sugar, you didn't know no better back then, but them grown men shoulda been hung by their heels."

Maybe she did know better. Maybe she just didn't care. She knew Jack was married, but he said his wife didn't treat him right. Told Veezie he loved her and claimed he wanted to marry her, soon as he got a divorce. "He lied to me, Beulah. I was stupid." Tears clouded her eyes.

"Nah, hon, you ain't stupid and I ain't neither, although some folks would have us to think it. Me and you is good as anybody and don't you never forget it."

Veezie's lip quivered. "Me, good? No, Beulah. I might not know much, but what I done was sinful as all git-out, and I reckon I knew it when I done it." The skin around her eyes tightened.

"Aw, but child, don't ya see? You ain't gotta live in the past. Glory be, my past ain't nothing to brag about, but according to my preacher, I done been justified. And Praise God, you is now also just-if-you'd."

"Just if I'd what?"

"Well, it's like this—remember the night me and you knelt by yo' bed and asked God to wash away all yo' sins?"

Veezie nodded.

"Well, he did, and when God forgives, he forgets. So now it's just-if-you'd never sinned. He's done slap forgot about 'em and you best forget about 'em, too."

If only she could.

Chapter Five

Veezie chewed on her thumbnail and pondered Beulah's words about loving the skin you're in. "Beulah, you love the skin you in? I mean have you ever wished—"

Beulah's face broke into a smile. "Ever wished I weren't colored?"

"Yeah."

"Well, I'll put it to you like this, sugar. I ain't never wished I lived on the moon, 'cause I never will. I ain't never wished I could fly, 'cause I ain't got no wings. And I ain't never wished I was in no other skin, 'cause this is the skin the good Lord wrapped me up in." She chuckled. "And I think it looks right good on me, if I do say so myself. Why? You ever wished you was black?"

"Uh-uh."

Beulah cocked her head and let out another hearty chuckle.

"You look tickled. You laughin' at me?"

"Nah, I wuz thinking since you done got all spruced up and nowhere to go, why don't you run over to Mr. Bullard's store and fetch me about two-and-a-half yards of yellow linen, so's I can make you a new dress. Can't nothing lift a woman's spirits like being fitted for a new frock. I'll call Miz Winnie at the Beauty Parlor, and get her to crimp your hair with them pretty little finger waves. She always done a fine job on Miz Ophelia, and you got that pretty corn silk hair like hers. Jest needs some fixin'." Beulah pressed her forefinger to her cheek and her laughter sounded like tiny bell's jingling. "Sugar, when I get through with you, ever'body for miles around is gonna say, 'Ooh wee! Why, that Miz Veezie, she is one fine lady.'"

Veezie's mouth gaped open. "Oh, Beulah. You think you can? Make a lady out of me, I mean?"

"Why sho', honey. I raised Miz Harper, didn't I? Oh, Lawsy, they ain't never been a finer specimen of a real lady, but she ain't got nothin' you ain't got, sugar. It's jest hid, but we is gonna find it."

"How we gonna do that, Beulah?"

"Well, I ain't saying it's gonna be easy. But the first thing I need you to do is go fetch a linen handkerchief out of the top bureau drawer and stop wiping your stinkin' nose on yo' hand. And when you done with that, come stand in a chair and I'm gonna straighten the seams on the back of your stockings. You got real nice legs but them crooked seams makes you look bowlegged."

Veezie slid behind the wheel of the shiny black 1935 Roadster. She grabbed hold of the fancy red glass knob on the steering wheel with her left hand and ran her fingers over the soft gray seats. It was hard to imagine such a fine automobile belonged to her.

The memory of Jack teaching her how to drive his old jalopy put a sour taste in her mouth. Unfortunately, driving wasn't the only thing the sorry so-and-so taught her, but her past was behind her and she was now just-if-you'd. Beulah said so.

Driving into town, the sun seemed brighter than she ever remembered. Two days ago, she wanted to die. Yet today, the exciting idea she could become somebody folks could admire, gave her a reason to live. She didn't know how the illiterate maid would pull it off, but somehow Veezie believed she would. In Goose Hollow, she was snubbed and called "that O'Steen girl," but she wasn't in Goose Hollow any more.

Recalling Beulah's instructions, she slung her shoulders back. *I'm a Harrington and I'm good as anybody.* She strode into Bullard's Store with her head held high and pranced over to the dry goods counter.

A man in his mid-fifties with bushy gray hair and a matching mustache said, "Good morning, miss. May I help you find something?"

"Why, thank you, kindly." She pointed upward. "I'm needing some o' that yellow linen on the top shelf. 'Bout two-and-a-half yards, if you please."

His eyes squinted. "The material you're pointing to is poplin, miss. Is that what you want, or are you looking to buy linen?" He reached under the counter and pulled out a bolt of beautiful yellow cloth. "This is linen. Which shall it be?"

Veezie twirled a shank of hair around her finger, feeling foolish. Any rich girl should know the difference between poplin and linen. "They're both mighty pretty, but I reckon I'll stick with the linen."

He smiled. "I don't think we've met. I'm Rufus Bullard. And you are—?"

"Why, I'm mighty glad to meet you, Mr. Rufus Bullard. I'm Miss Veezie Harrington. I 'spect you've heard of my mama. Her name was Ophelia." Veezie glanced around, hoping anyone in hearing distance would be impressed.

"Aw, yes, Miss Harrington. Ophelia was a regular customer of mine. Too bad she died in her prime. I knew her daugh . . . that is, I was familiar with Miss Harper, also. We live in a small town, so naturally, there's been talk, but I suppose all's well that ends well. And it certainly seems things ended well for you." He quickly added, "As it should have, of course. I always wondered where Miss Harper got her black hair, since neither of her parents had . . . I'm rambling. Welcome to Flat Creek. Now, how much material did you say?"

"Two-and-a-half yards, if you please."

He rolled the material from the bolt and reached for the scissors. Without looking up, he said, "I suppose you'll continue the Harrington tradition of a Memorial Day Party at Nine Gables? For years, it's been the social event of the season."

Having no idea what he referred to, but liking the idea of a family tradition, she simply nodded. Beulah could explain.

Mr. Bullard carefully folded the linen and then tore off a long strip of brown paper from a roll. He wrapped the cloth into a neat package and tied it with a string. The cash register drawer flew open and Mr. Bullard deposited her dollar bill and drew out forty-five cents change.

Veezie turned to see a nice-looking fellow standing near the bags of flour. Their gaze locked.

"Good morning." He smiled and tipped his hat.

She glanced from side to side. There was no other woman in the store. *He tipped his hat. At me?* "Uh . . . Good morning yourself."

He stepped toward her and her face flushed with excitement. He was a real gentleman, no doubt about it. Wearing a starched white shirt, striped tie and dress trousers, he didn't look like any of the men she knew.

He said, "I'm glad to see you're feeling better."

Her knees buckled. He sounded as if he knew her. *Impossible.* Yet there was something strangely familiar about the voice.

"I didn't introduce myself, Sunday, when I stopped by. You didn't seem to be in the mood to chat." He reached out his hand. "I'm Shepherd Jackson, pastor of Flat Creek Fellowship Church."

Her jaw dropped. His dark brown eyes sparkled and tiny wrinkles formed around the edge of his mouth when he smiled. His dark hair had the tiniest hint of gray at the temples, giving him a look of distinction. And though he was every bit as handsome as Beulah said, it wasn't his good looks that captured her and wouldn't let her go. It was the way he looked at her. With tender eyes. Like she was somebody. Her heart pumped faster at the thought of being justified. "Uh . . . glad to make your acquaintance. I'm—"

He smiled. "I know. You're Veezie. It's a very unusual name. I like it. It suits you."

"Thank you." If only she could think of something interesting to say to give her reason for staying a bit longer. She tucked the package under her arm. "I reckon I better get going," she stammered. Her shoulders drooped. Why did she say she had to go, when she wanted very much to stay?

A clever thought flitted through her mind. Beulah would no doubt be pleased if she brought home a few groceries. She opened her pocketbook and counted her money. One quarter, one dime and two nickels. She pulled out the quarter. "I reckon while I'm here, I might as well get a quart of sweet milk and a loaf of light bread."

Mr. Bullard grabbed a bottle of milk from the cooler, picked up a loaf of bread from the shelf, walked back and sat the goods on the counter. "Miss Harrington, that'll be twenty-three cents, please. Fourteen cents for the milk and nine cents for the bread."

Veezie handed him the quarter, and paid for a couple of licorice sticks with her two cents change.

"Ker-ching." The sound of the cash register brought her back to earth. With the package under one arm, and holding a grocery sack with the other, she could think of no other excuse to tarry. She turned toward the door and that's when the preacher reached out his hand and caught her wrist, sending shocks of energy through her body.

"I'm glad I ran into you, Veezie. It's good to see you up and about. Your rosy cheeks and bright eyes belie the fact you've ever been sick. So now that you're feeling better, I'd like to invite you to visit us at church tomorrow morning. Services begin at eleven o'clock."

No doubt her cheeks were rosy, for she could feel the heat rising to her face when she realized he was waiting for her answer. She wet her lips. "I used to go to church in Goose Hollow occasionally, but I ain't been to no church since I moved here. Maybe I will." Ridiculous fantasies danced in her head. "Eleven o'clock? Yeah, preacher. I just might do that."

Veezie jerked the hairpins out of her hair, shook it loose and let her long locks blow in the wind as she drove home. She sang to the top of her lungs "Fly in the Buttermilk, shoo fly, shoo, fly in the buttermilk, shoo fly shoo—" Beulah was right. Today was her starting point. There'd be no more yesterdays.

Veezie's pulse didn't slow down all the way back to Nine Gables, even though the fantasies flitting through her head were absurd. The man was simply being nice because that's what preachers are paid to do. That's how they wrangle people into the fold. She meant nothing more to him than another dollar in the coffers. He'd be stupid not to try and win her affection, knowing she was heir to the Harrington fortune. Besides, he was old enough to be her daddy. Well, that's what her head said; but her heart thumped out a different tune.

She parked the car and ran into Nine Gables, yelling, "Beulah? Beulah! Where are you?"

Beulah walked out of the butler's pantry with a jar of nine-day pickles in her hand. "Land sakes, child, what's all the hollering about? You sound like you seen a ghost."

"Maybe I have and she was me."

"Girl, you ain't making a dab o' sense. You ain't no ghost. My preacher says the only ghost is the Holy Ghost, and I believe 'im, but even if they was such a thing, you'd have to be dead to be one."

"Well, I *was*, dead, but I ain't no more." She twirled around, making her gored skirt swing away from her body. "Oh, Beulah, I done buried the ol' me and the woman you're looking at is the new me."

Beulah's face broke out in a wide grin. "I ain't got no way o' knowin' what kinda foolishness you're up to, but whatever it is, I pray hangs around for a spell. It's good to see you feeling so spry."

Veezie sat the sack of groceries on the table, and reached in the pie safe for one of Beulah's tea cakes. She stuffed half of the large cookie into her mouth, filling her jaws.

Beulah peeked into the grocery bag. "Land sakes, chile, what made you wanna buy a loaf of bread and a quart of milk, when we ain't got no need for nary one? You know the milkman comes three times a—" Beulah scratched her head. "You got a mighty peculiar look on yo' face. What you up to?"

Veezie couldn't get the words out fast enough. "Beulah, I'm gonna have me one of them Memorial Day shindigs like my mama used to throw. You know, when folks come here from far and wide to party. But we gotta hurry, 'cause we ain't got long to plan it."

Beulah shook her head. "My stars, who put that bee in yo' bonnet? Shug, that's about the craziest idea I ever heard tell of."

Veezie stiffened. Nobody was going to rob her of her joy. "Mr. Bullard just upped and said he reckoned I'd be pitching a party on Memorial Day, 'cause it was a Harrington tradition. And soon as he said it, I knew—" Veezie narrowed her eyes. "What's wrong? Why ain't you happy for me?"

Beulah stalled. She adjusted her apron bib, then untied and retied the back sash before giving her answer. "I'll put it like this: I'm mighty glad the dark cloud's lifted, sugar, but a *party*? That's plumb crazy. You ain't ready."

"Well, I'll get ready and you gonna help. Now, did my mama have a list?"

"A list?"

"Yeah, you know . . . all them folks she sent invitations to. Surely, she had a list. I'm gonna invite everybody back this year. Ain't no use in trying to talk me out of it, Beulah. I aim to prove to folks in Flat Creek that I ain't no little waif from Goose Hollow no more." She threw her chin in the air. "I'm Miss Veezie Harrington from Nine Gables and I'm gonna show people that I'm somebody.

You wait and see."

Beulah shook her head as she walked over to the large mahogany desk and pulled out Ophelia's guest list. She handed it to Veezie, along with a box of stationary edged in gold and embossed with the Harrington seal. Her mouth turned down. "Oh, sugar, can you even read and write?"

Veezie harrumphed. "Of course, I can read and write. I went all the way to the eighth grade before I dropped out to help with the chores."

Ophelia's list contained fifty-seven names, though most were couples, which made a total of—a lot of people. Math was never Veezie's best subject. She addressed two more envelopes with names that didn't appear on the list. The Rev. Shepherd Jackson and Dr. Flint McCall and Family.

She took the list to the veranda, sat at the wicker tea table and in her best penmanship, wrote fifty-nine times: *"Miss Veezie Harrington corjulie invites you to a party on May 30, 1937 at Nine Gables at six o'clock. Delishus refreshments will be served. There will be lots of fireworks. Please come."*

Veezie walked into her mother's bedroom and picked up a small black bottle of MY SIN perfume from the dresser and dotted each invitation with a tiny dab before sealing, exactly the way she saw the beautiful Myrna Loy do it in a picture show

Chapter Six

Sunday morning, Veezie snatched a thread-bare, slinky red dress from a hanger, and holding it with her index finger and thumb, dropped it into the trash can. She should've dumped it months ago.

Memories rushed through her head of the many Saturday nights she wore the skimpy dress to a juke joint in Goose Hollow. Cat whistles started the minute she stepped in the door of *The Silver Slipper*. Made her feel special the way the men looked at her. They'd race to the juke box and put in a nickel to play her favorite tune—"I Can't Give You Anything but Love, Baby." The fellows stood in line just for a chance to dance with her. They'd hold her close and fill her head with all the words she wanted to hear.

But she was no longer in Goose Hollow and she had no need for a juke-joint dress. Looking down at the crumpled red material in the metal can empowered her. She hadn't expected how freeing such a simple act could be.

If not for Beulah, she might still be looking back toward

Sodom. That's what Beulah called *The Silver Slipper*. Had something to do with a story in the Bible about a woman who looked back when God said look where you're going, not where you've been. Veezie never forgot it, for that was the night Beulah taught her all about sin. Sounding like a street-corner preacher, the roly-poly maid wagged her finger in a furious fashion and in a quivering voice, said, "Remember, honey, the good Lord never said sinning ain't fun, but He did say you can sho' count on regrettin' it later. When you lay a egg, you can expect to hatch a biddie."

Veezie cringed. She sure learned that lesson the hard way. From now on, she'd wear the kind of clothes that would make men tip their hats and say something like, "Good morning, Miss Harrington. You're looking mighty fine, today." She'd cover her mouth pretending to be embarrassed, bat her eyelids, and in a bashful-sounding voice, say something like, "Well, my, my, ain't you sweet to notice."

She browsed through the crowded armoire, determined to find the perfect outfit to wear to church.

Thirty frustrating minutes later, eight fancy dresses lay wrong-side-out in a mound on her bedroom floor. She finally settled on a delicate floral print—white with tiny pink rosebuds. With cap sleeves and a cut-lace collar buttoned at the neck, the dress was so sweet it was almost syrupy. Compared to the tight, low-cut red satin frock, it was as different as daylight and dark. And different was what she aimed for.

After a quick glance at her reflection in the armoire mirror, she made her way downstairs. She pushed open the kitchen door, and the tempting smell of country ham filled her nostrils.

Beulah wiped her hands on the tail of her apron and parted her lips. "Oh, my goodness, look at you in that pretty dress. If you ain't the perfect picture of a lady of means, I wouldn't know where to find one. Turn around, sugar and let me take a gander at you."

Veezie's mouth gaped open. "You mean it, Beulah? I really look like a lady?"

"Do I mean it? 'Course, I mean it, sugar. There ain't gonna be a better-looking woman in that church today. Miz Winnie done a fine job crimping your hair, yesterday. I ain't never seen nothing prettier. You go on into the dining room, now, and I'll fix your plate. When you finish eating, run on back up to your room, and I'll be pickin' you out a hat and a pair of gloves." Beulah's forehead knitted as she gazed at the ceiling, looking as if she might pluck a memory from the light socket. "If I recollect, Miz Harper had a nice straw hat with a pink ribbon she wore with that dress. It'll look real nice on you, too."

Beulah served Veezie's plate and then went to find the hat.

After breakfast, Veezie sat in her room on the round vanity stool in front of the big round mirror. Beulah brushed her hair and then placed the straw hat at a slight angle on her head.

Veezie's face pinched into a frown. "Ain't it whonk sided?"

"'S'pose to be crooked, honey. It's how ladies wear 'em." She reached up and fluffed out the big satin bow in the back and smoothed out two long streamers. "My, my, if you ain't purty, I ain't never seen purty."

No one—not even Sally O'Steen, who thought until her dying day she was Veezie's mama—had ever treated Veezie with such love. If God had allowed Veezie to choose a mother, she wouldn't have picked Sally and she wouldn't have picked Ophelia Harrington. No sirree, she would've picked Beulah. The woman could be cantankerous at times, that was a fact. And she definitely didn't treat Veezie like the head of the household that she was. No, Beulah treated her more like . . . more like a daughter. With a sudden urge to hug the maid and yet afraid Beulah would resist, Veezie crossed her arms around her own breast and squeezed. She whirled around on the vanity stool and looked up into the old woman's face.

"I love you, Beulah, and I ain't never said that to nobody else in my whole life." Though Veezie didn't mean for the words in her heart to gush from her lips, they rose to the top and overflowed like a pot of grits on high-boil. Her voice cracked. "I know you didn't want me comin' here and taking Harper's place, but you've been good to me, anyhow. For the life of me, I don't understand why, 'cause I've dealt you a heap of trouble. I been downright hateful at times."

Beulah reached down and cupped her hands on either side of Veezie's face. Eyeball to eyeball, she made a faint smile. "Honey chile, I can't deny I didn't want Miz Harper to have to leave Nine

Gables. Didn't seem fair. But then life ain't always fair. But I want you to remember something, sugar. Whatever happens, I don't never want you to look back and feel like I loved Miz Harper better'n I loved you. It just wouldn't be so. You is special. Mighty special." She turned away when her voice quaked.

Veezie didn't question her, though she mulled over Beulah's words. *Whatever happens?* It almost sounded as if she expected something bad to happen, sooner than later.

Veezie opened the car door and slid in. She took one last look in the rearview mirror to check her lip rouge before reaching for the starter. Beulah rushed out of the house, yelling and waving a Bible in the air.

"Wait, sugar. You take my Bible to church with you. But you need to get one o' your own next week. And when the plate comes around, be sure you put enough money in, so as not to look stingy, but not so much as to make it look like you showing off. Folks is gonna be watching."

"How much is enough but not too much?"

Beulah shrugged. "I'd say five dollars ought not to draw too much attention."

Veezie's heart was full. She opened the door and jumped out. Her arms wouldn't reach across Beulah's wide middle, but she stretched as far as she could and gave her a warm hug. "Bye, Beulah."

"Stop that foolishness 'fore you get all wrinkled. You gonna be late if you don't hurry, so git going."

Veezie parked in front of the church and reached up to touch her hat, making sure it was still sitting catawampus.

The minute she stepped out of the car, her pulse raced. Had she made a mistake by coming? What if word leaked out that she let a married man get her pregnant? Her insides quivered at the thought. No. No one here could possibly know. There were only five people in the whole world who knew her secret and none of them would ever tell. Not Flint, not Harper, not Beulah nor George, and surely not her. Well, there was one more. The father, Jack Hawk from Goose Hollow, but he had more reason than anyone to keep his mouth shut.

Veezie read the large sign on the front lawn. *Flat Creek Fellowship, Where Everybody is Somebody*. She gaped at the building with a dropped jaw. With her hand she shielded her eyes from the sun, leaned her head back and gazed at the tall steeple. Her head swayed from side to side, marking time with the bell in the tower as it rang out. But it was the brightly colored stained glass windows pieced together like giant jigsaw puzzles to form beautiful pictures, which stole her breath. She recognized a picture of baby Jesus in a manger and another one of Jesus with little children sitting in His lap. She chewed on her fist, imagining her baby girl, cradled in the arms of Jesus.

It was the most beautiful church she'd ever seen. But then, she'd only been to one other—Brother Charlie's Church in Goose Hollow. That wasn't the name of it, of course, but it's what everybody always called it—"Brother Charlie's Church."

Two men stood on either side of the wide double doors, shaking hands with all who entered. Accordion music rang out from the inside. With her shoulders back and her head held high, she strolled up the church steps and hoped she could remember all the instructions Beulah rattled off. A man extended his hand and mumbled a weak welcome. She stopped inside the vestibule and peeked into the sanctuary. Her heart beat so fast, it made her dizzy.

Beulah said lift her chin slightly, just enough to make her appear confident, but not enough to make her seem snooty. Too frightened to look around, she focused straight ahead, her gaze fixed on a cross carved on the front of the dark pine pulpit. Beulah said not to sit in the back, so Veezie walked all the way up the center aisle and eased down in a pew on the front row. The tight muscles in her shoulders relaxed. The varnished pews with gently curved backs were much more comfortable than the slatted pews at Brother Charlie's Church.

Were people really staring or was it her imagination? She rubbed her sweaty palms together. According to a bulletin board hanging on the wall, there were ninety-eight people in Sunday School who gave a total of thirty-nine dollars and fifty-two cents. Without moving her head she let her gaze shift from right to left before opening her patent leather pocket book. She pulled out a small change purse to double-check and make sure she had the five-dollar bill.

The musician's nimble fingers moved gracefully on the

accordion buttons as he pushed and pulled on the instrument. Veezie recognized the tune—"*Love Lifted Me*." The choir walked in and took their place in the raised loft. When the music stopped, Veezie fidgeted on the seat, then opened the Bible she held in her lap, and pretended to read.

Out of the corner of her eye, she glimpsed someone walk up. She glanced down at the floor and saw a man's wingtips. Then a vaguely familiar voice said, "I was hoping you'd come."

Her tongue twisted. "Uh . . . well . . . you *was*?" She lifted her head. When the Reverend Shepherd Jackson extended his hand, she responded with a feeble handshake. He turned, walked up three steps to the raised podium and stood behind the pulpit. The lady at the piano played softly, as he spoke.

The soothing tone of his voice made the hairs on Veezie's arms prickle.

"Before we begin worshipping the Lord in song, I'd like to welcome our visitors. Looking out among the congregation, I see only one new face this morning, and I shall be happy to introduce her, in case you haven't had the pleasure of making her acquaintance."

Her pulse raced. She glanced from left to right, hoping to see someone standing.

"Miss Veezie Harrington, please rise and let the good folks here at Flat Creek Fellowship get a good look at you."

If Veezie could've swapped places with a turtle, she would've done so gladly for there was nothing she wanted more than a shell in which to disappear. She stood, fiddled with her belt and without lingering, gave a short nod and took her seat.

As the preacher read his text, Veezie followed the words in the Bible with her finger. Knowing Beulah would drill her when she returned to Nine Gables, she tried hard to concentrate on the sermon, though her mind wandered down forbidden paths where she had no business going.

Veezie had known a lot of men in her twenty-two years, but not until yesterday when she walked into Bullard's store and met Reverend Jackson, had any man made her insides turn to mush, simply by flashing a mouthful of pearly-white teeth. She couldn't rightly put her finger on what it was about him that stirred her so. What a ridiculous notion—her, falling for a preacher. *Am I crazy*? She shrugged. *Maybe.*

Twenty minutes into the sermon, a dreadful thought flitted through her mind. What if he's married? The bitter taste of bile rose to her throat. Of course, he was married. Why wouldn't he be? She tried to follow his gesturing hands, as he flung them back and forth, emphasizing the points in his sermon. But it seemed his right hand did most of the gesturing and it was the left hand she wanted to see.

He closed his Bible and with arms uplifted, said, "Shall we stand and pray?" Seeing a shiny gold band, Veezie choked, as if she'd swallowed a pine burr.

At the sound of "Amen," her eyes clouded and she couldn't get to her car fast enough. How ridiculous to get so upset over the preacher having a wife. What difference did it make? Even if he wasn't married, he wouldn't be courting the likes of her.

Chapter Seven

Driving home, Veezie pulled off the side of the road, stuck her head out the window and yelled, "Hey, wanna ride?"

Beulah looked spiffy, all dressed up in her Sunday best, even though the blue straw pillbox hat looked too small for such a large head. But maybe it was stylish. Beulah seemed to know more about those things than she did.

Beulah shook her head. "You git on home, girl. I'll be there t'rectly."

"Don't be silly. It's hot out. Get in."

"I said git home."

"I ain't a goin' 'til you get in."

Beulah grumbled and opened the back door of the vehicle.

"Aw, shucks, Beulah. Why don't you get up front."

Beulah plopped down on the back seat and slammed the door. "I Suwannee, girl, if I'm gonna learn you how to act like a white lady, then you is gonna have to do like I say. Now, git goin'."

Veezie hoped Beulah wouldn't question her about the church

service. She wasn't in the mood. To avoid it, she decided to take over the conversation and keep the lead. She glanced behind her. "Beulah, how many folks go to your church?"

"Keep yo' eyes on the road."

"I can see where I'm going. How many?"

"I ain't never counted, but more today than usual, I speck. They is having dinner on the ground, but I left church early, knowing you was gonna be hungry."

"Shucks, Beulah, t'weren't no need in you doing that. I could fix a bite. I was used to fending for myself when I lived in Goose Hollow."

Beulah smiled. "But you ain't in Goose Hollow no more, and I'm gonna see to it you stop acting like you is. And sugar, one o' the first things we need to work on is the way you talk."

"What's wrong with the way I talk?"

"Well, for one thing, a lady would never say 't'weren't no need.'"

"But I meant it. Like I said, I can fend for myself."

"What I'm saying, sugar, is that ladies don't take short cuts when they talk. They drag out what they aim to say. Instead of saying 'T'weren't no need,' you say somethin' like 'It were not no need.' See the differ'nce?"

Veezie nodded. She saw a difference all right, though she didn't know why it should matter as long as she got the point across. But if becoming a lady meant changing the way she spoke, then she'd pay attention to Beulah's advice until she learned all she needed to know.

Mid-afternoon, Beulah walked into the drawing room with a glass of sweet iced tea and a plate of divinity—six beautiful little white candies with a half pecan stuck on top of each one.

"I brung you something, sugar. You seemed a little out o' sorts at lunch. Noticed you hardly ate. Thought a bite o' candy might perk you up."

Veezie feigned a smile. "Thanks, Beulah. I'll take the tea, but I ain't so hungry right now. Think I'll save it 'til supper."

"Honey, I been waiting to hear about yo' day, but you been awfully quiet. How did you enjoy the church service?"

She bit her thumbnail. "Fine. It was just fine."

"Where'd you sit?"

"Up front, like you told me. On the first pew." She took a sip of tea and hoped Beulah wouldn't feel the need to question her further.

"That's good, honey. But Lawsy, I didn't mean you had to go all the way up to the first pew. Just didn't want you sitting in the back. That's all. Midways will do fine, next time."

"I'll keep that in mind." Veezie rubbed her forehead.

"How you like the preacher?"

She shrugged, not wanting to let on. "He's nice. Real nice."

"He sho' is. I think the world of Brother Jackson. But oh my stars, that man's had his share o' troubles."

"Whatcha mean?"

"Having his wife took, the way he did."

"Took?" Veezie's brow lifted. "Who took her?"

"Not who but what, sugar. Consumption. I reckon it's been about two years now. Sad, sad it was. She was like a Princess out of a storytelling book. Was good to everybody, too. White or colored, made no never mind to her. Yes'm, Miss Jenny was a fine woman."

A widower. Veezie jumped up, grabbed two pieces of divinity, shoved one in her mouth and ran toward the door with the other in her hand.

"Where you going in such an all-fired hurry?"

"I gotta find something to wear to church tonight. You be pickin' me out a hat. Something real pretty."

"Don't need no hat. Ladies don't wear hats after six o'clock."

"Jeepers, Beulah. You sure know a lot about the dos and don'ts when it comes to being a lady. I want you to teach me everything you know. I wanna be like a Princess in a storytelling book."

Beulah picked up the candy plate and walked toward the kitchen, chuckling. "I sho' got me a challenge with this 'un."

At four-thirty, Veezie came tripping down the stairs wearing a pale blue suit. She twirled around. "How do I look, Beulah?"

Beulah squinted and rubbed her chin. "The color looks mighty pretty on you, but that jacket is so tight them buttons is gonna pop off and go sailin' across the room if you draw a breath. Hit don't look decent. Go back upstairs and find you a blouse to wear so's you don't have to button the jacket."

Frustrated that Beulah hadn't given her approval, Veezie plodded up the stairs and put on the blouse that had hung on the same hanger with the suit. She took a long look in the mirror and shrugged. It wasn't that she wanted to go to church looking like a floozy, because she didn't, but did she have to dress like an old-maid school teacher?

It seemed as if six o'clock would never come. When time finally rolled around, Veezie grabbed Beulah's Bible and left for church.

With her shoulders back and a spring in her step, she walked down the aisle, stopped midway and took a seat. The crowd was slimmer, but it seemed everyone who came through the door, walked straight to Veezie and told her how glad they were to have her visit. Maybe there was truth to the sign, *A Church Where Everybody is Somebody*. Could it be she'd finally found a place where people would accept her?

The preacher sprinted up to the pulpit, looked down at her and smiled. Veezie's heart fluttered. She held his gaze and returned the smile. He turned his head slowly, looking out among the sparse crowd, but her heartbeat slowed when she realized he smiled at everyone in the same way.

He took his text from the book of Ruth. Veezie hung on to his every word. What a beautiful story. She imagined she was Ruth, longing to win Boaz's heart. And her mother-in-law loved her so much, she was willing to help her come up with a plan to snag him.

Before the sermon ended, the names became confused in Veezie's mind. Not only was she Ruth, but Shepherd Jackson edged out Boaz and Beulah was now Naomi. It was such a romantic story. If only she could wake up the next morning, at the feet of Shepherd Jackson and he'd look at her tenderly and say "Blessed be . . . blessed be—" She flipped through to the book of Ruth and read the passage again from Beulah's Bible. *Blessed be thou of the Lord, my daughter: for thou has showed more kindness in the latter end than at the beginning, inasmuch as thou followedst not young men, whether poor or rich.* She thrust her hand over her heart. The preacher explained the kindness Boaz referred to was called virtue, and it meant purity of character—a characteristic to be admired in any woman.

Veezie's lip curled upward as she hung to every word. Seemed Boaz was saying since Ruth didn't chase after men, either rich or poor, it meant she had more virtue in the end than she did when she first came. Her hopes rose. She was a lot like Ruth, wasn't she? Though plenty of men chased after her at the *Silver Slipper*, didn't it count that she didn't chase after them? And if she understood the meaning of virtue, it was a fact she had more now than when she left Goose Hollow. Staying cooped up in her room for six months made it impossible not to feel a bit virtuous. In time, she would become so virtuous, Ruth would look like a fallen woman in comparison. Boaz took to Ruth. Was it possible the Reverend Shepherd Jackson could take to someone like her? She'd work on it. She wrote down a couple of words the preacher used that she didn't understand. One was 'sanctified' and the other was 'glorified.' She didn't have to write 'justified,' since Beulah had explained that one to her. Beulah knew a lot about the Bible.

The congregation stood to sing Amazing Grace. Veezie sang the words from her heart: "I once was lost but now I'm found, was blind but now I see." Her eyes had been opened wide and she liked what she saw. When the handsome preacher issued an invitation to join the church, she stepped out and boldly walked down the aisle. Her heart raced when he took hold of her hand.

"Welcome, my sister," he said, gripping her hand between his own.

Sister? She didn't want to be his sister. She wanted— He turned loose and her hand dropped, as did her hopes. Why did she allow ridiculous notions to flit around inside her head?

After the benediction, people filed around her to welcome her into the fellowship, like she was somebody special.

Monday morning Veezie arose early. There was so much to be done and so little time. She yawned as she entered the kitchen. The party was only a week away. "Beulah, where's George?"

"He's out in the patch gathering tomatoes, sugar. You don't need to be pesterin' George. He's got a heap o' things to do, trying to keep up these yards and the garden. Breakfast is almost ready. Go sit at the table."

"I ain't hungry. I need to talk to George. It's about the party next week."

Beulah's brow furrowed. "Oh, chile, I wish you'd forget that silly notion."

Why couldn't Beulah be happy for her? She finally had something to look forward to, but she needed Beulah to cooperate. Everything needed to look as it did when her mama pitched a party. "George says the parties were in the garden and he always strung lots of Japanese lanterns. Do you know where my mama stored them lanterns?"

Beulah nodded. "Yeah. I know. Now do like I tell ya, girlie, and go sit at the table."

Veezie plopped down in the dining room. "I don't know why I have to sit in here. Why can't I sit in the kitchen?"

"'Cause you can't, that's why. Now git them elbows off the table."

Veezie liked for Beulah to correct her. But learning how to become a lady would take lots of practice. She folded her napkin and placed it in her lap. "Well, when George comes in, would you tell him to check on them lanterns? I don't want to wait until the last minute and then have to run around like a chicken with a wrung neck, trying to find everything. I want him to barbecue a hog, the same way he done it in the past."

Beulah grumbled, as she put a small baker of biscuits on the table. "Seems like George done a heap o' talking. But I don't reckon he told you much about the last one 'cause they weren't much to say. Folks traveled far and wide to one of these parties when Mr. Gordon was alive, but Mrs. Ophelia had a way of rubbing folks the wrong way. I'd be lyin' if I said they was more'n a dozen folks who showed up last year. I 'spect you can count on far less coming this year. Forget it, sugar. It ain't a good idea."

"Oh, Beulah, don't be such a stick-in-the-mud. They'll come. It's gonna be the way George said it used to be. Think you might finish the yellow dress in time for me to wear it next Monday night?"

She rolled her eyes and muttered, "It's nigh about finished, except for sewing on the buttons and stitchin' a hem."

"Beulah, I need some quick lessons on how to act like a lady. You gotta help me."

Beulah nodded. "One o' these days, we'll get around to it."

"No. I can't wait. Start teachin' me now."

"Land sakes, chile. You act like I ain't got nothing else to do sides piddle with you. What's got you so keyed up all of a sudden?"

She giggled. "I'm thinking how swell it's gonna be, getting acquainted with all my mama's friends and I need to know how to act around 'em." She wrung her hands together. "I added two invitations of my own choosing."

"And who might that be?"

"I sent an invitation to Flint, Harper and the young'uns. And then . . . then I sent the other one to that preacher."

"You ain't talking about Brother Shep Jackson, I don't reckon, since you don't even know him. You mean the preacher from Goose Hollow?"

Veezie let out a grunt and changed the subject. "I can't wait to see little Callie. I reckon I'll always think of her as my baby sister. You know what's funny, Beulah?"

"What's zat, sugar?"

"Folks used to say Callie looked like me. Ain't that funny, since we now know that we ain't even kin?"

Beulah's face got all twisted, like she might've swallowed a big dose of castor oil. "Well, hon, would you be terribly disappointed if you found out them three young'uns really was yo' kin?"

"Oh, Beulah, I wish they was. I'd bring 'em here to live with me, and I'd dress 'em up in fine clothes and buy 'em candy and—"

"But sugarfoot, if they was really yo' kin, then wouldn't that mean you'd still be living in Goose Hollow?"

Veezie shrugged. "Well, since we just pretending, I'd rather play like all of us—me, Jim, Luke and Callie—all belonged here with you and George."

Beulah pursed her lips and nodded. "I reckon you got a point. But now, you need to find something to keep you busy and let me be. I got a heap o' things to do if we is gonna have a party." She walked away grumbling, "I jest wish ol' man Bullard woulda kept his mouth shut. The last thing you need is that bunch o' back-biting biddies nosing around."

Chapter Eight

Monday morning, Shepherd Jackson rose before daylight, packed his station wagon and took a second inventory. Tent, quilts, lantern, fishing equipment, two pair of rubber boots, iron skillet, coffee pot, tin plates, utensils, first aid kit and his clothes—it appeared he had everything.

His sweet Jenny had always taken care of the packing. She'd been so organized. He never had to worry about anything being left behind. This year, she'd be the only thing missing. His lungs constricted, making it difficult to breathe. Twenty-one years ago . . . or was it only twenty, when they eloped on Memorial Day and spent their honeymoon at Lake Cotawhatchee? He remembered their vow to return every year. And they had. Up until two years ago. His brow knitted together. Since her death, the days seemed so long, he often lost track of time.

This year, he promised his daughter he'd pick her up at college and take her to the special place where he and her mother spent so many wonderful vacations. The school was on the way to the lake.

He smiled as he drove. Sometimes God surprised him with pleasant memories, reminding him of what life was like before the void. Fishing adventures flooded his mind. His grip loosened on the steering wheel as weight lifted from his shoulders. Another mile sped past. He pressed harder on the gas pedal. Suddenly he couldn't wait to hook his bait and drop a line. Through the years, Jenny became quite the fisherwoman. He chuckled aloud, trying to imagine his girlie-girl daughter baiting a hook. Would she love the outdoors as much as her mother?

The trip took much longer than he remembered. In years past, he and Jenny would be so excited, they'd jabber the entire trip and the hours would fly by. It was a good time of year to go to the mountains. Already, the May humidity in south Alabama was stifling. It would be nice to camp out under the trees and feel the cool breeze blowing from off the lake.

The campus at Berry College in Rome, Georgia looked deserted. He supposed most of the students had already left for the summer. Gracie volunteered to stay two weeks after her last class, to tutor children at the nearby orphanage. Her tutoring class ended May 23rd, and the lake was less than forty miles from the school.

Jenny would be proud. For a fleeting moment, he envisioned his loving wife looking down from heaven with an approving wink. He'd take Gracie to the little greasy spoon where he and her mother ate their first breakfast together. He'd teach her how to fish for trout and cook over an open campfire, under the stars.

He parked under a street lamp and walked toward Gracie's dormitory. Seeing a silhouette running toward him in the moonlight, he squinted; then, smiled at the sound of her familiar squeal. She was beautiful. Took after her mother, with hair the color of a new penny and eyes so green, emeralds paled in comparison. Even her laugh reminded him of his sweet Jenny.

He ran to meet her.

She sailed into his open arms. "Oh, Daddy, I've missed you terribly. I've been counting the days. Aren't you excited? We're going to have such fun. I want you to show me all the things you and Mama did. I think she'd be pleased to know you're taking me there. Don't you agree?"

Gracie was right. Jenny would've been thrilled.

"Are we going to camp out tonight?"

"No, sweetheart. It would be difficult to set up a tent in the dark. I thought we'd spend the first night in a local motel. Besides, I've driven all day and I'm tired. After a good hot bath and a night's rest, I'll be much better company, tomorrow."

The next day, Shep was so busy setting things up and teaching Gracie how to fish for trout that he didn't have much time to miss what he didn't have. But when night came and he sat under the stars beside the campfire, the lump in his throat grew so large he thought he'd choke. Gracie was unusually quiet, but he supposed she was worn out from traipsing up and down in the streams, while weighted down in her mother's rubber waders.

"Daddy?" The light from the crackling fire illuminated her lovely face.

Shep glanced up and smiled. "Yes, punkin'."

"I know you get lonely, now that I'm away at college. Have you considered courting?"

"Considered *what*?" Surely, he misunderstood.

"Courting. But I think you called it spooning in your day."

His face burned and it wasn't from the warmth of the campfire. "Gracie! I consider that to be a crude and unladylike term and I'd thank you not to let such words proceed from your delicate lips." Shep didn't like the way she crinkled her nose and grinned. If only her mother was here. What a ridiculous thought. *If her mother was here, there'd be no need for such a conversation.*

"I'm sorry, if I embarrassed you, Daddy. But I want you to know if you ever decide to enjoy the companionship of a lady friend, I'm mature enough to understand."

"Honey, I loved your mother more than life itself. There could never be anyone who could take her place in my life." Jenny was the kind of wife any man would've been proud to claim. Not only beautiful, smart and sweet, but when she walked by, people took notice. And when she spoke, they listened.

He paused and looked toward the evening sky. "Gracie, there'll never be another woman like her. Your mother could've sat at the table with royalty. I don't know how to say it, but she was so—"

Gracie laid her hand on her father's arm. "Refined?"

What a perfect description. Though he and Jenny never had much money, she could take a flour sack, stitch up a dress and when she put it on, it looked like it came straight from a mail-order catalog. "Yes, honey, she was refined and I loved her so much." People said with time, the pain would lesson. They were wrong.

Gracie stood and stretched. "I hope one day to find a man who loves me as passionately as you loved Mama . . . but if I should die, I'd want him to keep on living. Daddy, sometimes it seems you died with her. I remember how you used to laugh."

"Gracie, Gracie. Don't feel sorry for me, honey. I'm fine. I still laugh."

"But it sounds hollow—not gleeful the way you laughed when she was alive. I'm saying if the right woman were to come along—"

Shep sat on the ground, his knees pulled up to his chest and his hands laced behind his head. How could he make her understand? "Gracie, the right one came along. It wouldn't be fair to another woman for me to marry again. I could never love her the way I loved Jenny."

"But Daddy—"

"Honey, I've told you how I feel and frankly, I'm not comfortable discussing the subject with my daughter." He picked up a long stick and punched at the campfire. "I don't mean to be sharp, but if you don't mind, I'd prefer to drop it."

"I understand. Goodnight, Daddy." Gracie went inside the

tent, where Shep had set up a cot for her.

No, she didn't understand. She couldn't, for she had never loved a man in the way her mother had loved him. Jenny's love broke all emotional, spiritual and physical boundaries. No man had ever experienced such incomparable ecstasy. Why would Gracie bring up the subject of courting, knowing how deeply he loved her mother? But even stranger, why did he keep seeing another woman's face in his dreams? He still loved Jenny and the idea of someone else invading his thoughts, terrified him.

As tired as he was, Shep was almost afraid to fall asleep. Afraid because he had no control over the recurring dream that began the night after he walked into Bullard's store and spoke briefly with Veezie Harrington. He hardly knew the girl. She wasn't much older than his daughter. *How would I feel if I knew some forty-year-old man was having dreams that included my little Gracie?* He tried to appease his conscience by reminding himself that he had no control over his dreams. Even so, he prolonged closing his eyes for fear the beautiful, youthful face would once again appear and the forceful pounding of his heart would awaken him—the way it happened last night and the night before.

The bright orange embers lost their glow and turned into crumbling gray ashes. An occasional spark would pop out of nowhere, float upward and then disappear into the darkness. It reminded him of his life. Once bright and full of fire. But when his Jenny died, the fire went out, leaving his life as void as a starless night. Gracie was the spark that kept him going. And as hard as he tried to dismiss the thought, he knew that one day she too, would find someone to light up her life and he'd watch her float away like spent ashes.

Chapter Nine

Veezie strolled down the antechamber and wandered into her favorite part of the house. Even Beulah couldn't explain why it was called a drawing room if no one ever drew in it.

Spacious enough to hold four log cabins the size of the one in Goose Hollow, yet the humongous room wasn't cold and uninviting like the front parlor. The wallpaper was dotted with tiny black harps on a stark white background and red velvet drapes hung in soft folds over the long windows.

Veezie wanted to believe that one day she'd sit down in front of the mahogany grand piano near the window, place her hands over the ivory keys and her fingers would know exactly what to do. It was only a fantasy, of course, for more than a few times she sat banging away, and it never sounded even remotely like the intended Blue Danube Waltz. In fact, the noise was more like a pack of 'coon dogs sniffing out a trail. One day, she'd take lessons and learn how to play such a fine instrument. Maybe even play in church. She glanced up when Beulah walked to the door.

"Telephone, sweet pea. It's Miz Harper."

"Harper?" Veezie sailed off the stool and ran upstairs to take the call in the privacy of her room. Her hand trembled as she picked up the receiver. "Hello? Harper? Zat you?"

"Hi Veezie. How've you been?"

"Fair to middling, I reckon. And you?"

After a couple of minutes of cordial small-talk, Harper thanked Veezie for inviting them to the party, but said regretfully, they wouldn't be able to attend.

Veezie's hand gripped the telephone receiver until her knuckles turned white. *I was right. Harper hates me.*

"Veezie? You still there?"

"Yeah. I'm here."

"As I was saying, I'm sorry we can't go but we've come down with the chicken pox."

With her left hand, Veezie reached across her body and massaged the tense, aching muscle in her right shoulder. She was almost glad Harper and the children had chicken pox. It was so much better than thinking they didn't want to see her.

"Lucas caught them first, then Callie, and tonight I broke out. Can you believe I went through childhood without having chicken pox? But I suppose it's understandable, since Mother . . . uh I mean Ophelia kept me isolated from other children whenever possible. Jim doesn't remember ever having them, so I suppose he'll come down next."

"Oh, Jim had 'em all right. Same time as me. I reckon he was too little to remember, but I ain't forgot. I was about ten and I reckon he was no more'n two or three at the time. Mama . . . well, Sally . . . she took some sulfur and mixed it with lard and rubbed all over us. It's supposed to be good for the itch. You might wanna try it." She snickered. "But I reckon being as how you're married to a doctor, you don't need no medical advice."

There was an uncomfortable pause. Then Harper said, "Veezie, I haven't spoken with you since . . . well, since you lost the baby."

Why did she say I lost the baby, like it was my fault? It ain't like I misplaced her somewhere. Veezie wiped the wetness from her face. "You mad with me, Harper?"

"Oh, Veezie, how could I ever be angry with you? You were willing to entrust me with the most precious gift anyone could ever give another. It was an unselfish act and I loved you for it. I still do. I'm sorry our little diamond wasn't strong enough to survive."

Veezie swallowed hard. "Did you see her? Did you look at her, Harper?"

"I did. She was already gone by the time I arrived, but I held her in my arms, and then Beulah laid her out in the pink wicker bassinet. She looked like a little doll, lying there."

"Harper, I've wished a thousand times I woulda looked at her and cuddled her. Does Flint still blame me?"

"Of course not, Veezie. He said she didn't stand a chance, she was so tiny. Her little lungs weren't developed."

"You called her our little diamond. That's what Flint kept

saying. Said she was like a perfect diamond."

"That's the name we put on her tombstone. Diamond."

Veezie's lip trembled. "I think it's beautiful. I've been afraid to ask what happened to her. I'm so glad she has a tombstone. Where is she buried?"

"She's resting in peace in the Goose Hollow Cemetery, Veezie. We buried her next to your . . . next to my mother, Sally O'Steen. I hope you don't mind."

Veezie bit down on her forefinger to keep from crying. "That's fine, Harper. I know I've said some right mean things about yo' mama, but she loved us young'uns in her own way, I suppose. It was like she was under Monroe's spell. If he told her not to feed us, then we went to bed hungry, so I faulted her for not standing up to him. No doubt he woulda beat the living daylights out of her if she'd a crossed him, though."

There was one question left unanswered. Veezie had hoped Harper would volunteer, but when she didn't, she had no choice but to ask. "Harper, I know you and Flint didn't have time to adopt her before the little thing died. Did you put the baby's name on the tombstone?"

"We did, Veezie."

Baby Girl Harrington? Her heart sank. It would only be a matter of time before everyone would know.

"It says 'Diamond Vee McCall, Born and Died May 7, 1937.' I spelled her middle name "V-E-E. You like it?"

She choked back the tears and nodded. Veezie had done a lot

of things in her life she wasn't proud of, but choosing Harper for her baby's mother was about the smartest thing she'd ever done. "Thank you, Harper. That's a real fine name."

Sunday morning, Veezie sat at the vanity in her petticoat and held a silver hand mirror in front of her face, while Beulah carefully unrolled strips of brown paper from her hair.

"Beulah, I ain't never seen nobody roll hair on tore up paper sacks before. You sure it works? I hope I didn't go through a sleepless night for nothing."

"Sho' it works. I rolled Miz Harper's hair on paper every Saturday night from the time she could walk until the night before she—" She paused. "All this talk makes me forget my business. You stop axin' so many questions and quit your squirmin'."

When Beulah pulled the last paper strip from her hair and brushed it out, Veezie stared at her reflection in the mirror and gently stroked the bouncy yellow curls that framed her face. A Princess out of a fairytelling book. That's exactly what she looked like.

Beulah picked out a black sleeveless sheath for Veezie to wear to church and insisted it fit her much better than it had fit Harper. Beulah always knew how to say the right thing.

But when Veezie couldn't pull herself away from the mirror, Beulah scolded her. Sometimes the *right* thing wasn't always the thing she wanted to hear. Her reflection was enough to convince her that with time and patience, Beulah could make her over into a head-turning, hat-tipping, tea-going sort of lady.

She arrived at church twenty-five minutes early. Perhaps the preacher would mosey into the sanctuary, see her sitting there and while waiting for others to arrive, he'd mention the party and how he looked forward to going. She'd smile, remember not to gush, and simply thank him for the kind words. Just like a real lady. And she wouldn't say t'weren't. Her gaze stayed focused on the back door of the sanctuary near the choir loft, where he made his entrance the week before.

She twirled a lock of hair around her finger. Today, she wouldn't rush out as soon as the service was over. She'd take her time and amble out slowly, in case anyone had a hankering to talk.

A pretty young woman, tall and willowy and looking quite dapper with bobbed chestnut hair, walked up, holding a chubby baby in her arms. Twin girls about the age of three, maybe four with pigtails and wearing matching sailor dresses, hung to their mother's coat tail. The kind-faced lady thrust out her free hand and in a sweet, sing-song voice said, "Miss Harrington, you got away last Sunday before I had a chance to welcome you. My name is Marcy Woodham. Do you mind if we sit with you?"

Veezie glanced at the door and wondered why it was taking the preacher so long. People began to fill the church. She smiled and slid over. "That's mighty kind of you to ask. I don't like sitting by myself." Beulah told her not to talk about herself, but show an interest in other people. "You got pretty young'uns. How old is the little one?"

"Thank you." She wiped drool from the corner of the baby's mouth. "He's six months." Her face beamed. "We got our boy this time. Named him Junior after my husband. Adolphus wanted a boy last time, but of course, he wouldn't trade his girls for a dozen boys." She turned and straightened a bow ribbon on one of the girl's pigtails. "And they're crazy about their daddy."

Veezie's heart raced. "'Scuse me. I don't think I caught your name."

"Marcy."

"And . . . and what did you say your last name was?"

"Woodham." The woman turned around and waved. "Over here, honey."

Veezie closed her eyes. She couldn't look. But when Marcy said, "Adolphus, I'd like you to meet Miss Veezie Harrington," she had no choice but to stand and face him. *Why, Lord? Why now?*

Adolphus Woodham's face lit up like a stoked up cook stove. He twisted his hat in his hands and mumbled, "Glad to make your acquaintance Miss O'—"

"Harrington," she blurted. Her knees wobbled.

"Oh . . . yes. Miss Harrington." He glanced at his wife. "Sweetheart, I've got a sick headache. Feeling kinda faint. You mind if we go home before the service starts?"

Marcy's brow formed a vee—the way one would expect a loving wife to respond to her husband's sudden illness. "Of course, we can leave, dear. I hope it's nothing serious."

He mumbled. "I'm sure it'll pass. Just don't feel like staying."

Veezie wanted to sink into the floor and be swept up with the rest of the trash when Marcy reached over and gave her a hug. "Sorry, we have to leave, Veezie. I hope you'll be back next Sunday so we'll have a chance to become friends."

Friends? She wouldn't say that if she knew the truth.

The Woodham family slipped out the door, moments before a strange man stepped up to the pulpit. But Veezie's mind was no longer on Shepherd Jackson. If condemnation could produce bruises, she'd be black and blue, from beating herself up. She recalled the night Adolphus picked her up walking home from the Silver Slipper. It was raining. She was soaked from head to toe. Appreciative that he was kind enough to take her home, Veezie owed him, and there was only way she knew how to pay. Now, she understood why he was hesitant to accept her gratitude. He had little to gain and much to lose.

I thought that was all behind me. Months ago, when she and Beulah prayed together, Veezie confessed her sins to God. She remembered calling Adolphus by name. And when she went to sleep that night, she had a sense of peace, knowing God had forgiven her. But she remembered something else Beulah said that night. *Sin often brings consequences, later on down the road.* Veezie had a feeling she was about to travel that road.

When Adolphus' wife learned the truth—and no doubt she would—she'd be devastated. She'd probably leave him and children who adored their daddy would be heartbroken. And everyone in Flat Creek would know why Marcy Woodham left her husband.

The stranger delivering the message must have given a reason for the pastor being away, but Veezie heard nothing after coming eyeball-to-eyeball with the hand-wringing, tongue-tied, red-faced Adolphus. She could put all romantic fantasies to rest. With a sordid past stalking her, no decent man could ever be interested in her and especially not a man of God.

At the close of the service, an announcement was made that Reverend Jackson was vacationing with his daughter and therefore evening services would be cancelled. The congregation stood and sang, "Are your garments spotless, are they white as snow, are you washed in the blood of the Lamb."

Her heart broke.

Chapter Ten

Shep couldn't shake the feeling he was in the wrong place. It wasn't that he thought it was sinful to take a vacation. He didn't. Time spent with his daughter was a good thing. Yet there was an unsettling gnawing in his gut that he couldn't explain.

After cooking supper over an open pit, he pulled out his marshmallow sticks—small limbs whittled to a sharp point. After each meal, he eagerly grabbed a bag of marshmallows and he and Gracie roasted the fluffy confections over an open fire, the way he and Jenny had always done it. He poked a piece of white candy on the end of a stick.

Her nose crinkled. "I think I'll pass, Daddy."

"Nonsense. This is all part of it. Your mother and I roasted marshmallows after every meal. She always knew exactly how close to get them to the fire and then she'd pull it back at the right moment. Always brown but never charred." He shoved the stick out for Gracie to take.

She held it, but seeing her mouth turn down while eating, he grinned. "Sorry. I shouldn't have forced you."

"It's delicious, really."

"Really?"

She turned her back and spit it out. "No." She wiped her mouth with her hand and smiled. "It's horrid. I hate marshmallows."

Shock turned to laughter. "Oh, honey, then why?"

"Because I love you, Daddy. And I knew how much you enjoyed it."

She cringed, wiping the sticky from her hands.

What a great job Jenny had done, raising such a sweet daughter. How could he feel such loneliness with his precious daughter by his side? Shep tried not to imagine how much worse it'd be when some young man would win Gracie's fancy and take her away from him. As far as he knew, she wasn't involved with anyone, but with her looks it wouldn't be long before she'd be walking down an aisle. *And whither he goest she will go. His people shall be her people.* He gulped. *Oh, dear Lord, I'm not ready.*

"Gracie, I know you've made a lot of good friends at school. But is there . . . I mean, do you . . . are you—?"

Her face lit up with a smile. "With all this talk about romance, are you having difficulty asking me if I might be in love?"

He grinned and nodded. "As I said, you are your mother's daughter. You both could always read me like a book."

"Frankly, Daddy, I don't have time to get romantically

involved."

Time? "I can't say that I'm disappointed in your answer, but honey, how much time do you suppose it takes to fall in love?"

"Well, I don't happen to believe in love at first sight. I think it takes months or perhaps even years to develop a lasting relationship. I don't know how I'll do it, yet, but my dream is to start an orphanage. I know it'll take money, courage, dedication and a lot of hard work. I can't allow myself to fall for a man. What if he didn't share my dream?"

Shep's heart swelled with pride. Gracie had good intentions. She wanted to save the world. But she was still very young. Given time, she'd realize how unrealistic those goals were. And by then, maybe he could let her go. At nineteen, she still had her head in the clouds.

Gracie stood. "Goodnight, Daddy. I think I'll go lie down in the tent and get some sleep. See you in the morning." She pecked him on the cheek and in a light-hearted whisper, said, "I have plenty of time to fall in love. You're the one who should start looking around."

Nights were always the hardest. Shep stretched out on an old army blanket, which he threw on the ground outside the tent, but sleep wouldn't come. He stared at the stars. Was Gracie serious? Date again at his age? Never. The idea was preposterous.

The minutes turned into hours. One thought led to another. He couldn't remember which thoughts led to the young woman at Bullard's store. What was it about the girl that infatuated him so?

Sure, she was beautiful, but there was something different—something pure and unassuming. A chuckle escaped his lips, remembering how Veezie's manner of speech stunned him when she first opened her mouth. He was accustomed to southern colloquialisms, but somehow the improper diction seemed natural coming from the lips of an aging farmer wearing faded, ill-fitting overalls. But she was no farmer and her clothes fit her extremely well. She was different in a refreshing sort of way. No frills. No put-on. Since losing Jenny, there wasn't a widow or old-maid between the ages of thirty and forty-five who hadn't tried to turn his head with any means they could conjure up. Some of their approaches were downright embarrassing. And why he hadn't come down with sugar diabetes was a mystery, with all the cakes and pies that showed up at his door.

His tongue stuck to the top of his dry mouth when he recalled the feeling he had last Sunday night when he looked down where Veezie sat and her gaze locked with his. It was at that moment he felt something he hadn't felt in years. But she felt it, too. He hadn't imagined it. He knew it. He wasn't sure how he knew it, but he did. Shep shot straight up on the blanket and drew his knees to his chest. His heart pounded like a woodpecker pecking on a tin roof.

Was he crazy? Where were these vain imaginations coming from? From Gracie, that's where. All that dopey talk about courting opened a door that he needed to slam shut. *I felt nothing and she certainly feels nothing for me. I'm forty years old. She's barely in her twenties.*

"Daddy?" Gracie stuck her head out the tent. "What's wrong?"

He winced. Had he said the words aloud? "What are you doing awake, sweetheart?"

"I was asleep but I woke up when I heard you groaning. Are you hurting?"

The muscles around his mouth twitched. If only she knew. The guilt and shame he bore made it almost unbearable to breathe. His heart belonged to Jenny. How dare he allow another woman to worm her way into a space that belonged to the love of his life. A stranger, at that. "I'm fine. Go back to sleep, punkin. Sorry, I woke you." He laid his head down on the wool blanket. With his arms wrapped around a favorite pillow, he clutched it to his chest and stared at the stars.

Groaned? Maybe he had.

Chapter Eleven

Sunday evening, Veezie sat in the wicker swing on the veranda and tried to shake Adolphus Woodham from her thoughts. Yet his face seemed etched on the underneath sides of her eyelids. She jumped when Beulah opened the door and walked out with a tall glass of sweet iced tea.

"You nappin', sugar?"

Veezie shook her head. "Nah, just thinking."

"Well, it's a mite warm out here on the porch. Thought you might wanna wet your whistle."

"Thank you. I could do with a cold drink."

When Beulah started back inside, Veezie caught her by the tail of her dress. "Don't go in. Sit out here with me for a spell, Beulah."

Beulah chuckled. "Well, I won't deny it'll feel mighty nice to get off my feet for a while. These corns are killin' me." She plopped down in the metal glider.

For several minutes the only sounds came from a dog barking in the distance and the squeaking glider as Beulah pushed back and forth.

"Sugarfoot, when you gonna tell me what's going on in yo' pretty little head?"

Veezie lifted her shoulders. "I dunno." She bit her thumbnail down to the quick. "Beulah, you wouldn't understand."

"Try me, sugar."

Beulah squeaked that glider like she had all the patience in the world.

A full five minutes passed before Veezie blurted, "Oh, Beulah, I might as well a'stayed in Goose Hollow. I don't belong here. I feel like a fish trying to swim without no fins."

"Sounds like you might be trying to have a pity-party. S'pose you tell ol' Beulah what's got you feelin' so glum."

"I'm too ashamed."

"Just spit it out, sugar."

She let her gaze fall to the floor. "Remember me telling you 'bout the time a man picked me up and it was raining?"

Beulah's brow furrowed. "I remember. You said you'd been hanging out at that ol' honky-tonk and was on your way home. But sugar, I want you to forget about it. You done and confessed all that mess to the Lord, and He don't want you dredging up them ol' past sins. You ain't the same girl you was the night you walked down that road. You keep reminding yourself that you is a new creature 'cause it's a fact. And don't let the ol' devil tell you differn't."

How could she make Beulah understand? "This morning for the first time in my life, I felt like a decent human being." She rolled her shoulders. "But I was dreaming."

"That weren't no dream, sugar, 'cause that's what you is. A decent human being."

"No, Beulah. Wishing don't make it so. White trash can't never be nothing but white trash."

"Hush yo' mouth, girl. That kinda talk comes straight from the devil and don't you forget it."

"Oh, Beulah, maybe it is coming from the devil, but I can't outrun him."

Beulah pushed off the glider and stood. "Let's go in the house and get to the bottom of what's eating you. It don't look right, me sitting out here doing nothin'. What if somebody wuz to drive by?"

Veezie rolled her eyes. "Who cares?" But at Beulah's insistence, she followed into the kitchen and plopped down in the wooden chair.

Beulah sat at the table, across from her. She reached over and gently patted Veezie's shoulder. "Now, tell ol' Beulah what happened to make you want to go back and dig up a past that's done been buried?"

Veezie propped her elbows on the table and sank her chin into her clasped hands. "Didn't dig it up, but it's come back to haunt me." She gnawed her trembling lip. "Beulah, I looked fine at church today with my hair all curled up and a pretty dress on. I did, didn't I?"

Beulah grinned. "You sho' did, Miz Veezie. You looked mighty good. But now, you ain't supposed to brag on yo'self. You save that job for other folks."

"Not bragging. I was trying to say I appreciate what you done to get me looking lady like. I reckon I looked as spiffy as any woman in that church. Maybe even more so than most. But I learned something about myself today."

"What's zat, sugar."

"You can cut off a rattlesnake's fangs, but if he slithers across somebody's foot, what you reckon they gonna do?"

Beulah cocked her head. "Well, I don't spect he could hurt nobody."

"That ain't the point. The point is, they ain't likely to smile and say, 'Well looky yonder at that pretty little creature, crawling over my foot.' No ma'am, they'll jump back and holler, 'Oh my, Lordy, it's a snake.' Don't you see? Nobody ain't gonna take the time to check for fangs. He'll still be what he was." Veezie could tell by the blank expression that Beulah wasn't following the conversation. She'd have to give her the details.

She told her about meeting Adolphus' family and the look on his face when he shook her hand. "Changing my outside didn't change what Adolphus saw when he looked at me, and I knew it. I could see it in his eyes. Beulah, I couldn't have scared him more if I'd been a rattlesnake."

"But sugar, it ain't just your outsides what's changed. You

done changed on the inside, where it counts. God knows you ain't the same girl you was then."

"Maybe God knows, but ain't nobody else gonna give me a chance to prove it. All my life I've been a nobody. Is it so wrong to want to be somebody, Beulah?"

Beulah's face twisted. "You *is* somebody, sweetpea. You is special. Why, I wager they ain't never been nobody what was more a somebody than you is, chile."

Why couldn't Beulah understand that in the eyes of others, she'd never be anything but a cheap little floozy? Her old life had suddenly boiled up from a cesspool of sin and destroyed any hopes of ever being respectable. She remembered Brother Charlie, the preacher from Goose Hollow, saying, "Be sure your sins will find you out." She didn't know where to find it in the Bible, but she knew it was true, because her sins had come looking for her and found her straight away. Veezie threw away her juke joint dress for naught. She might as well be wearing it.

Monday morning Shep paced back and forth in front of the tent where Gracie lay sleeping. It didn't seem right to wake her so early, but all night, something inside his gut nagged at him to return to Flat Creek. He unzipped the canvas and poked his head inside the tent. "Sweetheart, wake up."

She failed to budge.

"Wake up, Gracie."

She garbled a low grunt. Then nothing.

He eased inside and stooped down beside her cot. With his hand on her shoulder, he shook her gently.

She moaned. "Daddy? Is something wrong? It's still dark outside."

What excuse could he give for leaving so abruptly? Was it really because he couldn't bear staying at the lake without his Jenny? Or was it the guilt of leaving the flock that God entrusted to his care? Perhaps both were merely excuses—he couldn't say. He only knew he had to go.

"Get in the station wagon, sweetheart. You can sleep while I pack the gear. We're going home."

"But Daddy—"

He had to be firm. No more cowering to fluttering eyelashes. "No buts, sweetheart. Trust me, it's time to go." He hated to disappoint her, but he couldn't pack the car quick enough. How could he explain the urgency when he couldn't understand it himself?

The sun was up by the time he finished taking down the tent, packing the vehicle and cleaning up the camp site. The trip to South Alabama, allowing for two meal stops along the way, could take at least twelve hours. It would be dark by the time they arrived in Flat Creek.

As he drove out of the campsite, he glanced over his shoulder at his sleeping daughter. He knew how much she wanted to stay. Would she be terribly disappointed in her dad for being so mulish?

With his thumb, he twisted his wedding band around on his

third finger, while gripping the wheel tightly with his right hand. He fought bitterly against unwanted thoughts. *Get thee behind me Satan. In my heart I'm a married man. Always will be.*

Due to a flat tire on the way home, the trip took even longer than Shep anticipated.

Holding the wheel with one hand, he rubbed the back of his neck with the other. A loud puff blew out from his lips when he finally saw the sign "Welcome to Flat Creek."

It was after nine o'clock when Shep dropped Gracie off at her friend Lorene's house, where her friends had gathered to shoot off fireworks. He couldn't remember ever being quite so tired. Gracie said she'd have a friend drive her home, so there'd be no need for him to come back for her. Still, he offered once more, hoping all the while, she'd reassure him.

"Call me, sweetheart if you need me, and I'll come get you."

"Sure, Daddy. But I won't need you."

Shep knew what she meant, but still, the words cut through his heart. There would come a day—and it wouldn't be long—when she would no longer need him.

After a hot shower, Shep crawled under the sheets and tucked Jenny's picture under his pillow and closed his eyes. Startled by the telephone's loud ring, he jerked straight up in bed and jumped to his feet.

"Harper?"

"Oh, Brother Jackson, I'm glad I reached you. I tried to call earlier but no one answered."

"What's the problem?"

"You remember the young woman I asked you to pray for?"

His pulse raced. "Veezie? Has something happened to Veezie?"

"Oh, I forgot. Beulah told me you paid her a visit, so you do know her."

"Uh . . . well, not as well as I'd like to, but—" He flinched. "Well, I meant to say that she visited the church last week and I plan to call on her to let her know we appreciated the visit." He winced. Until now, he hadn't even admitted to himself that he wanted to see her. The reason he gave might fool Harper, but why try to fool himself? "What's going on?"

"I had a call tonight from Beulah. You remember, the maid."

He chuckled. "Most definitely. She's a delightful character."

"Well, she's frightened that Veezie may do something dreadful."

He detected a tremble in Harper's voice. "I don't understand. Like what?"

"Maybe even take her life. Brother Jackson, you were there for me when my daddy snuffed out his life. Beulah loved Gordon Harrington and she's frantic. She insists she's seeing familiar signs in Veezie that she saw in Daddy, only hours before he . . . before he—"

"I'm glad you called, Harper, but perhaps Beulah is overreacting. I'm sure finding your father the way she did, left emotional scars. Veezie looked quite happy in church last Sunday."

"No, preacher. Beulah isn't one to panic. I'm afraid it's serious. Seems the party was a flop, and Veezie is devastated."

"Party? Was today her birthday?"

"Oh, I suppose you didn't know, but she planned a big Memorial Day celebration at Nine Gables. Beulah said Veezie sent out over fifty invitations and yet only three people showed up and they all left shortly after arriving."

He supposed it would be disappointing to go to great lengths to plan a party and have no one come. But devastating to the point of suicide? Didn't make sense. Yet, Harper wouldn't have called unless—

"I know it's late and I hate to ask—"

"Please. What would you like me to do?"

"Beulah called and pleaded for me to go to Nine Gables to talk to Veezie but I can't leave. Flint's at the hospital with a patient and I have the chicken pox and two very sick children. I hoped maybe you could go counsel with her before she does something stupid."

"Sure thing. I'll go over right away, Harper. You take care of yourself and those kids. I'm sure everything will work out." But how could he be so sure?

"Thanks, preacher. As a word of warning, Veezie is a like a pair of tight-fitting shoes. She can rub you raw at first, but given time, she loosens up and wears well on you. So please, be patient with her."

"I understand." But he didn't—not really. How could anyone as sweet and innocent as Veezie rub someone raw? She reminded him of a soft, autumn breeze that made him want to inhale and hold his breath to enjoy the freshness. He'd never met a woman who radiated such purity. Perhaps it came from being raised in the country, away from everything worldly. He hoped the sudden wealth wouldn't change her.

Beulah opened the door to Nine Gables before Shep had a chance to ring the bell.

"Oh, preacher, I'm glad you came. She's in the drawing room, squalling her eyes out. I'm scared. Ain't no telling what she's likely to do in the state she's in."

He whispered, "Harper said she's upset because no one came to her party. Is that all there is to it?"

Beulah's brows knitted together. "All? Why preacher, that chile is devastated and for good reason. Oh, Lordy, I tried to get her not to send out them invites, but her mind was made up. I feel like takin' a broomstick to ever' single person on that list who didn't show up."

He flinched when Beulah glared at him as if somehow he was to blame for people failing to respond. "Can you show me the list, Beulah?" He wasn't sure why he asked and was glad when Beulah didn't question him.

She walked over to the desk and pulled out an envelope. "I can't read nor write, preacher, and right now I'm thinking it's a good thing. I might wanna go wring some necks if I knew whose necks to wring."

He skimmed the list and then stopped on a single name. His jaw dropped. No wonder the maid glared at him with daggers in her eyes. "Oh, Beulah, my name is on here. But . . . but I've been away all week and haven't had a chance to check my mail. I feel terrible."

"Well, you is forgiven, preacher. I didn't know."

He waved the list in the air. "Beulah, I've lived here for years and I've never even heard of half of these people. Who are they?"

"Friends of Miz Ophelia's, but I think most of 'em lives out of town and I mostly stayed in the kitchen in years past and never got acquainted with 'em. When Mr. Gordon was alive, it was a different story. Folks came from far and wide to attend the party. But last year, only about a dozen folks showed up. I tried to tell Miz Veezie, but she don't wanna believe it. She thinks they didn't come 'cause o' her. Preacher, she's just so down on herself."

"Point me to the drawing room, Beulah, and I'll see what I can do."

Chapter Twelve

Veezie lay face down on a settee. "Go away, Beulah," she squalled. "I told you I don't want to talk about it."

"It's not Beulah, Veezie."

She jerked her head up and quickly dabbed at her swollen eyes. "What are you doing here?"

He knelt beside the settee. "Is that any way to talk to your guest? I was under the impression you invited me to a party. Sorry, I'm late. I've been camping all week with my daughter, and just got back in town."

She sat up, but wouldn't look at him. "There ain't gonna be no party."

He reached and took her by the hand. "Oh, no you don't. You can't get by with that. You and I are going to have a party." He stuck his head out the door and called for Beulah. "Beulah, I'm starved. Would you mind setting a table for two in the garden? I saw the beautiful decorations when I drove up, but tell George the

Japanese lanterns must have gone out. If he'd be so kind as to light a string over our table, Miss Veezie and I would be most pleased."

Beulah's gold tooth glittered. "We'll take care of it right away, preacher. We'll have the food out in a jiffy."

Veezie buried her face in her hands. "Why are you doing this, preacher?"

"You can call me preacher on Sunday morning. But on the other six days of the week, why not call me by my name. My—"

"I know your name."

"Well, of course you do. But I was about to say my friends all call me 'Shep.'"

She dropped her hands and slowly lifted her head. "Well, what should the rest of us call you, preacher?"

He reached up and brushed a lock of hair from her face. "I was hoping I could count you among my friends. You invited me to your party. I take that as proof enough that we're friends."

"Humph! Don't prove nothing. I didn't invite my friends." She hung her head. "Well, 'cept for you and Harper. All the rest was my mama's friends."

His gaze locked with hers and his lip turned up at the corner. "So you admit that both Harper and I are counted among your friends. As a friend, I won't allow you to cancel a party just because some high-brow acquaintances of your mother's chose not to come. Frankly, I'm glad. I think we'll have more fun without them."

Beulah came to the door. "Preacher, yo' table is set up in the garden, but if you'll kindly 'scuse Miz Veezie, I 'spect she wants to take a few minutes to freshen her face and touch up her hair before dinner."

"I don't mind waiting. Take your time." He reached down and offered his hand to help Veezie off the settee.

Warmth spread through her when he squeezed her hand, but perhaps it was nothing more than an unintentional reflex.

Beulah whispered, "I'll meet you upstairs, sugar."

Veezie ambled up to her room, her emotions so jumbled she wondered if her mind was playing tricks, the way it happened before. She rubbed her temples. Was Shepherd Jackson really waiting for her in the drawing room?

Beulah's face beamed. "Sugar, that yellow linen looks right pretty on you, but it got a mite wrinkled with you wallowing around on a sofa. Quick, put on this one."

Veezie's eyes widened at the lavender chiffon tea-length gown, slung over Beulah's arm. She'd admired the dress from the first day she moved into Nine Gables. It was strapless, yet too sweet to look naughty. Veezie didn't claim to be an expert on what a lady wore, yet she was well versed on the naughty. And this wasn't it. "But ain't this a party dress?"

"Sho' is, but you having a party, sweetpea. Now hurry." Beulah helped Veezie into the gown and zipped it. "This here was Miz Harper's favorite party dress. She bought it in New Orleans for the debutante ball. But red was her color. Somehow, lavender never did look right on her and I told her so. But now, with your pretty blond hair, you was made to wear lavender." Beulah zipped her and turned her around. "Well, now if you ain't looking like a princess, I ain't never seen one."

Veezie tried to conceal her smile. "You ever seen a real live princess, Beulah?"

"Maybe not, but I reckon I know what one looks like, and you is it." She brushed out Veezie's hair and said, "Wait sugar. A little dab of lip rouge, and you'll be ready."

"Beulah, why you doing all this?"

"Why? I reckon 'cause he's such a nice fellow. He went to a lot of trouble to be here for a party and you ain't got no cause to disappoint him. Wouldn't be ladylike, and you always harping that you want to be looked upon like a lady. Now, you go on down and let him know you 'preciate him a coming. And sugar, let him do most of the talking."

Veezie started down the stairs and stopped midway when she saw Shep at the bottom, gazing up at her. She'd been looked at by men in the past, but no man had ever looked at her with such tenderness. Her knees crumpled beneath her and she grabbed hold of the rail to keep from falling. It wouldn't be long before word would spread about her tainted past. And when that happened, he'd never look at her the same way again. She turned, ran back up to her room and fell across her bed. "I can't do it, Beulah."

Beulah plopped down beside her and gently patted her on the back. "Now, honey, you dry them tears before you go and mess up yo' face again."

Veezie turned over and jerked her head up. "Beulah, it ain't right."

"What ain't right, sugar?"

"Me deceiving him like this. Acting like something I ain't."

"Why, you ain't deceivin' him. This is you, shug." Beulah picked up a hand mirror from off the bed and held it in front of Veezie's face. "Look at this pretty woman. This is who you is. You're on yo' way to being a real lady. And right now, you have a gentleman friend downstairs who's come a calling. A genu-ine lady wouldn't leave him standin'."

"But Beulah, you act like he's come a'courtin'. The only reason he's here is cause he got an invite. I never shoulda sent it. He's a preacher. He ain't interested in nobody like me."

"Maybe he is, maybe he ain't. He may be a preacher, but he's a man and he ain't blind. Love is like a rose, sugar. Ain't never seen one what started out in full bloom. But if you nip the bud before it has a chance to open, you ain't never gonna know how beautiful it coulda been."

"Humph. I've seen rosebuds that never opened. They just withered up and died, 'cause they was infested with bugs. That's like me, Beulah. I'm infested, and you know it. What's gonna happen when he learns about my past?"

Beulah's mouth flew open. "Yo past? Yo *past?* What past, sugar? You ain't got no past. God done slung them sins as far as the east is from the west. Remember? And me, nor you, nor the preacher and not even the man who picked you up coming from the juke joint can pull back what God's done got rid of. Now, we ain't got no business up here gabbing when you got a guest a waitin'. Git yourself back down them stairs. And when you git to the bottom, hold out your hand and in a low voice, say somethin' real sweet, like 'Sho hope I didn't keep you waitin' too long.'"

Veezie snubbed and with the back of her hand, she wiped the dampness from her upper lip. "I'll try."

Shep took one look at Veezie standing at the top of the stairs and his heart pounded. No woman since Jenny had been able to take his breath away. He was afraid to blink for fear the beautiful illusion would disappear. He took in the way her hair fell on bare shoulders. His gaze followed her as she slowly descended the stairs. The hair on the back of his neck bristled. Had he lost his sanity? She was young enough to be his daughter. He was still in love with his wife. He'd always thought of himself as having a sound mind, but suddenly all sense of logic seemed to have escaped through a hole in his head. He licked his dry lips.

She held out her hand. He took it in his and then shrank in embarrassment realizing his hand was sweaty and turned loose. Of course, it was sweaty. It was the end of May in Alabama. Why was he building this up to be more than it was? The only reason he was here was because Harper indicated the girl was depressed. That's why he came and it's why he stayed. Standing mute, like a pimple-faced kid on his first date, he glanced at his watch. Eleven-fifteen, yet he seemed strangely rejuvenated. Perhaps he'd gotten his second-wind. He tried to think of something to say, other than, "You look fabulous," but his mind went blank. He breathed a sigh when she spoke first.

Her moist eyes twinkled. "Hope you didn't get tired of waiting."

"Not tired at all." He extended his hand. "Shall we go to the garden?"

She nodded.

What was going on inside her head? Though he tried to deny it, Shep knew the thoughts taking place inside his, and it scared him to death. What was it about the girl that he found so fascinating? He ran his fingers through his hair and tried to assess the situation. *What I feel for her is nothing but . . . but pity.* Yes, that made perfect sense. Poor little backwoodsy creature trapped inside a beautiful body. Her education probably didn't exceed sixth grade. As a pastor and minister of the Gospel, his job was to convince her she had something to live for. But glancing around the grounds at Nine Gables made him wonder why she needed convincing.

Together, they walked toward the garden and when they reached the table for two, Shep pulled out her chair. George had placed a small lantern on the linen-draped table and the flattering glow from the flame would've made Mammy Yocum of Li'l Abner fame look good, but Veezie's exquisite features in the soft, flickering light made it difficult to draw his eyes away from her. When he did, he glanced at the kitchen window and gave a nervous chuckle at the sight of Beulah peeking out. When the nosey maid's eyes met his, she snatched the curtains together, though Shep had no doubt she'd find another venue.

George brought two plates filled with barbecue pork, baked beans and corn on the cob and set before them. "Thank you, George," Shep said. He unfolded his napkin and placed it in his lap.

Veezie wrung her hands.

He pretended not to notice. Truth be known, he wanted to wring his also. Shep prayed over the food and took a bite of the shredded pork. "Delicious."

She shrugged.

He turned his head and coughed in his hand. "George sure knows how to barbecue."

She nodded. "I guess." Her voice was so low, he could barely hear.

Why was she being so quiet? Perhaps this wasn't such a great idea. If only he could think of something clever to talk about. Clever? At the moment he'd settle for boring, but for the first time in his life, he seemed to be at a loss for words. He blotted the beads of sweat accumulating on his upper lip, with the back of his hand.

He glanced up at the kitchen window again. Now there were two faces. George and Beulah appeared to be fighting for a glimpse of what was taking place—or rather what was *not* taking place.

It was then that George came limping out with a basket full of fireworks. "It's almost midnight," he announced. "Preacher, if you and Miz Veezie will kindly follow me down to the lake, Beulah says it'll make a heap prettier sight, shooting 'em off over the water."

"Sounds like a great idea, George. Thank you." He stood to pull out Veezie's chair, but she shoved back and was on her feet before he had a chance.

The terrain was uneven. Would it be too awkward to reach for her hand? Simply for the purpose of protection, naturally. But what if she read more into it and thought he was being fresh? Absurd! He thrust his palm toward her. "May I hold your hand?" Rocks seemed to roll around in his stomach. "There are holes in the field. I wouldn't want you to fall." Would he expect a man—any man— to do less for Gracie? It had nothing to do with Veezie being a beautiful woman in the moonlight. He would've done the same if she were a wrinkled old lady with earlobes tickling her shoulders and snuff dripping from the corners of her mouth. As a gentleman, it was the right thing to do to protect a lady from falling.

She shrugged.

George pulled a blanket from the basket and spread it out on the lawn near the water. "Beulah said y'all gonna need a place to sit."

Shep gave a short nod. "That was very thoughtful. Thank you, George. And thank Beulah."

"Yessir." Hunched over with his left hand on his hip, the tall, lean, caretaker's dark face grimaced with every gouty step he took.

Shep waited for Veezie to sit. She plopped down on the blanket and pulled her knees up to her chest. She wrapped her arms around her legs, laced her fingers together and stared up into the heavens. Layers of lavender chiffon surrounded her on the blanket. What a striking portrait she made, with blond curls gracing her bare shoulders and the silvery moonlight illuminating her lovely face. He thought of telling her so, but the fear she might misinterpret his intentions gave him pause. What a silly thought. To Veezie, he was nothing more than a nice man. A nice *old* man. He winced. And a preacher, at that. He chewed the inside of his cheek and tried to sort out his feelings. Should he be pleased or dismayed that the notion of him having romantic thoughts would never enter her head?

Shep fiddled with his wedding band. It wasn't like him to get so stirred over nothing. The idea that he'd be interested in courting her would never cross Veezie's mind. And it shouldn't. Because he wasn't. So why did such absurd thoughts keep wedging their way into his head?

Plenty of older men at church complimented Gracie on her gorgeous looks and not once had he—nor did Gracie—ever suspect any of them of being forward or out-of-line. In fact, it made him quite proud when anyone paid his daughter compliments.

His purpose in being here was to lift Veezie's spirits and nothing else. What could lift a woman's spirits quicker than for a man to pay her a nice compliment? He'd do it.

George ambled away, walking nearer to the water's edge. He untied a canoe, and pushed off.

Shep held up flat palms. "Where's he going?"

"The island I reckon."

"Island?"

"Yeah. Mostly a small sandbar in the middle o' the lake, but I suppose that's where he's headin'."

He squinted. "I think you're right. I can see it, now."

George stepped out of the canoe onto a patch of land, holding the basket of fireworks. He placed the basket on the ground and Shep assumed he was trying to find something to light. Time seemed to drag. "I wonder what he's waiting on. Maybe he forgot the matches."

Veezie gave another shrug.

He twisted the napkin in his hands while trying to think of an appropriate compliment. Nothing too broad, yet he needed to be specific. Something that would make her feel as gorgeous as she looked. Maybe that's the word he should use. Gorgeous. No, that was a bit strong. Though it was true, he needed to tone it down. Beautiful? Still too bold. Lovely? *Yes, lovely.*

He flinched when she turned and caught him staring. He groped for a way to lead up to the compliment. "I was admiring all the stars. Look at them."

"Uh-huh."

He licked his lips. She didn't look impressed or depressed. She simply looked bored. He couldn't blame her. But Beulah knew

Veezie better than he did, and if indeed she was down in the dumps, he hoped it wouldn't take long for her to snap out of it. Exhaustion was causing him to have weird thoughts. He needed to get this done so he could go home and crawl under the covers. Shep sucked in a lungful of air. "Veezie?" He ran his fingers through his hair. "You look real good." The minute the words leaped from his lips, he wanted to draw them back. *Good? What happened to lovely? I'm such a rube.*

She mumbled, "Okay, I will."

He cocked his head so far, his ear almost rested on his right shoulder. "I beg your pardon?" Which one was from another planet? Him or her? "I'm sorry. What are you talking about?"

She threw up her hands. "You told me to look at the stars. So I did. Then when you said, 'Look real good,' I thought I missed something. So I scrooched my eyes and looked again, but I didn't see no difference."

"Never mind." He wiped his sweaty brow. If he ever got away from here, he'd never let himself get hooked into a similar situation again. Hooked? He wasn't hooked. He came because as a minister of the gospel, he was called to a situation where a young woman was suspected of being suicidal.

Why was George taking his time? How long did it take to light a bottle rocket? He squirmed, ashamed for not having sympathetic feelings but even more ashamed for having impure thoughts. Impure? Were they? Maybe not for some men. But he wasn't just any man. He was a married man of God. Even though Jenny was dead, in his heart he was still as married as the day he put a ring on her third finger, left hand.

A whistling sound blared, breaking through the silence and the whole sky lit up in an electrifying display of color.

Veezie's head tilted toward the sky. "Oh, look! Ain't that pretty?"

With her distracted by the blast of sparks against the dark sky, the tension eased and no longer did conversation seem so vital. He gazed at her silhouette. "Very pretty," he whispered,

After the fireworks' grand finale, Shep stood and helped lift Veezie from the ground. They walked back toward the big house, but this time he didn't offer his hand.

"Veezie, you've been very quiet, tonight. Is something bothering you that you'd like to talk about?"

"Nope."

"That's fine. I understand. I realize I haven't said much, either. But I'm not always like this."

"Only when you're with someone like me. Right?"

His mouth dropped. "No. No, you have it all wrong. It has nothing at all to do with you." Guilt jerked at his conscience. *Really? Nothing at all?* Knowing she waited for an explanation— and knowing he couldn't lie, he rolled the words around in his head before answering.

"I've been roughing it for several days in the Georgia Mountains, and drove all day to get home. I think it's understandable that an ol' fellow like me would be tired. Maybe you and I can try this again sometime when I'm rested."

She jerked her head around. "You mean it?" Her face lit up for the first time all night.

What did he say to bring about such a change? "Uh . . . sure. Why not?" He could think of a dozen reasons to answer his why nots.

"You ain't, you know."

"I don't understand."

"You said you was an old man. You ain't old. Least I don't think of you that way."

He smiled and walked her to the door. "Thank you for inviting me to your party. It was a lovely evening."

"No, it wasn't. I was a bore."

He smiled. "It's never boring to be in the company of a beautiful lady. Good night, Veezie."

Shepherd walked out to his car and drove away at twelve-forty-five. Holding the steering wheel with his left hand, he ran his right hand over his left shoulder and massaged the aching muscle. He hadn't intended to stay so late. But it was all in the line of duty. What kind of pastor would he be if he wasn't available when called upon in a crisis situation? Maybe the next mission the Lord chose for him would be easier than this one. Going into the jungles of Africa would be less frightening.

What was it about Veezie Harrington that scared him so?

Chapter Thirteen

A few hours rest proved to be all Shep needed to clear his foggy head.

He tucked his shirt into his slacks and walked into the kitchen. Though he couldn't forget the events of the previous night, he'd file it away as a learning experience. It was the first time since Jenny died that he'd looked upon a woman—any woman—as desirable. A hot flush rose to his cheeks. So he noticed. So what? He was a man before he was a preacher. And she was one of God's magnificent creations. There was no harm in recognizing beauty. It wasn't as if he was a college kid on the prowl, because he wasn't. He was a mature man—the father of a woman not much younger than Veezie Harrington.

The smell of country ham filled his nostrils.

"Good morning, Daddy." Gracie reached up and with the back of her hand, wiped sweat from her forehead. Standing over the stove with Jenny's white apron on, she'd never looked more like her mother than at that moment.

He leaned over and pecked her on the cheek as she cracked another egg in a large crockery bowl. "My beautiful daughter, you'll make some man a good wife one day, but I pray it isn't anytime soon."

She giggled. "You have nothing to worry about." She fanned her hands in his face. "Shoo! Go sit on the porch. I'll call you when breakfast is ready."

The conversation during breakfast was minimal. Not only was Gracie like her mother in looks and personality, but she had a way of sensing when he was troubled, even when he tried hard to pretend otherwise. But there was one big difference between his wife and his daughter. With Jenny, he could always share his intimate thoughts. Of course, if his wife had lived, he wouldn't be having these troubling thoughts.

Gracie's voice drew him back. "Daddy, I didn't get home until twelve-fifteen last night. I was surprised not to find you here. I thought you were going to bed. Where were you?"

Shep bristled. "That almost sounded like an accusation, as if you think I was out carousing around."

"Daddy! I wasn't accusing you of anything." She cackled. "What a ridiculous notion. The thought of you carousing, as you put it, would never enter my mind." Gracie smeared fig preserves on a biscuit and handed the Mason jar to her daddy. "I didn't mean to be nosey. You seem worried and I thought maybe you might want to talk about it."

"I'm sorry, sweetie. Didn't mean to snap at you. I'm a little edgy from lack of sleep. I received a call last night that someone was in trouble and needed my help."

Her brow lifted. "I thought as much. Who was it?"

Shep's muscles tensed. "A woman who recently moved to Flat Creek."

"What was the problem?"

"I'd rather not say, sweetheart. Some things a pastor must keep confident." He ran his hand through his hair. *Confident—or hidden?* Changing the subject, he said, "Did you have fun last night?"

"We had a swell time. The whole gang was there."

"I'm glad, honey. Enjoy these years. They'll pass quickly and before you know it, you'll be as old as your ol' man."

"Daddy, I won't mind getting old if I can manage it as gracefully as you. You look great for your age."

For my age? He squirmed. Why should he be surprised that his daughter thought of him as a relic?

Gracie took a bite of toast. "Daddy, someone at the party said Harper Harrington was cut out of her mother's will and forced to move away with little more than the clothes on her back. Do you know anything about it?"

"I've heard various versions. Many people in Flat Creek have vivid imaginations."

"I heard a girl from the sticks moved in and took over the whole shebang. They say . . ."

"*They* say?" The hairs on the back of his neck bristled. "Took over? You make it sound as if something illegal took place. Maybe you shouldn't listen to the town gossips, Gracie. And furthermore, I'm surprised to hear you speak of someone coming from 'the sticks' as if that somehow makes her a lesser individual."

"Sorry, Daddy, I was merely repeating what I heard. I'm sure there's not more than a grain of truth in all the talk. It sounds too illogical to be true." She shrugged. "But, jeepers, it's nothing to me. I didn't mean to rile you."

His jaw flinched. "Rile me? That's silly. I'm not riled. I simply don't understand why people want to start rumors about someone they don't really know. She's a very nice person."

"So you know the girl?"

"Yes. We've met. And she's not a girl. She's a woman." Shep cringed. What made him make such a numbskull remark? Feeling the blood rush to his face, he stood and picked up his tray. "I enjoyed the breakfast. I think I'll go inside and study."

Gracie put her hand over her mouth and chuckled. "If I didn't know better, I'd think—never mind."

"What?"

"Nothing, Daddy. It was a silly thought. You'd laugh hysterically if I told you what just ran through my mind."

And you'd laugh even harder, if you knew what just ran through mine.

Chapter Fourteen

Veezie trudged into the kitchen. "Beulah, why you reckon he ain't called? You don't suppose he's sick, do you? Think maybe I ought to check on him?"

"No, sugar. It ain't yo place." Beulah continued shelling a mess of Little Lady Finger Peas in a porcelain dishpan sitting in her lap—the first pickings of the season. She snapped as many as she shelled, but Veezie didn't mind, since she was partial to peas with lots of snaps, anyway.

Beulah stopped and rubbed her chin as if pondering a deep thought. "I don't mean to drown yo' hopes, chile, by throwing dirty dish water on 'em, but to tell the truth, this all seems mighty sudden to me. You sure you ain't just wishing and a hoping the preacher is sweet on you? Not that I was spying or nothin' but at times I happened to be in eye-range last night and I didn't see a whole lot going on betwixt the two of you."

"What's the matter?" Veezie's teeth ground together. "You think I ain't good enough for him? Well, maybe I ain't. But I can be. And you gonna help me, Beulah. You done promised."

"Course I is. You gonna be good enough. You is gonna be a real lady, and one day some fine man is gonna take notice. But it'll take time, shug. I don't want you setting yourself up for a letdown. I worry about you. That's all."

"Beulah, I know how you feel. I thought the same way while we sat watching the fireworks. I couldn't even talk to him, 'cause I thought he felt sorry for me, being as how I didn't have nobody to show up for my party. And they ain't nothing I hate worse'n pity. But you should've heard the sweet things he said right before he left." A blush heated her face at the mere thought of such romantic words coming from the lips of Shep Jackson. "He was smitten, Beulah. Ain't no doubt about it."

Beulah ran her hands through the peas, picking out the blights. Without looking up, she said, "If you don't mind telling, exactly what *did* the preacher say, sugar, to make you think he is took with you?"

"Ah, Beulah, I don't mind telling you. Fact of the matter, I like dwelling on it. Here's the way it went." She muffled a giggle with her hand. "Me and him walked to the door, and he said he was dog-tired, being as how he'd been on the road all day. But it t'weren't so much what he said but the way he looked at me Beulah, when he said, real sweet like, 'Me and you gonna try this again sometime when I ain't so tired.'"

The furrow remained on Beulah's brow. "He wanted to try it again, did he? So what did you say to that?"

"I said, 'You mean it?' I was pretty sure he did by the look in his eyes." A long sigh escaped her lips. "Oh my lands, you shoulda seen his face. That man was swallowin' me whole."

Beulah frowned. "I don't want to hear no vulgar talk. Git on with what he said when you asked him if he meant it."

"Yeah, that's the good part. He looked at me like a kid eyeing stick candy, and it's the honest truth." She flinched. "Sorry, Beulah. But would you say it's vulgar if I tell you he was practically drooling when he gave me his answer?"

"I declare, chile, if you don't beat all. You ain't gotta draw me no pictures. I just wanna know what he said."

"Well, it was so good I ain't wanting to rush it. Instead of plowing through it with a team o' mules, I rather give it to you slow, like digging a garden row with a spoon."

"For crying out loud, I ain't got time for yo' silly dilly-dallyin'. I got—"

"Okay." Her shoulders slumped. "He said, 'Why not?' That's exactly what he said when I asked if he meant it. 'Why not?'"

Beulah's frown weakened. She massaged her forehead with her thumb and two fingers. "I see. Well, it sho' sounds like he mighta been took with you, all right."

"I know it's hard to believe, Beulah. It was for me too, at first. But it was wrote all over his face. If only he woulda told me earlier how he felt, I coulda told him I was crazy about him, too. But how was I to know someone like the Reverend Shepherd Jackson would give a frog's eye about me."

A sudden memory caused Veezie to grimace. Why did Adolphus' face have to appear every time she started to feel good about herself? If only he wasn't a member of Flat Creek Church. Her chest heaved.

Beulah stood and picked up the pan of peas. "Well maybe the preacher does give a flip and maybe he don't, but I ain't got time to sit around trying to figure it out. You get on outta here and find somethin' to occupy yo' time. I got chores to do."

"But they ain't nothin' for me to do here, Beulah. Why don't you let me help you with the wash? I like being with you."

Beulah's face wrinkled up like a prune. "Cause it ain't fitting that's why. What would folks say if'n they drove past and saw a rich little white gal like you, standing over an old iron pot with a scrub board in her hand?"

"Beulah, you tell me to pay no mind to what folks say, and now you say I ought to worry. Which is it?"

Beulah swatted Veezie on her backside. "Stop jabbering and find you something to do, girl. With all them books sittin' in the library, go git you something to read. Miz Harper spent hours with her head stuck in a book. It's what uppity ladies do and you always harpin' on wanting to be a real lady. Now git!"

Veezie grumbled as she ambled down the long hallway toward the library, a large room with rich pine paneling. Two walls were lined from floor to ceiling with shelves of beautiful, leather-bound books. Since it seemed everything worth taking was always out of her reach, Veezie climbed the ladder and slid a bright red book from its resting place on the top shelf. It was neither the thickest nor the thinnest, but it happened to be the one directly in front of her. Besides, a book with a red cover was bound to be more interesting than a dull, brown book.

Descending the ladder, she trudged over to the damask-covered settee near the window. Sprawled out on the French provincial furniture, Veezie opened the book and read the author's name. Nathanial Hawthorne. She'd never heard of him, but with such a romantic-sounding name, the book was bound to be more interesting than a story written by a man with such a simple name as Mark Twain. Even the title, *The Scarlet Letter*, stirred her interest, as she imagined a story about a passionate love letter written on perfume-scented, scalloped-edged, flaming red stationary with a gold monogram at the top. Maybe she'd send Shep a scarlet letter one day soon.

The lovely thought soon vanished. Barely into the second chapter, and feeling dreadfully sorry for the main character, Veezie caught a tear oozing down her cheek. She wanted to stop reading, but she had to know what happened next because this could be the story of *her* life. She could be Hester Prynne. Veezie sniffed as she pictured all the accusing eyes staring at the young woman as she buried her face in shame.

Her hands trembled as she read the following lines: "People say," said another, "that the Reverend Master Dimmesdale, her godly pastor, takes it very grievously to heart that such a scandal should have come upon his congregation."

Veezie slammed the book shut with a bang, flung it to the floor and then stormed out of the library. What a horrible story. She walked out to the porch, sat in the swing and tried to empty her mind of the image of poor Hester, with the townspeople glaring as she clutched her baby next to the bold red letter on her breast.

The haunting words from the Scarlet Letter blared in Veezie's head, like a warped record on a turned up Victrola. She sucked a heavy puff of air into her lungs and slowly exhaled. Would the Reverend Shepherd Jackson take it grievously to heart if her scandalous past should become known to *his* congregation? The notion of wearing the letter "A" embroidered across her breast sent prickles up her spine. Veezie groaned. Why was she tormenting herself? Beulah said not dredge up the past. God forgot it. She had to forget it, too.

But what about Adolphus? He hadn't forgotten. What if he blabbed? He had as much to lose as she did. He couldn't tell. Not now.

Veezie walked into the church early Sunday morning, even before the deacon rang the big bell in the vestibule. She sat on the right side of the aisle, hoping Marcy would choose to sit on the left, where they sat last week when Adolphus walked in feeling poorly.

Seemed most regular church-going folks generally adopted a favorite pew. Veezie wanted to adopt one as far away from the Adolphus Woodham family as she could get.

She wrung her hands until her knuckles ached. She needed to stop fretting over Adolphus and dwell on more pleasant things—such as the tender look on Shep's face when he walked her to the door. Regardless of what Beulah thought, his interest wasn't something she dreamed up. It was real and Veezie had relived it over a thousand times in her mind, the way he said, "Thank you for inviting me to your party. It was a lovely evening." His eyes sparkled and deep dimples caved into his cheeks, and then he said, "It's never boring to be in the company of a beautiful lady." He talked so proper. She had to learn how to talk like a lady, so she wouldn't embarrass him in front of folks. Beulah would teach her all she needed to know.

Veezie turned when someone from behind nudged her on the shoulder. An attractive lady in her mid-thirties smiled and extended her hand over the back of the pew.

"Hello, my name is Rachel Crawford and this is my friend, Marie. I don't believe we've met."

Veezie reached over and shook her hand. "Veezie Harrington's the name and I'm mighty pleased to meet both of you."

Marie raised an eyebrow. "Harrington, you say? Are you the girl Mrs. Gordon Harrington . . . well, what I meant was . . ."

Veezie shrugged. "It ain't no secret. Yeah, I'm the one she gave away. But I'm back where I belong, now."

"I'm sorry. I didn't mean for it to sound so rude."

"Don't matter. I reckon they ain't no other way to say it."

Pleased that the two ladies seemed to want to make her acquaintance, yet eager to turn around and face the front in time to see Shep walk through the door, Veezie wrung her hands, trying to imagine how Beulah would advise her to handle the predicament.

Before she could come up with an answer, Rachel said, "Well, if Mrs. Harrington had any inkling that you'd turn out to be such a beautiful young lady, she wouldn't have taken a million dollars for you. The joke was on her."

Veezie's jaw dropped. What if she'd turned her back and missed the best compliment anyone had ever paid her? She wanted to crawl over that pew and hug Rachel Crawford. "That's the sweetest thing anybody's ever said to me, Mrs. Crawford. You're a mighty nice lady."

"Please, call me Rachel. And it's the truth. Welcome to Flat Creek Fellowship Church, Veezie. We have a wonderful pastor. Have you visited before?"

Veezie nodded. "Yeah, I been a couple o' times."

"Well, I'm glad you've come. I've been away for several weeks."

Veezie thanked her and turned to face the front. What a grand day this turned out to be. The anticipation of waiting for Shep to enter, combined with the thrill of hearing someone say such nice things about her, made her day.

In the stillness, she heard Shep's name mentioned in the conversation taking place behind her. With her back pressed firmly against the pew, Veezie expected to hear nothing but glowing words coming from such nice ladies. She almost wanted to turn back around and get in on a discussion having to do with her favorite subject.

"Shep came by twice this week," Rachel said. "We've decided to try and work things out."

A hard knot formed in Veezie's stomach. She brushed her hand across her lips. There had to be an explanation. It wasn't the way it sounded. But her shoulders slumped when Marie said, "Oh, I'm so happy for you, Rachel. You two are perfect together."

Veezie couldn't breathe. Needed air. Fiddling with the buttons on her blouse, she unbuttoned the top two, though Beulah surely wouldn't have approved. Drawing a deep breath, she sucked air into her deflated lungs and exhaled in time to hear Rachel's response.

"He's wonderful, Marie. I don't know what I'd do without him. And to think we almost broke up."

Veezie held her hand tightly over her mouth to trap the groaning pushing to come out. But who could she blame? Not Rachel and not Shep. Marie was right. They'd make a perfect pair. Rachel was beautiful, sweet and a real classy lady. The kind of wife a church would want for their pastor. And he was everything a woman could want in a man. There was no one to blame but herself. She should've known better than to think she could land a big fish like Shepherd Jackson. He was too good for her.

When the pianist struck the first chord, Veezie stood and slipped out the door, without waiting for Shep to enter.

For no particular reason, or at least none that she was aware of, she headed the car toward Goose Hollow, and wound up in front of her old church. A small clapboard building with plain windows, a tall steeple and a bell. That was as fancy as it got. It wasn't a fine brick building like the one at Flat Creek Fellowship, but it was beautiful in a simple sort of way. She walked up the steps and peered through the open door. Everything looked the same. Same pews, with slats too far apart to be comfortable. The congregation was singing *Peace like a River* and old man Jonesy Jimmerson could still belt out the bass when they got to the words '*wonderful, wonderful peace.*' She was glad the people were standing, since it made it less noticeable when she slipped in.

She trudged down the aisle, and when five-year-old Lucas saw her, a half-moon smile flashed across his dimpled face. He punched Harper, who turned to look. Harper whispered to Flint, and they all shifted down the pew and motioned for Veezie to sit with them.

Veezie had almost forgotten how beautiful Harper was. Even in a plain calico dress and with her long, black hair pushed away from her face in a simple sort of a way, she was still quite a looker.

Charlie Yancey, Veezie's former pastor, who knew her well when she lived in Goose Hollow but loved her anyway, spotted her in the sparse crowd. His gait was much slower than when she saw him last, but he finally reached her pew.

Wrapping his feeble arms around her, he said, "Good to have you, home, Veezie."

She choked back the tears as he ambled up to the podium, holding tightly to the rail. The congregation sang the first and third verses of *Bringing in the Sheaves*.

Veezie's body jerked with sobs that couldn't be quenched. Harper held her tightly and whispered, "What's wrong, sweetie?"

"Brother Charlie," . . . she snubbed, "welcomed me home."

"Well, of course he did. We all welcome you back."

"But I ain't got no home, Harper. Not in Goose Hollow. Not at Nine Gables."

The singing stopped and Harper whispered, "You're coming with us after church. We need to spend time together and talk."

Veezie nodded and dried her eyes. Harper didn't seem surprised that Veezie didn't feel at home at Nine Gables. Was it because she understood? Had she never felt at home there, either? It was a beautiful, humongous house with elaborate furnishings—but it wasn't a home.

Five-year-old Lucas scrambled over and crawled in Veezie's lap. All through the sermon, she could feel his little eyes staring up at her. Occasionally, he'd reach up and pat her cheek, ever so gently. He cupped his hand over her ear and whispered. "I still love you, Veezie even if you're not my sister, anymore."

Veezie gave him a squeeze. She glanced down the pew and couldn't deny a tinge of jealousy, seeing Harper cradling Callie in her arms. If she could live her life over, she'd stay home on Saturday nights and look after the kids, instead of traipsing off to juke-joints and leaving them with a drunken father and a mother who was incapable of taking care of herself, much less three helpless children. But it was too late for regrets.

Flint and Harper's new house beside the clinic was a neat little white bungalow with dark green shutters. Clay pots lined the porch with all sorts of pretty flowers—petunias, geraniums, and some that Veezie couldn't name. A little red wagon was in the neatly swept yard. It was the perfect picture of a happy home.

The smell of roast beef cooked with carrots, onions and potatoes greeted them as they entered the house. Two bib aprons hung on a nail beside the kitchen sink. Harper slipped one over her head and handed the other to Veezie, along with a knife and a bowl of fresh vegetables to cut up for salad.

Grease popped and sizzled as Harper poured a few cups of fine-ground cornmeal from Mr. Pollard's grist mill into a large green bowl. She mixed the white meal with water and a little salt, shaped the pones with her hands and quickly dropped them into the hot iron skillet.

Flint reached for a mitt and a hot pad and lifted the roasting pan from the oven, then called for Jim to get a bowl of butterbean dumplings and a pecan pie from the Hoosier cabinet, which Harper had prepared before leaving for church.

Veezie's mouth watered. It wasn't hard to guess that Harper spent a great deal of time in the kitchen with Beulah, while growing up. Even the golden-fried cornbread rivaled Beulah's. Fifteen-year-old Jim pulled out a chair for her to sit at the table.

"Have a seat, sis."

Sis? She glanced at Harper and wondered if it made her jealous for Jim to still think of her as his sister.

Jim's nose crinkled. "Lucas and I are outnumbered. We now have three sisters. You, Harper and little Callie."

Harper looked over at Veezie and winked. Her smile gave evidence that there was no room for jealousy in her heart. Instead, she appeared to be proud of Jim.

After asking God's blessings upon the food, Flint passed the roast to Veezie. "You look great, kiddo. I hardly recognized you when you walked into the church."

"Thank you." She forked a slice of roast and passed it. "I reckon I can thank Beulah if I look different. She's done real good at learning me how to dress and now she's working on learning me how to talk proper. She's gonna make a lady out of me."

Flint gave a quick shrug. "Good for you. We should always strive to better ourselves."

Veezie dipped out a hefty portion of butterbean dumplings. "Beulah's learnt me a lot. I don't even say t'weren't no more."

Jim smiled and glanced toward Harper who must've understood what he wanted before he had a chance to say anything, because she grabbed a piece of cornbread and poked it toward his mouth.

After dinner, Harper picked up Callie who'd fallen asleep in her high chair. "Veezie, as soon as I put the baby to bed, you and I will go sit on the porch and catch up."

Veezie's lip trembled. *The baby.* She knew Harper referred to three-year-old Callie. But Veezie couldn't help thinking that if she hadn't been so stubborn and refused to cuddle her little girl, perhaps Harper would be putting another baby to sleep today. Regardless of what Beulah said, Veezie knew she killed that baby as sure as if she'd poked arsenic down its little throat. The thought sent shivers down her back. "You go ahead, Harper and do what you need to do. I'll clean up the kitchen."

Jim stood and grinned. "No you won't. That's *my* job."

Veezie's eyes widened. "Your job? Since when?"

He glanced down at the floor. "Since I stayed out past curfew on Memorial Day."

Though he was not her brother, she was proud of Harper and Flint for doing such a good job raising him. A short while ago, he was on the road to becoming a hoodlum, but it seemed almost overnight he'd turned into a fine young fellow. He must've grown six inches since she saw him last. No doubt he got his height from Monroe. Veezie prayed that was all he got from his wayward father. "I'll help you, Jim."

Flint smiled. "No, you don't, Veezie. No one helped him slip in the house at eleven-thirty, Monday night."

Jim had a sheepish look on his face. "But it was Memorial Day and even the girls at the party got to stay out later than I did."

Veezie lifted her shoulders and giggled. "Well, I reckon that's reason enough for me to help him, since I stayed out later'n that." She quickly picked up on the disgusted look on Flint's face. "It ain't what you think, Flint."

"And how do you know what I'm thinking?"

"You're thinking I'm up to my ol' tricks of hanging out at jukes. But you're wrong. You want to know where I was?"

He shrugged. "You don't owe me an explanation."

"Maybe not, but I want you to know. I ain't . . . I mean, I haven't been to a juke since leaving here. Hadn't wanted to go, neither. Flint. Didn't I tell you about Beulah praying with me and asking the Lord to take my sins and throw 'em as far as the East is from the West? Well He did, and I ain't got no reason to doubt it. Beulah says I'm justified. Just if I'd never done them things. I bet a year ago, you wouldn't have believed I could change, but I did. I'm not the Veezie you used to know."

Harper walked back into the room, with a pie in her hands. "Veezie, I overheard and I'm so proud of you. Have you met new friends in Flat Creek, who've had an influence on you?"

"I reckon you might say I have." Eager to tell Harper about last Monday night, Veezie assumed her best friend would be pleased that a fine, upstanding man of the highest caliber spent time with her and called her beautiful. And if he wasn't already spoken for, Veezie had no doubt he would've been knocking on her door last week. He was smitten with her, and she knew it.

Harper sliced the pecan pie and served the plates. "Maybe I know this new friend who has you smiling. What's her name?"

"Ain't no *her*. And you know him, all right." Veezie bit her lip to hide the smile. "It's Shep Jackson."

Harper dropped her fork and shot a disapproving look toward her husband.

The warmth in the room quickly dropped to a shivering low.

Chapter Fifteen

Veezie's heart sank. It was evident that Harper and Flint not only disapproved of her hanging out with the preacher, but they appeared horror-struck.

Harper took a deep swallow of iced tea and almost spit it across the table. "*You*? And Brother Jackson? Are you serious?"

"Is that so terrible?"

"Oh, I didn't mean it the way it must have sounded. Brother Jackson's a fine man and a great pastor. It's—well, I don't know how to say it."

She didn't have to say it. Veezie knew what she meant. Harper found it impossible to believe that any decent man, especially a man like Shep, could have feelings for an ill-bred hick like her.

The skin around Harper's eyes tightened. "Veezie, there's something I find a bit peculiar. You call him Shep?"

"Does that upset you?" She stiffened, expecting an affirmative response.

"Upset me? Well, no, but he was my pastor when I lived at

Nine Gables and I know him well—and yet, I wouldn't think of calling him by his given name."

Harper glanced toward Flint as if hoping for backup, but with his head hung low, he didn't appear to want to enter into the discussion. Harper picked up her napkin and dabbed at her lips. "Veezie, I don't mean to be critical, but perhaps it would sound more respectful if you'd refer to the preacher in a more formal manner. The parishioners call him Brother Jackson."

Veezie's hopes plummeted. "Oh, I understand. You think because I'm white trash, folks might get the wrong idea, if a little floozy is on a first name basis with their preacher?" She flung her napkin on the table and grabbed her glass of tea, when it wobbled. "I thought you'd be happy for me, Harper."

"Oh, sweetie, I can see I've upset you, and that wasn't my intent. But I know how much you want to make a good impression, and I'm only trying to help you. It seems you're being a bit too familiar. A nickname is reserved for close friends and family and a man of the reverend's distinction should be given due respect."

Bumfuzzled by Harper's peculiar attitude, Veezie shrugged. "I meant no disrespect. It was his idea for me to call him that."

Harper's brow lifted. Whether from surprise or disbelief, Veezie didn't know.

"I wasn't implying you did anything wrong, Veezie. It's just . . . well, why don't you and I go sit on the porch and talk? I'm interested in knowing how the friendship came about."

Veezie pushed her chair back, stomped out to the porch and

plopped down in the swing.

Harper pulled up a metal glider. Her eyes squinted into tiny slits. "Now, tell me how you came to know Brother Jackson so well?"

After viewing the displeasure in Harper's eyes, Veezie was no longer sure she wanted to share her thoughts. But other than Shep, Harper and Flint were the only friends she had left, now that she'd cut herself off from the people who frequented the Silver Slipper. She held her head back and closed her eyes, as if trying to remember, although she recalled quite well, every hour, every minute, every second spent in his presence. "Harper, you remember when you called the preacher and asked him to pray for me?"

She nodded, approvingly. "And I knew he would. He's a real prayer warrior."

"Well, that Sunday after church, he came up to my room and stood in the doorway and he prayed for me, just like you asked."

Harper's eyes widened. "Oh, Veezie. I'm so sorry. I didn't mean for him to make a visit. I only asked him to remember you in prayer. I was concerned about you. I don't suppose I said it, but I thought he understood you weren't ready to receive visitors. I feel terrible."

Veezie shrugged. "No harm done."

"So that's how you came to know him."

"No. That ain't when it happened. I was all wrapped up in my troubles the day he came by and being as how I couldn't get past the pain, I wouldn't even look at him." She grinned. "I reckon if I'd had any inkling he was so good looking, I would've stared him down. But he didn't tarry. Just prayed and left."

"I see. So how *did* you get to know him?"

"Well, first time I laid eyes on him—I mean *really* saw him for the first time—was two days later at Bullard's store when I went to buy material. He was standing next to the counter and he tipped his hat at me."

Harper squinted. "That was it?"

"No. There's more." Veezie only paused because she wanted it to sink in that a man looked at her and tipped his hat. "I didn't recognize him, of course, but he told me who he was and he invited me to his church. Said he was glad I was doing better."

"That was nice of him."

"Oh, he was real nice. But then something awful happened, Harper."

Her brow formed a vee. "What?"

"Well, I don't want you feeling bad, 'cause I know you had a good excuse . . . but only three people showed up for my party and when they saw weren't nobody else coming, they upped and left. Didn't eat nothing. Didn't wait for the fireworks. Just upped and left."

Harper winced.

"Well, I wanted to die. And it wasn't the first time I ever thought about it, but this time I was ready to do it. The idea of everybody laughing at me, talking behind my back was killing me.

But then he showed up and everything changed. He was late 'cause he'd been camping all week. And you know what? Even though he was dog-tired, he come right on over, soon as he could."

"Veezie, I don't want you to misunderstand what I'm about to say, but I hope you aren't letting yourself fall in love with him. I'd hate to see you hurt."

Veezie lifted her shoulders. "Hurt? Why do you think he'd want to hurt me?"

"I'm not saying he'd want to. But I'm afraid you're so vulnerable after all you've been through, that you might misunderstand compassion for love. Even if the two of you had anything at all in common, which I don't suppose you do, the vast difference in your ages would make it impossible for a real romantic relationship to develop. But I'm sure you realize that."

She bristled. "You're wrong, Harper. Age ain't got nothin' to do with true love."

Harper raised one eyebrow. "True love?" Her lip curled, slightly, but not so slight that Veezie didn't catch on.

"Well, I can see you don't believe me, but it coulda been love, if only—"

"Go on."

"Ain't no doubt in my mind that he was taken with me, but I found out this morning him and his girlfriend been broke up and now they gonna work things out. I won't lie to ya, it hurts—but I reckon it's for the best."

Harper let out a sigh. "I agree, Veezie, and I'm glad you see it that way."

"But Harper, if he hadn't already found him somebody, something in his eyes told me it would've worked between us. A spark was there that me and him coulda lit into a flaming hot fire."

Harper blushed and then stammered, "One day the right man will come along, Veezie. One near your own age. One you can relate to."

Veezie stood. "It ain't the age difference that bothers you, is it Harper?"

"What do you mean?"

Her lip quivered. "Saying all that stuff about finding me somebody I can relate to, boils down to the fact you don't think I'm good enough for him."

"That's not true."

"Yeah, it is. And you'd be right in thinking it." She walked over and leaned against the porch post. "Because truth is, I *ain't* good enough. But it don't keep me from wishing I was. That's the only reason I'm not aiming to fight for him, though Shep Jackson's a man worth fighting for. But I met his girlfriend at church today and she's a real fine lady—the kind o' woman he deserves." She shrugged. "I want him to have the best, and she's it."

"Oh, Veezie, you're sweet. Trust me, you're doing the right thing by not pursuing him. I knew his wife, Mrs. Jenny. I've never known two people to be so in love. They were compatible in every way. Be patient and one day you'll find someone with common interests, and that's important for a relationship to thrive."

Tears came to her eyes. She stood and bit her quivering lip. "I'll go in and fetch my hat and pocket book, then mosey on towards the house. Thank you for dinner. It was real good."

Harper's brow furrowed. "I can see I've hurt you. I'm sorry. I didn't mean to."

Veezie swallowed the pain. "I know you didn't. Bye, Harper."

"Please don't rush off, Veezie. Why not wait until Lucas and Callie wake from their naps? They'll want to tell you bye."

She shook her head. "Kiss 'em for me and tell 'em I had to get home. Will ya?"

"Of course." Harper walked over and hugged her tightly, though Veezie pulled away.

Sunday after church, Shep shook hands with the congregation as they filed out of the sanctuary. After the last couple walked out the door, he glanced up at the darkening sky and decided to pull down the windows in case of a cloud burst. Hearing the sound of a ladies high heel shoes on the wood floor, he tugged at a jammed window and said, "You'd better wait for me in the car, honey. I have a few things to take care of before we leave, and you may get wet if you wait. Looks like we're in for a downpour."

"Well, how sweet of you."

Shep jerked around. "Rachel! I thought you were Gracie."

"Now how did I know that? Maybe, the affectionate term, 'honey,' gave it away." Her eyes twinkled when she laughed.

She had such a sweet laugh. Not boisterous, not cackling, but almost melodious, like birds singing in harmony. Shep reached out and took her hands in his. "Oh, Rachel. I'm glad you stayed. I was hoping we could talk." He winked. "Happy?"

"Oh, Shep, I'm happier than I've been in years. You're wonderful."

"You keep saying sweet things like that and we may stay here until we both get wet."

"You don't know how much you mean to me," she said.

"So things are good?"

"Very good. I almost made a serious mistake and had it not been for your wise counsel, I would have. But I did what you said. I agreed to go away with him Friday night and listen to his side, without interruption. We drove to Long Beach near Panama City, and over dinner he explained how the whole mess happened. The account in the paper was inaccurate."

Shep grinned. "Didn't I tell you? I knew there had to be a mistake."

"It wasn't Rob that night. His brother had taken our car and it was Hugh who had the accident, not Rob. And the woman in the car was Hugh's date."

"I knew there had to be an explanation, Rachel. The man is crazy about you. But how did Rob's name wind up in the paper?"

"Hugh has never been the reliable sort. His license had expired and when he had the accident he pulled Rob's license from the glove compartment and handed to the police. And that's how the mix-up happened. I almost lost a wonderful man because I was too stubborn to give him a chance to explain. I'll never doubt him again."

Shep looked around. "I was hoping to see him with you this morning. Has he not moved back in?"

She beamed. "Yes, he's back where he belongs. I missed him so. The baby's teething and he stayed home with her this morning." She laughed. "Little Lucy is crazy about her daddy. I don't know which of the two missed the other the most. But Rob insisted I come and thank you for getting our family back together."

"I'm glad I could help, Rachel. Rob's a good man. You two are perfect together."

"That's funny. Marie said the same thing this morning."

Gracie waited for her Daddy in the station wagon. "Who was the lady you were talking to?"

"Name's Mrs. Rachel Crawford."

"She's very attractive. I noticed there was no man with her and she waited a long time for everyone to leave. Seems to me she wanted to be alone with you." She winked. "Is there something you'd like to share with me, Daddy?"

"Gracie, I'm her pastor, for crying out loud. Not her boyfriend. I met with her for counseling last week and she wanted to thank me for getting her and her husband back together. And that's all there was to it, little Miss Romantic."

"Well, who was the young woman sitting in front of her?"

Shep shrugged. "I don't remember seeing anyone on the pew in front of her. Her friend Marie sat beside her."

"No, before the choir came in, there was a pretty young woman sitting all alone. I've never seen her before. I wondered if you'd met her."

"Gracie, sweetheart, don't you ever quit? I told you to give it up. Why can't you understand that I don't need a woman? I've had the best. The memory of your mother will last me a lifetime. So stop riding that horse, will you?"

Gracie giggled. "No, you misunderstood. She was much too young for you, Daddy. I was just curious, since she looked to be around my age and I'd never seen her before. She walked in, took a seat and when she turned around and shook hands with Mrs. Crawford, I gathered by their actions that the girl was a visitor. When I looked back, she was gone."

"What did she look like?"

"Like I said, she was beautiful."

"Can't you give me a better description than that?"

"She wore a pretty black linen sheath, spectator pumps and—"

Shep's brow furrowed. "For crying out loud, Gracie. I don't care what she wore. What color was her hair? Was it long or short? Was she short or tall, fair-skinned or dark? Large or petite?"

"Jeepers, Daddy, why are you getting so upset?"

He flinched. It was a logical question. If only he had an answer.

Chapter Sixteen

Hurt? Angry? Sad? Veezie's emotions reeled as she drove back to Flat Creek. Maybe Harper was right and the only kind of man who'd fall for her would be one with similar interests who could relate to her. But why would she want to fall in love with an ill-mannered, ignorant nincompoop?

She ran up the stairs at Nine Gables and fell across her bed, feeling sorry for herself. She'd almost drifted off to sleep when the doorbell rang. She sprang up. Something inside her whispered, "What if?" What if she only imagined the conversation on the pew behind her this morning? What if Shep was not in love with Miss What's-her-name, but he loved her, instead and had come to tell her so? The air seeped from her lungs, leaving her deflated. Why did she keep torturing herself by pretending he cared? Her shoulders slumped. She didn't claim to be very smart, yet she had sense enough to know it was time to stop dreaming.

Beulah's heavy feet clomped across the marble floor, causing an echo. Veezie eased off the bed and tiptoed to the hallway outside her bedroom door. Standing near the top of the stairs, she cupped her hand over her ear. At the sound of unfamiliar female voices, she shrugged. Since Veezie had made no friends in Flat Creek, she assumed the guests were looking for Harper. With the bedroom door open, a woman's shrill voice made it impossible not to hear.

"It's nice to see you again, Beulah. The club sure misses your chicken salad."

"I thank you, Miz Cotter. I reckon I oughta invite y'all in. But I know you ain't here to eat chicken salad and I ain't quite sure why you is here. You mind statin' yo' business?"

Veezie giggled and expected to hear them ask for Harper.

"We've come to get acquainted with Ophelia's daughter, the young Miss Harrington."

"Can't help wonderin' why you just now showin' up. If I ain't wrong, and I seldom is, you three was invited to come get acquainted with Miss Harrington last Monday night. But I don't recollect seeing nary one of ya here."

Flattered that her mother's friends had come to meet her, Veezie wanted to believe they had a good excuse for not showing up at the party. Of course, they did. They'd come to apologize. She'd accept graciously, the way a real lady would. She cringed when one of the women screamed at Beulah.

"How dare you speak to us in such a manner. I declare, Ophelia would turn over in her grave if she heard her help acting so high and mighty. Stop standing there like a ninny, Beulah and announce us!"

Veezie's pulse raced. Imagine that. High society ladies refusing to leave until they could make her acquaintance. She opened the door to the armoire and rummaged through her clothes, trying to decide what to wear. This was her chance to make a good impression on the right kinds of people. She jerked on a crisp, pink taffeta dress and was brushing her hair when Beulah clomped into her room.

The cook's mouth fell open. "And where you think you is going?"

"I have callers. I'm going down to meet 'em. But I can't zip this dress. I'll suck in and you pull it together."

"Sugar, them ain't callers. Them is three rattlesnakes, coiled up in that parlor. And they is full of venom. You stay up here and I'll go down and tell 'em you is feeling poorly and ain't up to visiting."

"No, Beulah. I speck they come to apologize for not coming to my party. Hurry. Zip me."

"Goodness knows, I might as well be sending you into a snake pit as to send you downstairs with them three. Sugar, you best stay up here. Ol' Beulah will get shed of 'em."

"Beulah, do like I tell ya. Go tell 'em I'm fixing to come soon as I straighten myself up a bit. And make us some hot tea in them fancy little cups and serve it with some o' them apple tarts you fried yesterday."

"Sugar, them left-over tarts done been throwed away, and don't nobody want nothing hot to drink in this heat. I'll sit out a pitcher o' cold water."

"Stop being so contrary, and do like I tell you. I'm gonna have me a tea party."

"Oh my soul, chile, don't you know when you lie down with dogs you bound to get up with fleas? You might as well start scratchin' now, 'cause them three ain't nothing but a pack o' dogs." Beulah was still grumbling when she stomped out.

Veezie smeared on a little lip rouge and traipsed down the stairs. She slowed as she reached the drawing room door. If she ever wanted folks to look upon her with respect, these women were the kind of friends she'd need. The kind her mother had. *I'm a Harrington. No need to be scared. I'm good as anybody.* She entered with a smile. "Good afternoon, ladies. How nice of y'all to come a calling." When they attempted to rise, Veezie motioned them down with her hand. "Aw, shucks, no need to stand on my account." She heard Bette Davis say that, or at least something similar in a picture show once. It sounded good.

A heavy-set lady with salt-and-pepper hair sat nearest the door. Her hairdo, with all its tightly crimped finger waves gave the appearance of a freshly furrowed field ready to be seeded. It wasn't hard to catch on that this was the self-appointed leader of the group, the way she took over. She tipped her head at Veezie and in a nasal twang, said, "Miss Harrington, my name is Mrs. Ebenezer Waters."

Veezie walked over and extended her hand. "Howdy do, Mrs. Waters."

The woman appeared pleased, for she grinned and nodded toward the other two ladies. "May I introduce Mrs. Woodfin Parker, III and Mrs. Bailey Cotter."

Veezie sized them up. They reminded her of the story of the Three Bears. Mrs. Waters was too fat; Mrs. Parker, too skinny; Mrs. Cotter was just right—though a mite on the short side. "Beulah's fixing us some hot tea. I wish she hadn't throwed away them apple tarts she made. I'm sorry we ain't . . . uh, I mean, we don't got none left."

The skinny one with a mule's face said, "Tea is fine."

Veezie ran her fingers through her hair and glanced back toward the door. "Beulah will be out d'rectly." Noticing how the short lady looked at the other two and smiled, Veezie knew right away they were all three fond of tea.

Mrs. Waters, the one with the finger waves said, "We were your mother's closest and dearest friends, so you can't imagine our shock when we discovered Ophelia's secret. You poor darling. I can't imagine how dreadful it must have been to learn your own mother gave you away." She clicked her tongue in a little tsk-tsk sound.

Mrs. Parker, the mule-faced lady, spoke up. "But it's certainly understandable why Ophelia felt the need to do such a thing. I for one, cast no stones. I'm sure any of us would've done the same thing had we been led to believe our child would be–"

She stopped and coughed in her hand. Glancing at her cronies, she finished, with "Flawed. It wasn't poor Ophelia's fault the doctor gave her a false report."

Veezie thought it odd to hear the words "poor" and "Ophelia" used in the same sentence. She turned and stared at the third lady, waiting to hear what Shorty would have to say.

Mrs. Cotter resembled a rodent. She was less than five-feet tall, and wore her hair in a bun. But it was the long nose on such a tiny face that gave her a mousy appearance. Even her voice was squeaky. "Miss Harrington, we came to invite you to become a part—"

She was cut off by Mrs. Waters who shot her open palm in mouse's face. "Why don't we wait for another time to discuss that idea, Flossie. I think I hear Beulah coming down the hall with our tea."

Mrs. Parker nodded in agreement. "Excellent idea, Flossie."

Veezie cocked her head and smiled. "Now, what was you about to say? Somethin' about an invitation?"

Mrs. Water's face turned the color of an overripe persimmon. "I think you misunderstood, dear. I believe Mrs. Cotter meant to thank you for inviting us to have tea with you, and look . . . here's Beulah now."

Beulah stomped in the room looking madder than a run-over dog. She carried a silver platter, with a china teapot, sugar, creamer and four dainty tea cups. She glared at the three visitors before plunking the tray on the coffee table.

Veezie stammered, "Beulah didn't you bring us nothing to eat?"

"Ain't got nothing." Her nostrils flared. "Didn't know they was a coming."

"Well, go stir us up some chicken salad." Didn't Beulah understand how important this visit could be?

Mrs. Parker spoke up. "Not for me, dear. Thank you. I'm fine."

Mrs. Cotter glanced over at Mrs. Waters, who covered her mouth with a lace handkerchief. Veezie heard a slight giggle. Then another.

"What y'all laughing about?"

Mrs. Waters took one swallow of tea and then sat her cup on the end table near her chair. With a straight face, she said, "I was thinking how delighted Ophelia would be if she could peek in and see us all sitting here, chatting with her delightful offspring."

When a snort escaped Mrs. Cotter's lips, she covered her mouth with her fist. With a half-shrug, she turned to address her hostess. "Sorry, my dear. I didn't mean to laugh, but such an endearing thought is bound to bring a smile to one's face. What a shame your mother didn't live long enough to get to know the darling child she gave birth to." More snickers followed.

Veezie caught on. There was nothing funny. They were laughing at her. All her life people made fun of her. She thought it'd be different now that she lived in a big house and had nice clothes. But it didn't make one iota of difference. She was nothing but a joke. Harper was right. Shep Jackson was too good for her.

With a sudden desire to be alone, Veezie glanced toward Beulah, who stood in the doorway with her hands folded tightly across her chest. Their gaze locked. Veezie tucked in her bottom lip to stop the trembling and it appeared to be the cue Beulah had waited for. The stone-faced maid shuffled across the room and tugged on Veezie's sleeve. "Miss Harrington, if you is ready to go back upstairs and finish whatever it was you was a doing, I'll be more'n happy to see yo' guests out the same door they come in."

Veezie stood and hung her head so no one could see the tears welling in her eyes. "Thank you, Beulah." Her shoulders curled over her chest. "Begging your pardon, ladies, I wish to be excused."

Without waiting for them to respond, she turned and ran up the stairs and fell across her bed. Lying on her stomach, she buried her face in the pillow and beat her fist on the mattress. "I wish I was dead." She rolled over on her back and sobbed. "God . . . if you can hear me, please just let me die."

Chapter Seventeen

Veezie likened her life to that of a cheap, tasteless novel that no one cared to read. Who could possibly be interested in such a shallow character? Though the heroine's devoted maid wept, slaved and prayed over her, the weak plot was disgusting. The book was nothing more than a trashy novel with steamy chapters. Why expect the ending of such a miserable story to be better than the beginning? If only she could slam the book shut.

Monday morning, she did.

Nothing mattered anymore. Beulah sat for hours by Veezie's bed, holding her hand. Occasionally, she'd squeeze. Veezie longed to return the show of affection, though she lacked the strength to tighten her grip.

George knocked on the door. "How's she doing, Beulah?"

"Come on in. I ain't sure she even knows she's in this world, George. She ain't spoke a word since them witches left, three days ago."

"Is she eatin'?"

"Not on her own. I have to force food down her. I shoulda kept her up them stairs Sunday, even if it meant hog-tying her to the bedpost."

"Ain't yo' fault, Beulah. From what you said, she was dead set on going down ."

"God bless her, she's still too fragile from losing that young'un to have to deal with another blow. And I declare, them three ol' hags couldn't a been meaner if they'd been vying to win a hateful contest. I tried my dead-level best to keep Veezie from going down them stairs, but she's a stubborn little cuss."

When Veezie closed her eyes, Beulah gently pulled the sheet over her arms. "If only—"

George's neck crooked when the cook's voice lowered to a whisper. "Only what?"

"Well, as crazy as it sounds, the night of the party, I was holding out hopes that Brother Jackson would show half as much interest in our little Veezie as she showed in him. But I reckon I was expecting too much."

"Ain't he a lot older'n her?"

"Shucks, what differ'nce does a few years make if you in love."

"You think he's in love with her, do you?"

"Ain't you been listening to a thing I been saying, George? No, I don't reckon he's in love with her, ignoramus, and that's the problem. 'Cause they ain't no doubt in my mind that she's in love with him. But seems like she gets knocked back down ever' time she tries to get up. Po' little thing waited all week by the telephone, hoping he'd call. And I was a hoping with her."

George gave a short chuckle. "Well can't nobody accuse you of not trying, Beulah. You made it mighty cozy for 'em down by the lake, sending the blanket and all. And I stalled and took my time before lighting the first bottle rocket, like you said do. But they is just some things you can't make happen and I reckon love is one of 'em."

Beulah jumped up and leaned over the bed. She brushed her hand across Veezie's face, then held up her forefinger. "George, look."

"What you pointin' at?"

"I ain't pointing, dimwit. It's wet. My finger's wet. Don't you get it? She's a crying."

He shrugged. "Prob'ly just her eyes watering."

"Maybe. But George, I sometimes get the feeling she can hear."

He shook his head. "Nah, you wrong. She ain't hearing nothing in the state she's in."

"How ya know?"

"Well, look at her. She ain't moved a lick. I hear tell some folks just go slap crazy when bad things happen. I reckon that's what—"

"Shush yo' mouth, ol' man. She ain't crazy. And she ain't gwina be."

"Now, I didn't say she was. I merely said I heard tell of it happening in times past."

Beulah bent over so close that Veezie could feel her warm breath in her face. "Po' little thing. Can't help feeling sorry for her. She didn't stand a dog's chance growing up the way she did, and then coming here was like dropping her off on another planet. God bless her, I don't reckon she knows where she belongs."

George made a clicking noise with his tongue. "Beulah, you a good woman. A friend to every stray dog, cat or pitiful young'un that shows up at yo' door. Be careful and don't get so close to her that you let her break your heart."

"That advice comes a little late, ol' man. If you coulda seen her face when she caught on that them ol' biddies was laughing at her, it woulda tore you up, too. I felt like takin' a broomstick to all three of 'em and beating the living daylights out of 'em. Now, I wish I had."

"And, where would that a gotcha? I'll tell you where. In jail. And then what would our little waif do?"

Veezie lost track of time, but she was ever aware that Beulah seldom left her side and if Beulah wasn't there, George was. Sometimes they both hovered over her. Watching. Waiting. Maybe George was right. Maybe she was losing her mind. Why couldn't she move her limbs? Or speak?

George said, "Beulah, I'm thinking maybe we oughta call Doc McCall and tell him she's having another one of them . . . what did he say it was? 'A get-her-tonic stupid spell?'"

"I ain't a gonna call him, George. Medicine ain't gonna cure what ails her. Doc said she pulled inside herself this way 'cause of being so let down over losing that young'un. And now, thanks to them three witches, she's been let down all over again. But she come back to us last time, and ain't no reason to think she won't come back this time." She let out a loud grunt. "Besides, it's *you* what's having the stupid spell."

"Why you say that?"

"Doc called it a cat-a-tonic stupor."

"Well, what's the difference?"

Beulah chuckled. "One is what you *is* and the other is what our baby has."

"Beulah, is you ever been sorry we stirred up the hornet's nest? Reckon we shoulda kept our noses out of it?"

She hem hawed around before answering. "Nah, George." A long silence followed. "'Course, I never figured on loving this young'un the way we loved Miz Harper. But I reckon it's her being so needy and all that kinda pulled her into our hearts. I've thought long and hard about us sticking our noses in it, yet I reckon it was the right thing to do. But, oh Lawdy, I'd sho' hate to lose her, now. I never had me no young'uns of my own, and this po' little creature kinda wormed her way into my heart, 'fore I knew what was happening." She paused. "George, we done the only thing we could do. We told the truth. Now, it's up to God to sort out the pieces."

Veezie wanted to shout, "I can hear y'all talking about me."

She wanted to ask what George meant by stirring up a hornet's nest. But the words in her head couldn't seem to find a pathway to her lips. Did it matter? Why should she care if she never spoke again? All she wanted to do was sleep.

Veezie had no idea how long she slept, but she opened her eyes to see Beulah sitting in the rocker by the bed, listening to Lum 'n Abner on the radio. "Beulah, what day is it?" The sound of her own voice startled her.

The old woman's jaw dropped. She switched off the radio and jumped up. "Glory be, you is a talking, sugar." She grabbed her heart. "It's Friday, baby. 'Nigh 'bout sundown."

Veezie nodded. "Friday?" She squinted. "Beulah, do you know how to make nanner puddin'?"

"Nanner puddin'?" She cackled. "Why sweetpea, that's one o' my specialties. Ain't I never made you none?"

She shook her head.

Beulah laughed and sobbed at the same time. "You want ol' Beulah to stir you up some puddin'?"

Veezie nodded once more.

Beulah ran to the door, yelling. "George, git over to Mr. Will Redd's store and bring me back some 'niller wafers. Our baby's craving her some nanner puddin'."

"How you know?"

"She told me, George."

"You mean she's talking?"

"Well, she ain't jabbering away by no means, but she did tell me she wants some pudding. Now, you stop stalling and if Mr. Will is closed, you go next door to his house and beat on the door and tell him you is got to get in. It's a 'mergency."

George chuckled. "I ain't sure he's gonna think so when I tell him what I'm aiming to buy."

"Well, we ain't gonna worry 'bout that. You just get it and get back soon as you can. Hallelujah, God done and heard our prayers."

Chapter Eighteen

For ninety minutes Shep Jackson sat motionless in his living room listening to two babbling women—Mrs. High and Mighty and Mrs. Negativity—dispensing what they referred to as Godly wisdom. A spiritual-sounding cloak for grave warnings.

He lifted his eyes toward the ceiling and sighed. For the first time in his life, he understood fully Proverbs 21:9: "It is better to dwell in a corner of the housetop than with a brawling woman in a wide house." What he'd give for a ladder.

The moment one woman took a breath, the other one jumped in ". . . And as long as your dear wife was living, preacher, this was not a problem. But having gotten wind that you've been visiting the widow Barnes on a weekly basis, Sister Dobbs and I could no longer, in good conscience, sit back and say nothing. Must I remind you that the Bible says we are to avoid all appearances of evil? It would serve you well to adhere to that admonition."

Shep chewed the inside of his jaw. The widow Barnes was a

Godly woman and dying of dropsy. She was so swollen, she was hardly recognizable. Did these two hens actually think he was having an affair with her?

Mrs. High and Mighty, spoke up. "Another thing—Sister Cora and I have observed inappropriate smiling from the pulpit."

Shep scratched his head. "Inappropriate smiling?"

"Perhaps ogling is a better word. Preacher, I'm sure you realize you're considered quite handsome by some, and when you look down from your lofty perch and smile in such an alluring way, you're planting wicked, immoral thoughts in the minds of women weak in the faith."

To that, Mrs. Watts gave a hearty nod. "That's a good point, sister."

Shep glanced at the mantle clock from time to time, hoping the hint wouldn't go unnoticed.

Mrs. Dobbs reached over and patted his hand with a sanctimonious smile. "We're simply saying, beware of the way you allow Satan to use you. Those intimate hugs at the close of the service are very inappropriate for a man of your position. Don't think people aren't watching."

At nine o'clock. He stood and yawned. "Thank you, ladies. I think I understand a lot more now than I did before your visit."

They glanced at one another with an approving look. Mrs. Dobbs rushed toward him with open arms. "God bless you, preacher, for being so receptive."

He jumped back with his hand clutching his heart... "Please, madam, I had no idea you were speaking from personal experience. The next time you feel an urge to hug me, say, 'Get thee behind me, Satan,' and I'm sure God will help you overcome those evil desires."

Her jaw dropped at the same time her arms did. "Well, I never!"

"And I pray you never will again." He walked to the door and opened it. With a sweep of his hand, he muttered, "Goodnight, ladies."

Shepherd shut the door to his bedroom and fell on his knees. "Oh, Lord, I'm not proud of the way I reacted. But God, I'm so weary from worrying about what people say. You tell me to be anxious for nothing but with prayer and supplication, make my requests known. I've been almost afraid to make my requests known, Lord, for fear of what people might say, if my request is granted."

Shepherd jumped to his feet and glanced about the room. He didn't hear an audible voice, but the words from Ephesians came to him as plainly as if God had written the scripture on the wall. "Redeem the time, because the days are evil."

He whispered, "I hear you, Lord." He walked into the kitchen in time to see Gracie reach in the oven and pull out a baker of cookies.

"Daddy, are your guests gone?"

"Yes, sweetheart, and I have a call to make. Don't wait up."

Gracie giggled. "I was about to give you the same advice. I'll be out with the gang. We're going to the picture show and plan to hang out at Mary Lou's afterward."

Shep pecked her on the forehead. "Have fun."

"Thanks. Where are you going, Daddy?"

"I'm going to redeem the time, sweetheart, because the days are evil."

"Huh?"

He smiled, winked at her and rushed out the door.

When Shep rang the bell at Nine Gables, Beulah opened the door and let out a loud, "Thank you, Jesus!" She stepped aside. "Come on in, preacher. Where you been?"

"Where have I been?" His knees wobbled. "You sound as if you were expecting me. Is something wrong?"

"Oh, my stars, they sho' is something wrong. Po' Miz Veezie, she done—"

Shepherd grabbed Beulah's shoulders when she broke down sobbing. "Calm down, Beulah and tell me. Is she all right?"

George stepped in the room. "Nah, preacher. Miz Veezie ain't all right. I reckon she done and lost her mind and I fear Beulah's gonna be next if she don't get hold of herself."

"What do you mean, she lost her mind?"

"Gone slap loco, preacher. She lies there in bed not knowing daylight from dark. She come out of it for a few minutes, then she pulled away from us again and I ain't knowing if we can ever bring her back."

Beulah pulled a handkerchief from her apron pocket and blew her nose. "Yeah, we can. With your help, preacher, I know we can save her from her demons. I was a praying you'd come and God's heard my prayer."

"Have you called the doctor?"

George looked at Beulah. "At's what I reckon we oughta do."

Beulah scowled "Well, you reckon wrong, ol' man, because we done know what's wrong with her. This ain't the first time, preacher. Doc came last time it happened and he calls it a stupor. Says traw-matic situations brings it on and they ain't no medicine what's gonna cure her. If them old witches—" Her voice trailed off.

Witches? Shep raised a brow. "Okay, let's have a seat in the parlor, Beulah. Suppose you start from the beginning, then I want to see her. But first, I need to know what's going on."

"The beginning?" Beulah and George exchanged glances. "I reckon you done know the whole story about Miz Ophelia Harrington swapping Miz Veezie for Miz Harper when the young'uns was first born."

He nodded. "I've heard bits and pieces. Go on."

"Well, a body woulda thought Miz Veezie would've been tickled to find out she inherited all this, but I reckon once she thought about it, it made her right sad."

George leaned forward. "Being in her condition when she come here, didn't make it any easier for her, since she—"

Beulah yelled, "Hush yo' mouth, George and let me do the talking."

George lowered his head like a whipped puppy. "Meant no harm, Beulah. I reckon I weren't thinking."

Shep groaned. "Stop your bickering, both of you and get on with the story. Beulah, you spoke of traumatic situations in her life. What did you mean? Tell me everything."

George and Beulah exchanged peculiar glances. But it was evident from the look that George got, that he was not to be the spokesperson.

"Well, preacher, it's like this. From the first day she come to us back before Thanksgiving, I knowed she was fragile like, but I didn't foresee nothing like this a coming. Then she had that first spell where she sort of sunk into her own little world. Didn't talk much and when she did, it was . . . well, kinda creepy sounding. But it didn't last long."

His muscles relaxed. No doubt Veezie was sleeping peacefully upstairs and Beulah and George were a couple of superstitious old people, talking nonsense about witches and creepy sounds. Nevertheless, the poor old souls were obviously worried, and it was up to him to calm their fears. "What do you mean, creepy?"

"Well, about thirty minutes before she had the first spell, I noticed she started talking crazy-like. I got the willies when she wouldn't take her eyes off o' the window. Then her voice got raspy-sounding and she went on and on about birds and how she wanted to fly with them birds. I know it don't make no sense, but I had the feeling, she just might try it."

George said, "Peculiar thing, preacher. Sometimes they weren't no birds out there, but she talked like she could see 'em."

When Beulah glared at him, George mumbled, "Go ahead, Beulah, you tell it. I just wanted to make mention 'bout them birds. That's all I was gonna say."

Beulah gave a hearty nod. "Well, George is right. She saw things what t'weren't there. And I got fearful she might decide to jump out the window and try to fly away, if I didn't keep an eye on her day and night."

Shep rubbed the back of his neck. "When was this, and exactly how long did it last?"

Beulah looked up at the ceiling as if the answer could be found in the chandelier. "Well, let me see, now . . . she was as sane as me and you when she come here, but then she started gettin' all weepy a couple weeks later . . . but it weren't until after she had the—" Beulah's wide eyes teared up.

"Finish, Beulah. What were you about to say?"

She looked at George and blurted, "The bemoanies. Yessir, that's what she had, all right."

"The *what*?"

"The bemoanies. It's where a body kinda gives up. That's what was wrong with her when Harper told you to pray for her, and you come and prayed. 'Member that?"

Of course, he remembered. Shep sensed there was something these two were holding back. In a few minutes, he'd march upstairs and see for himself what was going on in this household. "I had hoped to see her at church last Sunday, but—"

"Oh, she went, but po' little thing didn't stay."

"Why?"

"I ain't quite sure, and don't reckon it's my place to tell you what I think was in her mind. That ain't neither here nor there. It's what happened next that flung her back into a fog."

He blinked several times in an effort to stop the twitching in his eye. "What do you mean, Beulah? What happened?"

"Three ol' buzzards come to see her Sunday afternoon for no other reason but to have something to gossip about. And Miz Veezie—well, she ain't never had no learning—not that she's dumb, mind you." Beulah's chuckle had a sad ring to it. "Law, no, that baby's far from being dumb. She caught on real quick-like they come to gawk and poke fun at her. Broke her heart, it did." Beulah pulled up the tail of her apron and wiped a tear trailing down her cheek. "God bless her, it was too much for my baby to handle, her being in such a fragile condition, already. She took to the bed and po' little thing ain't been up since. Seems like she ain't got no will to live no more."

"Has she said she doesn't want to live?"

George shook his head. "She ain't said nothin' until about three hours ago, she asked Beulah for some nanner pudding, but when I got back from the store with the wafers, she'd done crawled back in her shell. Beulah poked it down her, once it was made, but I ain't sure she woulda knowed any difference if chopped liver had been on the end of the spoon. And our baby hates liver."

Shep heard all he could stand. He wiped his sweaty hands on his pants. "I thank you both, but now I want to see her."

Beulah shoved the flat palms of her hands in front of him. "Well, hold your taters, preacher. I'll have her ready in about two shakes."

"What do you mean, ready?"

"Well, no woman wants a man to see her not looking her best, especially a man she has fond feelings for. I ain't gonna let you go up there 'til I have a chance to comb out her hair and freshen her face. I'll come git you when I'm ready for you to see her."

George excused himself and Shep paced back and forth as he waited. What did Beulah mean when she said, "'No woman wants a man to see her not looking her best, especially a man she has fond feelings for?" He closed his eyes and prayed, "Oh, God, I knew I wasn't wrong. She does love me. Please, Lord, don't let me lose her, now."

"Preacher, we is ready for you. She sho' do look purty, too."

Chapter Nineteen

From listening to Beulah and George, Shepherd expected to find an emaciated, pale figure in the bed, but she couldn't have been more beautiful.

Long, silky blonde tresses cascaded over a white satin pillow and though her skin had a cleansed, natural appearance, the rosy cheeks and pink lips, were no doubt Beulah's doings. He'd never noticed how long her lashes were. Wearing a pink silk negligee, she reminded him of a sleeping angel.

Beulah's hand rested on his shoulder. "Go up to her, preacher and let her know you're here. George don't think she can hear, but I got a feeling she knows more'n she lets on."

"Veezie?" He bit his lip. Easing up to the bed, he reached for her hand. "Veezie, can you hear me?" Why did he wait so long? He should've told her how he felt from the beginning. Not wanting George and Beulah to hear the intimate things he needed to say, he motioned for them to leave the room. Even if she couldn't hear, his heart would burst if he held back any longer.

He pulled a chair to the edge of her bed, sat down and gently ran his fingers through her hair. "Oh, Veezie, I've been such a fool. I told myself it wouldn't work. We're from different worlds. People talk. But I don't care anymore. Let them talk." The words rushed from his lips like water from a flowing well that couldn't be tapped. "One of the reasons I fell in love with you was because there's nothing phony about you. You're like a fresh drink of water from a cool spring. So pure. So sweet. And so rare. Don't ever change, my love." He stroked her cheek with the back of his hand and laid his head next to hers.

The Grandfather clock in the parlor at Nine Gables struck three times. Shep jumped up, his pulse racing as if he'd run a marathon. How could he have fallen asleep, with his head on her pillow? His heart pounded. *Oh, God, what have I done?* If word should leak that he spent the night in Veezie's room, who would believe a plea of innocence? He swallowed hard. *They'd believe it if they knew Veezie the way I know her.* He paused. Seemed strange to think he knew her so well, since he'd only been acquainted with her for such a short time. But there was a naivety about her. One would only have to listen to her talk to know she was incapable of impure thoughts or actions. Perhaps that's what drew him to her. Since losing his wife, he'd been appalled by women flaunting themselves in front of him. Women he would've least suspected of being immoral had disappointed him. But Veezie wasn't like the others. What man couldn't fall in love with someone so sweet and innocent?

He took one last look at his sleeping angel and rushed out the door, down the stairs and prayed no one would see him leaving. He raced to his car, and with his hands trembling, he clutched the steering wheel, and heaved a sigh. It was silly to worry. Who'd be out at such an hour?

Upon arriving home, he tiptoed in the house, hoping not to awaken Gracie. If she should hear him come in, how would he explain? He wasn't ready to tell her he was in love with another woman. Would she be hurt and feel he no longer loved her mother? Could he convince her that his falling in love with Veezie had nothing to do with the love he still held for his Jenny? Maybe he was being overly anxious. After all, wasn't it Gracie's idea that he start courting?

Sunday morning, Shep looked out over the congregation, and Mrs. High and Mighty and her friend Mrs. Negativity were sitting in their usual pew near the front. His troubles were far from being over as long as the two busy-bodies were there to keep the pot stirred.

He sensed beady eyes following his every movement. He dared not let his gaze linger for even a second on a female parishioner, lest it provide the two nosey women with the fuel they sought to ignite suspicion and ruin his ministry. Sweat gathered on his upper lip. He pulled a handkerchief from his pocket and swiped his face. "Let us pray." With a bowed head, he lifted his voice toward heaven. "Oh, Father God, I lift up the psalmist's words this morning and choose to make them mine. 'Create in me a clean heart O God, and renew a right spirit within me. In Jesus name, Amen."

For the next several minutes Shep stood without speaking. A buzzing sound like swarms of bees could be heard among the befuddled, whispering congregants. He pursed his lips and looked out among the questioning faces. "I had a three-point sermon ready for today, but the message I prepared arose from a hasty, bitter spirit, so I shant preach it." When his voice cracked, he paused once more. "Instead, I shall read the text that's pricked my heart. He opened his Bible. Proverbs 29:20: Seest thou a man that is hasty in his words? There is more hope of a fool than of him."

Shep looked out through glazed over eyes and lifted his arms. "Please stand and sing the first stanza of *Trust and Obey,* and we'll be dismissed."

Before the pianist hit the first chord, Mrs. High and Mighty stood and furiously waved her hand in the air as if trying to hail a taxi. She shouted. "Preacher, I for one came to hear a sermon. I believe that's what we pay you to do. If you aren't prepared, then I should think you'd be honest enough to admit it instead of giving some hocus-pocus kind of excuse."

"Sit down, sister, you're out of order." The pianist began to play and Shep belted out the first words to the song, *"When in fellowship sweet, we shall sit at His feet..."*

###

Gracie didn't ask questions on the way home, nor did she question him at lunch. She was like her mother, that way. Jenny wasn't the pushy sort. Shep recalled the verse he read in church and envisioned a finger pointed at two nosey women. Yet, reflecting on his hasty response to Eunice Dobbs, he now imagined three fingers pointed back at him. No doubt about it, the woman was out of order. But did his admonition come from Godly counsel or from a bitter heart? He wasn't sure.

Gracie sat quietly, eating her dinner. He owed an explanation to his daughter, but how could he tell her what was in his heart? If only someone could explain these feelings to him. *Why, Lord? Why did I have to fall in love?*

He'd heard the talk around town, even before he met Veezie. People spoke of her as if she were an imbecile. "The doctor was right after all. Ophelia gave birth to a little idiot," they said. "You should hear the way the girl talks. A real hick." He burned inside, remembering the image he formed in his mind from listening to the gossip. How wrong he was.

Beulah and George said Veezie seldom ventured outside the gates of Nine Gables. Those spreading the biggest tales had never even met her. All it took for the nasty stories to circulate was for a couple of ol' hens to be offended by Veezie's folksy ways and from there, the wheels of the rumor mill spun half-truths into whole lies.

He swallowed hard. God called him to preach. Of that, he had no doubt. What would the parishioners say if they found out their

178

pastor was in love with Veezie Harrington? He knew the answer. He'd be packing his bag before the sun set. He grimaced.

"Daddy, are you okay?"

Shep blotted his lips with a napkin. "Okay? Why wouldn't I be okay, sweetheart?"

"I'm not sure. But I sense there's something troubling you. If you don't want to talk about it, I understand. Just remember— whatever the problem, it's not as big as our God."

He gave her a wink. "You sound like your mother. I'm so thankful for the influence she had on you." He rubbed his chin. "I hope you know how much I love you, sweetheart."

"And I love you, too, Daddy." She stood, picked up the empty plates and placed them in the sink.

He was more confused than ever. He needed someone to talk to. Someone who could give him Godly advice. But his daughter? He rubbed his sweaty palms on his trousers. No. Some things a father couldn't discuss with his daughter, and this was one of them.

Chapter Twenty

Sunday afternoon, Shep walked out on the porch, where his daughter sat reading a book. He bent down and with his head cocked, read the title. "Grapes of Wrath?" His brow knitted together.

Gracie shrugged. "I can see you don't approve."

"No, I don't approve. I've read reviews and John Steinbeck is said to have a vulgar vocabulary. Gracie, I forbid—" He bit his lip. She was nineteen years old. A grown woman. Her mother was married at her age. When did his right to forbid her from doing something and her right to make her own decisions—whether right or wrong—begin and end? He didn't know. If only Jenny were here. She'd know.

"Daddy, I could explain why I chose to read this particular book, but I don't think it would make any difference to you." She closed it and laid it beside her. "I'll take it back to the library, tomorrow."

Shep shook his head. "No, angel. I'm your daddy, not your

Holy Spirit. I spoke before I thought."

Gracie giggled and gave her father a wink. "Seest thou a man that is hasty in his words? There is more hope of a fool than of him. Proverbs 29:20."

Gracie quoting the verse back to him made him chuckle. "Well, maybe no one else heard what I said this morning, but at least my daughter was listening." He picked up the book and placed it in her hands. "If this is not for you, you'll know it. I trust your judgment."

He walked down the door steps. "I have a visit to make. Not sure how long it might take. Don't fix supper for me, hon."

When Shep arrived at Nine Gables, Beulah opened the door and with tears in her eyes, shook her head. "Ain't no change, preacher. You can go on up. The door's open."

"Thank you, Beulah."

He could tell Beulah had been expecting him by the way she had Veezie all dolled up in a gown the color of fresh-churned butter, matching her hair. Her pink lips and blushing cheeks against flawless skin gave meaning to peaches and cream complexion. The scent of fine perfume filled his nostrils as he leaned over her bed and planted a kiss on her forehead. "Hello, my sweet," he whispered. If only she'd open her eyes and acknowledge his presence.

He gently brushed his fingers through her golden hair. "I brought my Bible. I know how much you enjoyed the book of

Ruth." He pulled up a chair and sat. "I thought you might like it if I read the whole story to you. It's a rather short story. Only four chapters."

He fought the tears as he neared the end of Chapter Four. "So Boaz took Ruth, and she was his wife: and when he went in unto her, the Lord gave her conception, and she bare a son."

Shep closed his Bible and placed it on the bedside table. He pulled his chair closer to the bed and laid his head on her pillow. He sucked in the alluring scent of perfume and with his face near hers, hummed softly the tune to *The Very Thought of You.*

"Shep?"

He stopped humming. Had he only imagined the sweet sound of her voice? He lifted his head. With his elbows propped on the bed and his chin resting on folded hands, he stared into her face, wanting to believe he'd not dreamed it. She seemed to be sleeping peacefully. He eased his head back down on the pillow.

Minutes later, he thought he heard her say, "What was the little boy's name?"

He jerked up, cupped her face in his hands and stared at her closed eyelids, longing for them to open. "Veezie? Veezie, can you hear me?"

Beulah, rushed to the door, holding a feather duster. "Is you all right, Brother Shep?"

He nodded. "She spoke, Beulah."

She shook her head. "Nah, preacher. You likely was dreaming. Miz Veezie ain't moved a muscle. Po' little creature is in a world all her own."

"But she did, I tell you. She asked about a little boy."

"Sho' nuff? What little boy?"

"I don't know." Shep shrugged. "Maybe you're right, Beulah. I suppose I wanted to hear her voice so badly, that I imagined it. Still, I have a feeling she's about to emerge from this dark hole that's swallowed her."

"Yessir, you keep on believing, Brother Shep, and one o' these days, my baby will be back with us, good as new." Beulah walked out slowly, with her head hung low.

Beulah said what he wanted to hear, but her tone was far from convincing. Shep stood, and pushed the chair back with his foot. He hated to leave, but it'd soon be time for church to start. He leaned over and kissed Veezie on the forehead.

When he turned to walk out, Veezie said, "Did you tell me his name?"

His heart pounded like a jackhammer. He rushed back to her side. When he reached for her hand, her eyes opened.

"Do you know his name, Shep?"

"Who, honey?"

"The little boy."

"Whose little boy, Veezie?"

"Ruth and Boaz. I wanted you to keep reading. You said that Boaz took Ruth and she was his wife. And she had a son. Do you know what they named him?"

Making no attempts to control his sobs, Shep cried, "You

heard me. You understood."

With tears welled in her eyes, she nodded. "I once had a little—" Her voice trailed off.

"Obed, sweetheart."

"What did you say?"

"I said the little boy's name was Obed."

"Obed?"

"That's right." Shep pulled out a handkerchief and dried his face.

Except for moist eyes, her face seemed void of expression. Her weak voice was barely above a whisper. He leaned in to make sure he understood every word.

Veezie bit her lip. "I wonder if folks said nasty things about Ruth."

"Nasty things? Why would they?"

"Maybe they didn't believe she was good enough for him. He was rich and respected. And she lay down at the foot of his bed. Wouldn't that make folks think she was . . . was like me?"

His tears turned to laughter. "I imagine she was very much like you. A sweet, faithful, humble young woman with more love in her little pinky than most people have in their heart."

"You reckon he was older than her? I mean a lot older?"

His turned up lip trembled. "I figure he was probably about twenty years older, and that he loved her with all of his heart . . . just as I love you."

"Then, I didn't dream it? You do love me?"

"With every cell in my body. I adore you."

The confused expression on her face disappeared. Her eyes lit up and her lips parted in a smile. "You like nanner puddin'?"

He laughed. "I love banana pudding."

"Beulah made some."

Beulah, who had slipped in when she heard the commotion, chuckled. "Sugar, I done and throwed it out. Them nanners don't keep long, but I still got the makings. I'll make another one soon as I can git 'er done. I sho' will." She walked out laughing. "My baby's back and she's gonna have her some nanner pudding."

Shep picked up her hand and kissed it. "Wish I could stay and enjoy the pudding with you, but I'll barely make it to church on time, as it is. Welcome back, baby."

Chapter Twenty-One

Shep made it to church on time, with not a minute to spare. His heart overflowed with love. Love for God, love for his daughter, love for his flock, and love for a beautiful young woman who renewed something in him that he thought was lost forever. He preached one of his finest sermons. Or so he thought.

When he called on Deacon Watts to give the benediction, the big, burly man stepped up on the podium.

"Preacher, before we adjourn, I need to call the church to order."

Shep's brow furrowed. "Sure." He walked down the steps and took a seat on the front pew.

After following Robert's Rules of Order, the deacon laid out the purpose for the special called meeting. "It has come to my attention that there's sin in the camp."

Shep waited for an explanation. Why wasn't he consulted before bringing a charge to the church? Perhaps he could've counseled the guilty party and eliminated the need to address the whole congregation.

Buster Watts stood behind the podium with his hands gripping the sides of the pulpit. He popped his knuckles as he talked. "I've learned from a reliable source that our pastor's Station Wagon was seen leaving the house of a certain unmarried woman at the ungodly hour of three a.m. Saturday morning. Perhaps that explains why he was ill-prepared this morning."

Shep heard a chorus of gasps.

Horace Jones jumped up. "That's a lie. I don't know where you got your information, but I'll guarantee you, there's not one grain of truth in it."

Another member stood. "Now, I won't go so far as to say you're lying, Buster, but I will say you are gravely mistaken."

One after another stood in defense of their beloved pastor. Then Deacon Watts' wife, Cora, stood. "Well, I've sat silent as long as I intend to. But I won't allow you ignorant people to call my husband a liar. All I can say, is 'let those with ears, hear. And let those with eyes, see.' Sister Dobbs and I saw this coming. We even approached him and pleaded with him to repent, but he showed absolutely no remorse."

The buzz in the church stopped. The stillness was eerie. Heads turned when a child flipped the pages of a songbook, stirring the silence. His mother grabbed the hymnal and gave her son a slap on his thigh. The focus once again centered on Cora Watts' scowling face. Her husband said, "Cora, if you wish to be recognized, you'll need to come up to the podium."

"Aw, Buster, why can't I just say what I got to say where I'm standing."

"Now, Cora—"

She reached down and gave her girdle a jerk, before clomping down the aisle and making her way up the steps. She leaned over the pulpit. "I'm here to tell you, it's a sin what's been going on right before our very eyes. Folks, we got us a womanizer for a pastor, and it's time for us to do something about it."

A tall, thin, pimple-faced young man in the back of the church jumped up and blurted, "You're crazy, woman. Tell her to sit down and shut up, preacher."

His mother jerked on his shirttail. "Sit down, son." The buzzing whispers returned.

Mrs. Watts shook a finger at the young fellow. "One more outburst like that, Arnie, and I'll demand the deacons escort you out of this church and ban you from ever setting foot in here again. I've got something to say, and I intend to get it out." Once again, silence settled on the room.

"As I was saying before I was so rudely interrupted, Sister Eunice Dobbs and I have been made aware that our preacher has a roving eye. Now, I'll admit it came to our attention before many of you had a chance to pick up on it, since Sister Eunice and I have the gift of discernment. But lately, it's been so evident, that one would not have to possess the gift to see what's happening in front of your noses. The way he stands up behind that pulpit and lets his blue eyes dart from one pretty face to another—married or not—

doesn't seem to make a speck o' difference to him. And if you've been observant, you've noticed how he has a way of letting his lip curl slightly, in a provocative manner that would bring a blush to any decent woman's face. And then as soon as church is over, he rushes back to the door to make sure he doesn't fail to hug every single woman he ogled while he stood behind the pulpit."

Deacon Watts laid his hand on his wife's shoulder. "I think you've made your point." He looked straight at Curtis Dobbs. "Would someone please help my wife down the steps?"

Cora shrugged. "Well, there's much more that I could say." She looked up from the top of her wire-rimmed glasses. "If there weren't young children in our presence, I could tell plenty that I've seen with my own eyes, as certain women wait their turn every Sunday morning to get mauled by this man."

Shep's elbows rested on his knees and he covered his face with his hands. It was like being caught between a mountain lion and a tarantula. Would he be chewed up quickly, or was he in for a slow, painful death?

"I don't blame you preacher for hiding your face. You have much to be ashamed of."

Deacon Watts grabbed her by the elbow, "Step down, Cora. You've said quite enough."

Cutis Dobbs rose from the front pew and walked up to the base of the platform. He held out his hand to Cora as she waddled down the steps. The back of her dress hiked up over her bulging hips and she gave it a yank before taking her seat.

The Chairman of the Deacons said, "At this time, we'll take questions from the floor."

A distinguished-looking fellow, wearing a double-breasted suit, stood.

"The floor recognizes Oscar Dalrymple. What's your question?"

"It's two-fold. First, what makes you so sure it was Brother Shep that was seen, and second, where did you get your information?"

Deacon Watts rocked back and forth on his heels while grasping the edge of the pulpit.

"Those are fair questions. No doubt it was our preacher, because his is the only 1932 Ford Woody Station Wagon in Flat Creek. And the answer to your second question is confidential. But if you don't believe he was spending the night at Nine Gables Friday night, sneaking out at the ungodly hour of three a.m., why don't we give him the opportunity to stand and deny the allegations?"

The deacon stretched out his hand toward the front pew. "Reverend, I call you to come forth and answer the charges that have been levied against you."

Shep's legs felt too heavy to move. He was guilty of nothing. But what good would it do to try and convince anyone nothing happened? Who would believe him? No. For Gracie's sake, he wouldn't allow the nonsense to go on any longer by trying to argue himself out of this mess. Enough mud had been thrown.

He'd planned to tell Gracie about Veezie, but now that these awful allegations had been brought before the church, how could he ever make her understand? She'd have no reason to believe in his innocence, no more than anyone else in the church.

If he tried to tell her now, that he was in love with the woman he spent the night with, she'd think he was a hypocrite for preaching to her about purity and holiness. He shuddered to think of how this could affect her morals. He could almost hear her saying, "What's good for the gander is good for the gosling."

Deacon Watts' voice boomed. "Preacher, should the record show you refused to come forth to rebuke the charges?"

Shep stayed seated. "I've done nothing I'm ashamed of. Therefore, I refuse to stand and turn this into a fiasco. Do with me what you will."

"Well, I must admit, I expected you to stand and try to wriggle out of this, but I thank you for not dragging this out further. If the deacons will pass out the slips of paper and pencils, I believe enough facts have been provided. We will now take a vote on whether or not to relieve Reverend Shepherd Jackson of his duties as pastor of Flat Creek Fellowship Church. Mark 'No' if you favor his dismissal. 'Yes,' will be a vote to keep a proven womanizer as pastor of this congregation. But I have confidence you'll all do the right thing."

Gracie ran down the aisle and threw her arms around her daddy, then stood and faced the congregation. "What's wrong with you people? You all know my father. He's a good and decent man, who loves the Lord with all his heart."

Shep whispered, "Sit down, sweetheart."

"My father would never do what you're accusing him of. He's still in love with my mother. He hasn't looked at another woman since Mama died."

"Gracie! Please. Don't defend me."

The papers were passed down the aisle and handed back to the chairman. The congregation appeared paralyzed as the bits of torn sheets were unfolded one by one and counted.

When the last vote was counted, Deacon Watts coughed in his hand. "Well, when the Shepherd of the flock wanders away, the sheep will go their own way. That's what we've seen here tonight. A wayward shepherd and sheep gone astray. The count is seventy-three 'yes' votes to keep him and four 'no's' in favor of dismissal."

Eunice Dobbs jumped up. "Well, I am disappointed that only two couples—my husband and I and Brother and Sister Watts—appear to be concerned about the spiritual direction of this church." She waved a finger at the man sitting across the aisle from her. "And you . . . Lud Snodgrass, you're the very one who told my husband that you saw Brother Jackson with your own eyes, sneaking out of that woman's house in the early morning hours. And yet you didn't vote for his dismissal. What kind of two-faced weasel are you?"

"You're wrong, Eunice."

"Are you now denying that you said when you were delivering milk that you saw Brother Jackson come out of the door of Nine

Gables at three in the morning and get into his car?"

"I'm not denying I said it. And I'm not denying I saw it. But I do deny voting for him to stay. I cast a 'no' vote." He glanced over at Shep. "Sorry, preacher. But I saw what I saw."

Eunice's nose crinkled when her brow formed a vee. "Then I call for a recount, Buster, because that makes five. No telling how many more we might find on a recount."

Buster shrugged. "The votes have been counted three times by three men, Sister Dobbs. And it's not like we're looking at a tie. A dozen more votes wouldn't make a difference. The count stands."

"Well, it makes a difference to me, but I think I'm beginning to see the light, you mealy-mouth hypocrite. You voted for that skirt chaser to stay, didn't you?"

Cora Watts screamed. "You watch your mouth, woman. That's my husband you're calling a mealy-mouth hypocrite."

Curtis Dobbs stood. "Shut-up, Eunice." He dropped his head. "No need to holler at Buster. You can yell at me when we get home. I voted for him to stay. For thirty-four years, I've done what you've told me to do, gone where you told me to go—and voted the way you've told me to vote. But, I couldn't go along with you, this time, Eunice. I don't pretend to understand what happened at Nine Gables Friday night, but mine was a vote of confidence for a man—a man I know very well. And that man has never acted inappropriately toward a single member of this congregation. Yes, he's a hugger. He hugs women. And men. And little children and he'd probably hug your pet dog if you asked him to." Curtis grinned and glanced at his son, sitting in the back of the church. "Why, he even hugs grumpy teenagers." A few heads looked back and chuckled when the Dobbs boy stood and took a bow, to the apparent delight of his peers.

"That's the only hug some of us get all week." Curtis nodded toward the preacher. "I'm sorry, Shep that you had to sit through this, but at least you've learned the majority of us know you to be an honest, upright man."

Deacon Watts eyes darkened. "Well, Curtis, I guess even the elect can be fooled, but you would've been the last one I would've suspected of going along with the crowd. Before we adjourn, I wish to turn in my resignation as Chairman of the Deacons. I refuse to be a part of a church who winks at sin. Consider this my last task as I call the church to stand to repeat our benediction."

People shuffled to the floor, and recited in unison, "May the words of my mouth, and the meditation of my heart, be acceptable in thou sight, O Lord, my strength and my Redeemer. Amen."

Chapter Twenty-Two

Monday morning Veezie awoke to see Beulah standing over her. Her lip quivered as she looked into the old woman's eyes.

Beulah lifted her arms in the air. "Thank you, sweet Jesus for waking my baby."

Veezie rubbed her eyes. "Beulah, what you reckon's wrong with me?"

"Sugar, I don't rightly know, but Doc says you've had too much bad stuff to deal with and yo' brain just kicks off. I couldn't wait for you to wake up this morning to see if you was still with us."

"You know what I think?"

"Tell me."

"Well, I believe that doctor what told my mama she was gonna have a lunatic for a young'un knew what he was talking about. I reckon it takes some folks longer to get there than it does others."

"Oh, sugar, you ain't crazy."

"Maybe I am. I'm scared, Beulah. Shep's in love with me. Did you know that?"

"As a matter-o'-fact, shug, I happened to be dusting the stair rails outside your door and couldn't help overhearing him say all them sweet words to you." Beulah covered her mouth and chuckled. "Yes'm, that man sho' does love you, all right. Ain't no doubt about it."

"Well, that's what scares me."

"But I thought that's what you wanted."

"I do. I want it more than anything in the whole world. But what if I'm going loco, Beulah? All that time I was lying flat o' my back, not saying nothing, I could hear people talking, but it was like I couldn't talk back. It weren't 'cause I didn't want to. But they weren't no words inside me. Sometimes I wanted to speak, but by the time them words got from my heart to my mouth, they shriveled up and died. If that ain't crazy, what is it?"

"Sugarfoot, I ain't no expert, but here's how I see it. The good Lord makes our heads big enough to hold so much good stuff and so much bad. And when the bad overflows into the good, then I reckon it's like putting a bad apple in a barrel o' good uns. Before long, the whole lot starts to stink. But now, if you take out the bad apple and throw it in the slop pot, you've just made more room in the barrel for the good apples."

"So you thinking God might've shut off my brain for a spell, so I could empty my head of the rotten to make more room for all that's good?"

"Sounds like as good a reason as any, to me, child. How you feel, this morning, sugarfoot? Feel like going downstairs and eating a bite?"

Veezie slung the satin comforter back, sat up and stretched. "I reckon I do. What's for breakfast? I'm starving."

"Oh, sweet pea, ain't no words to tell you how proud I am to hear you say it. Up'n 'til last night, I thought you done and left us for good this time. But I got a feeling, you is gonna be fine—now that Brother Shep done got sweet on you. Hit's gonna be all good from here on out."

Veezie threw her legs off the side of the bed. "Oh, Beulah. I ain't dreaming, am I? He really was here last night and he really did say he loves me. Didn't he, Beulah?"

She chuckled. "Well, from where I was standing, it sho' did sound that way to me. Now get on your clothes and come on down to the table. I'll have breakfast ready by the time you gets down."

Beulah's explanation as to why Veezie wasn't able to communicate for a whole week made perfect sense. She could see it now, as clear as the globes on the chandelier. It was no coincidence that she got her voice back when Shep read that beautiful love story to her. God had reached in and flipped the switch so she could take in the good and crowd out the bad. It worked.

After breakfast, Veezie walked into the drawing room, sat down at the grand piano and banged on a few ivory keys. Beulah had mentioned hearing the late Mrs. Jackson play the piano at a funeral, and according to Beulah, it sounded like music coming straight from heaven.

Maybe she could find someone to teach her to play. Her lip turned up at the notion. She wouldn't tell anyone—no one except George and Beulah, of course. She'd wait until she could play everything in the church hymnal before letting Shep know. He'd be proud of her. Yes, that's exactly what she'd do. She swirled around on the piano stool. But how could she find a teacher, without anyone knowing what she was up to? Harper would know who to contact. Veezie sighed. It was time to get over being miffed. Harper and Flint had been good to her. She didn't want to lose their friendship. Besides, there was no need to be mad at Harper. What she'd said made perfect sense, even if it wasn't something Veezie wanted to hear. But now she couldn't wait to tell her she was wrong. Shep loved her. He said so.

Veezie would call her later in the day and ask her to recommend a music teacher.

Monday morning, Shep was on the porch when the sun came up. He'd spent most of the night in prayer. If ever he needed Godly wisdom, he needed it now. He'd rather die than to hurt Gracie.

Last night after church, he'd expected her to ask him to deny the allegations, but she didn't. They were both silent all the way home. He knew she didn't want to believe the milkman, although Lud Snodgrass was probably the most honest man in that church. Shep rubbed the back of his neck. Perhaps he should've told

Gracie the whole truth, how he fell in love with Veezie the day he first met her. How hard he fought against it, but it happened. He should've explained Veezie went through a severe culture shock and she had a difficult time adjusting. But with love and care, he had no doubt that God would heal her in mind and body.

And he should've admitted to Gracie that he accidentally fell asleep with his head on Veezie's pillow, although his body never left the chair he sat in. Would she believe him? Sure, she would. She'd believe him, but he might as well stab a knife through her heart, because she wouldn't be able to forgive him when she learned the woman he loved was only a couple of years older than her. The same woman she saw in church and said matter-of-factly, "Oh, Daddy, the woman I'm talking about was much too young for you."

His chest heaved when he sucked air into his lungs. No, he was wrong about Gracie. Sure, she might have questions, but she'd understand. After all, she was a real romantic like her mother. She'd encouraged him to start dating, and even said he was too young to spend the remainder of his life alone. He had plenty of things to worry about, but his sweet little optimist was not one of them.

It was time to turn in his resignation. God was not the author of confusion, and after that horrible scene at church last night, shouldn't he pack his things, move on, and allow the church time to heal? Tears flooded his eyes. He'd debated what he should tell Gracie, and what he should tell the church—but not once had he considered what he should tell Veezie.

Gracie opened the screen door and brought out a breakfast tray. "I thought we'd eat on the porch. It's a lovely morning."

Shep slid over in the swing to make room for her to sit down. As they ate, she babbled about everything from the classes she planned to take in the fall, to her opinion of Roosevelt's New Deal. They discussed everything except the subject that occupied both their minds.

He picked up his napkin and blotted his mouth. "Honey, we need to talk." He chewed his lip. How should he start? "Gracie, you know how much I loved your mother."

"I do, and that's why I know there's no truth to the vicious lies."

She was making this even harder than he'd anticipated. "Listen to me, sweetheart. I not only loved your mother when she was living, I still love her as much as I did the day she died. But the truth is, I've fallen in love with another woman. It doesn't mean I love your mother any less, because I don't."

Gracie's face paled. "Are you saying it's true? You're in love with that Harrington girl? But Daddy, they say—"

Shep gently placed his closed hand over her lips. "Ask me anything you want to know, honey, but don't ever repeat what 'they say.' Gossip always begins with those two words."

"Okay, Daddy. Start from the beginning and tell me what this is all about?"

He popped his neck and twisted his shoulder, stalling for time. The swing creaked back and forth. Start from the beginning, Gracie had said. So that's what he did. He told her about the phone call from Harper, saying Veezie was sick—and how he went to Nine Gables to pray for her. Then he met her at Bullard's store, and although he couldn't say it was love at first sight, he couldn't deny there was a strange attraction to this delightfully refreshing, yet backwoodsy-talking young woman. He swallowed his embarrassment and admitted to his daughter that his heart palpitated that following Sunday when he looked down from the pulpit and saw her sitting on a pew—and how he could hardly wait until that evening to see if she'd be back. He smiled when he talked about the look of wonder on Veezie's face when he shared the love story from the book of Ruth.

"Honey, I can't explain it, but believe me, the last thing I wanted was to fall in love again. Then the night you and I returned from the camping trip, I received a call from Harper, urging me to go to Nine Gables, because Veezie was in a depressed state of mind."

Gracie rolled her eyes. "Daddy, I'm beginning to think you may be the naïve one."

Shep could see he wasn't doing so well. But he was in too deep to back out now. He had to make her understand.

"Gracie, you remember how tired I was that night, but I drove over to Nine Gables to counsel a hurting individual. I didn't go courting. Honey, I don't expect you to understand, but something happened to me that night as we sat under the stars. And it wasn't anything she said, because she hardly said anything."

"Daddy, I don't know how to ask this, but did you . . . you didn't—?"

His jaw dropped. "No! No, honey. Of course not. I promise you, it was nothing like that. Veezie is a very sweet, gentle woman of impeccable character."

"Daddy, you've known her such a short time. How could you possibly know what kind of woman she is?" Her voice trembled.

He smiled. "Gracie, she's not like any woman I've ever known. She has a naivety about her—almost as if she's been transported from the last century."

"You mean like the prim and proper Victorian women?"

Shep shook his head and chuckled. "No. Definitely not the prim and proper type. I was thinking more along the lines of the Puritan woman. Delicate and untouched by the evils of the world."

"I can see she's charmed you. But I can imagine how sitting alone with a beautiful girl in the moonlight could make you feel young again. It's understandable that Satan would want to lure you into temptation, you being a Godly man. And it's also understandable that if you found yourself yielding to temptation, you'd naturally choose to believe you were in love with her."

"Gracie, that was the one thing I *didn't* want to believe. Trust me, I fought it."

Gracie's voice was barely above a whisper, "Do you think she's in love with you?"

His trembling lip curled slightly. "Yes. I know she is."

"And you? You're in love with her?"

He rubbed his temples with his hands and nodded. "I am, sweetheart. Does that hurt you, terribly?"

She leaned over and laid her head on her father's shoulder. "Daddy, you know how much you mean to me. I want you to be happy, and if I honestly thought this girl could make you happy, then I'd wish you both well. But I'm so afraid for you."

He lifted her chin with his hand. "Afraid for me? But why?"

Gracie was silent.

"What are you afraid of, honey?"

"Shall I be honest?"

"I've never known you to be anything else. What's troubling you?"

"Well, they say—" She stopped and rolled her eyes. "Okay, but I know of no other way to explain why I'm worried. I've heard she's the same age as Harper. You're old enough to—"

He interrupted. "Old enough to be her father? Yes, I am. Is that what's troubling you?"

"Maybe. I don't know. But I don't want some young girl making a fool of you. She could cause you to lose your ministry. Is she worth it, Daddy?"

Shep wrapped his arm around his daughter and swung back and forth. Ignoring her question, he mumbled, "It's gonna be a scorcher today. Not even eight o'clock and already the thermometer reads eighty-six degrees."

With no further prodding, Gracie laid her head on her father's shoulder.

The creaking swing seemed to grow louder as it rocked to and fro. After a long silence, Shep said, "I have an idea."

Gracie lifted her head and looked into his eyes. "What?"

"We'll invite her to dinner, next Saturday night."

Her brow furrowed. "You mean that Harrington girl?"

He flinched. Why did Gracie insist on calling her a girl? Was she doing it to try to make him admit he was being a silly old man?

"Yes, I'm talking about Veezie. It'll do her good to get out, and I know you two will get along great."

"Oh, Daddy, I don't know. Maybe that isn't such a good idea. Not until I know how I feel about the situation."

"Well, how can you decide whether or not you like her, if you don't know her? How about cooking your Dad up some of your famous chicken and dumplings, and baking a pound cake? I'll call her tonight and tell her that I'll pick her up at five o'clock next Saturday."

Gracie chewed her bottom lip. "Does it really mean that much to you?"

"It does, honey. I want you two to get to know one another."

"Whatever you say." Gracie slid from his arms. "Excuse me, please, I have lots to do. I should get busy."

Her somber voice lacked the cheerfulness that always brought a smile to his face. Optimistic by nature, Gracie's pessimistic attitude had taken him by surprise. He was prepared for her to feel a little disheartened. It would be natural for her to fear her mother was being pushed from his mind. But he thought once she understood that his love for Veezie had nothing to do with the love he carried in his heart for Jenny that Gracie would wish him well.

Shep wondered if his daughter slammed the screen door intentionally when she went into the house, or if the spring was lose on the door. But there was one thing he did know—he'd gotten himself in a fine mess by falling in love.

Chapter Twenty-Three

Veezie ran into the kitchen with her pocketbook hanging over her shoulder. "Beulah, I'm gonna drive over to see Harper. If I'm not back by suppertime, fix me a plate and take it to my room. I'll eat soon as I get back."

All the way to Goose Hollow, Veezie practiced what she'd say to Harper. The first thing she'd do would be to apologize for the way she left in a huff Sunday, after Harper and Flint were good enough to invite her to eat dinner with them.

Callie was outside chasing Needa, the cat, and came running up to the car as soon as Veezie parked. Veezie opened the door and held out her arms.

Callie looked up and grinned. "You pretty, Veezie."

Her heart swelled. Grown-ups lie. Children don't. If Callie said she was pretty, then it must be true. Veezie pulled a compact out of her pocket book and took a quick glance in the mirror. She smiled at her reflection. Callie was right and Veezie had Beulah to thank. She remembered how dull her dishwater blonde hair looked when she first moved to Nine Gables. But after Beulah washed it with a concoction mixed with lemon juice, it turned out bright as a daffodil. Beulah said it was the same mixture that Veezie's mother, Ophelia, used on her own blonde hair.

Harper opened the door and seeing the friendly smile on her face, Veezie knew right away there were no hard feelings. Still, she must apologize.

"Harper, I reckon I owe you an apology."

"Nonsense." Harper gave her a warm hug. "Come on inside, Veezie. I'm so glad to see, you. I've had you on my mind."

They walked into the kitchen and sat down at the table. Veezie glanced about. "Where is everybody?"

"Flint is at the hospital on call. And Jim took Lucas down to the creek to teach him how to fish."

"Funny, I still think about them young'uns like they really was my brothers and little sister. I reckon it ain't easy for them to understand what happened. Do they ever think about me? Do they, Harper?"

"Sure, Veezie. They miss you."

"I don't know why they would. I didn't do right by 'em, but I really did love the little stinkers. I just didn't know how to show it. They've got a right to hate me."

"Veezie, the kids are fine. It's you I've been worried about. When I realized you misunderstood my intentions, it broke my heart. You're very sweet."

"Well, I ain't mad at you, Harper, even if you was saying I don't deserve a man like Shep, 'cause it'd be the honest truth." Her heart thumped faster at the very thought of Shepherd Jackson. "But Harper, I didn't make it up. He told me flat out that he loves me." She placed her right hand on her heart and raised her left hand. "I ain't lying, neither."

Harper walked over and draped her arms around Veezie's shoulders. "Oh, honey, that's wonderful. I'm happy for you."

Veezie could hardly wait to tell the whole story from beginning to end. When she finished, she said, "And I want to learn to play the piano. So will you call that music teacher, Mrs. Wood, for me?"

"I'll call her now, while you're here." Minutes later, Harper walked back into the kitchen. She lifted both shoulders in a shrug. "I'm sorry, Veezie, but she has no openings. She suggested you call back in the fall."

"Oh, no. That ain't soon enough. Ain't there nobody else? 'Scuse my English. I mean *isn't* there nobody else?"

"Not to my knowledge. Why is it so important?"

"Why? Because I want Shep to be proud of me, that's why. I want to learn how to play *What a Friend we Have in Jesus.* That's my favorite song. Beulah sings it to me when I'm feeling down and out, and it makes me feel good all over to hear about a friend who bears all our sins and griefs, like they was his own. And goodness knows, I got plenty of both. Don't you love that song, Harper?"

Shep rocked back and forth in the porch swing. He could hardly wait to introduce the two women who meant more to him than anyone else on earth. His darling Veezie and his precious daughter.

Frank Tucker pulled up in the yard, and Shep could see two other men sitting in the cab of the pickup truck. He stood and waved them in. "What do I owe this visit to, fellows? Get out and come sit on the porch. It's a beautiful day. He recognized the other two fellows as Lomax Mundy and Cecil Hornsby. Y'all been to the Farmer's co-op?"

Lomax shook his head. "No, preacher, we're here to talk to you about something that's troubling us and to offer a little advice."

Shep's knees wobbled. *What now?* "Well, have a seat and tell me what's on your mind."

Lomax and Cecil gave Frank a nod and he seemed to take it as the go-ahead. "Well, preacher, I don't have to tell you how the folks at Flat Creek Fellowship feel about you. I think that was made plain last night. You're about the best preacher we've ever had in these parts."

Shep sat with his tongue stuck in his cheek. "Get on with it, guys. What's up?"

Frank pulled off his baseball cap, and rolled it around in his hands "Well, preacher, we feel what went on Sunday night was a real shame. It's easy to see how that kind of talk could wind up hurting not only you, personally, but such rumors could literally destroy the church. We still owe money on the building, and the last thing in the world we need is a church split."

Shep scratched his head. "I agree that if I'd been found guilty of the charges, a lot of damage would've been done. But I wasn't. So what's the problem?"

Lomax spoke up. "It's not the problem, but the potential for a problem that concerns us."

"Potential? I'm not following you?"

"Well, everybody knows Cora and Eunice are two self-righteous gossips and their actions were despicable, but the episode Sunday night brought some things to light."

Shep's pulse raced. "Such as?"

Cecil, who had sat quietly, blurted, "We think you ought to get married."

Shep let out a puff of air. "Is that all? That's why you're here?" He threw his head back and cackled. "Fellows, I thought you came here to toss me out on my head. Get married, huh? I agree with you. What a swell idea. That's exactly what I should do."

Frank wiped his forehead. "Whew! I was worried that you might not understand. I'm glad to see you're in favor of the idea. We love you, pastor, and we feel by having a wife, you won't be a target for the kind of vicious rumors you had to endure, Sunday night. You need a mature, Godly woman who is stable and equipped to teach Bible classes and take on other duties expected of a preacher's wife. We've gone over the list, and frankly, there are no single women with those qualifications in Flat Creek. But Maude Jacobs has a sister-in-law, named Willie Mae Dozier and you two would make a fine couple. She'll be perfect for you."

Shep's nose crinkled. "Are you talking about the woman who visited the church while on furlough? I thought she was married. But that can't be her. That woman is fifty if she's a day."

"That's the one. She and her husband served as missionaries in China until he died a few years back. She's a mighty good woman, preacher and we feel—"

Shep chuckled. "Wait a minute, fellows. Slow down—I'm capable of finding my own wife and besides, this Willie Mae probably has no thoughts of remarrying."

Lomax nodded emphatically. "Oh, yes, she does. In fact, we've already approached her and she was delighted at the prospect. Now, I'll be the first to admit, she's not the best-looking apple in the barrel, but we all know the sweetest apple is not always the prettiest *or* the one with the best shape. It's what's inside that counts. When you peel away the outer covering, I think you'll find Willie Mae to be a suitable companion."

Shep bit his lip to keep from smiling. Dare he confess that when he picks an apple it's his custom to pick the best looking one in the bunch? He stood and the other men rose. He wrapped his arm around the closest, which was Frank. "Fellows, I appreciate your concern. I really do. But when I marry it'll be because I love her and for no other reason." He grinned. "And if it makes you feel better, I've picked her out already."

Frank hugged his pastor. "Are you serious? You mean you've already found somebody?"

Lomax's jaw dropped. "But what are we gonna tell Willie Mae?"

Cecil, who had said very little, shrugged. "Who is she, preacher?"

"You'll know soon enough."

"Do we know her?"

Shep's smile stretched so far it made his face hurt. "Not like I know her."

Veezie drove back to Nine Gables and was walking in the house, when she heard Beulah's voice. She ran down the hall and saw the cook holding the telephone to her ear.

"She sho' is, preacher. She just this minute walked in the door."

Veezie grabbed the phone. Her heart pounded so fast, she could hardly speak. When she hung up, she ran down the hall squealing. "Beulah? Where'd you go?"

"My goodness, you gonna bust a gut hollering like that. What's going on?"

"He invited me to go to his house next Saturday night to meet his little girl. He wouldn't ask me to do that unless he might be thinking about marrying me, would he?"

"I ain't no mind-reader. Got no inklin' what he's thinking, but that girl of his ain't so little. 'Course now, I ain't seen her since 'fore her mama died, and I can't recollect how old she is, but I'm thinking she's getting on up there."

Veezie was in another world, and stopped listening. "What should I wear, Beulah? The yellow linen?"

"It does look right nice on you. I reckon that ought to do just fine."

Veezie had lost her own little girl, but God was giving her another chance. She'd have an opportunity to help Shep raise his child. Six months ago, she wouldn't have been ready for such a grave responsibility, but she was a changed woman. She could be a good mother, and she would.

"Beulah, I want to take his daughter a present. What you reckon I ought to carry?"

"Well, sugar, if that's what you want to do, why don't you pick out a book?"

She hardly got the words out of her mouth, before Veezie ran down the hall and into the library. She didn't want to pick out anything too difficult, and since she wasn't sure what grade the little girl was in, it presented a problem. After pulling out countless books and shoving them back into place, she found the perfect gift. A book by Margaret Sidney, called *Five Little Peppers and How They Grew*. If the child was too young to read it, Veezie would read it to her.

Children seemed to take to her, even when she didn't try to win their affection. Jim, Lucas and Callie—when they thought she was their sister—loved her, even though she paid them no mind.

She'd been too wrapped up in her own selfish world. But that was the old Veezie. She was a new creature. The Bible said so.

Shep would be pleased to see how quickly she would bond with his child. And pleasing Shep had become the desire of her heart.

Chapter Twenty-Four

Shep couldn't understand Gracie's rotten attitude. She sulked all week and when he tried to ease into the subject of Veezie, she always found an excuse to leave the room. But he'd convinced himself that she'd soften before the week's end.

Now, that Saturday had come, she showed no signs of changing her mind. Maybe it was a mistake to invite Veezie for supper. But how could he have anticipated Gracie's uncharacteristic behavior? He'd never seen this stubborn side of her before.

At four o'clock, he could smell a pound cake baking in the oven, and though she'd carried out his requests, he got the message that she wasn't happy doing so. The way she banged pots and pans in the kitchen, it sounded like an out-of-tune marching band. He wanted to call the whole thing off, but he was afraid of hurting Veezie.

He stayed out of the kitchen, and yelled from the hall. "Honey,

I'm going to pick her up. We'll be back in a jiff."

There was no response.

Veezie was ready when Shep drove up. She didn't wait for him to ring the doorbell, but ran out to meet him, in spite of Beulah's insistence that she allow him to come in.

With the book tucked away in her large purse, she grabbed his hand. He smiled, leaned over and pecked her lightly on her lips. "You look fabulous, honey."

The hairs on the back of her neck tickled, and she twisted her head around. "Aw, shucks, you say the sweetest things. Shep, you reckon she'll like me?"

"Like you? She'll love you. You're perfect."

Perfect? Veezie wanted to pinch herself to make sure she wasn't dreaming. This time last year, she was being shoved back and forth by a bunch of drunks in the Silver Slipper. And now, here she was, her past behind her. And looking like a Princess out of a fairy-tale book, it was still hard to believe that a handsome, well-respected preacher could be in love with her.

Minutes later, Shep pulled up in front of an attractive house with a big, wrap-around porch. Purple crepe myrtle trees bloomed in the yard. "Jeepers. Pretty place, you got here."

He smiled. "Thanks. It belongs to the church."

Why did she get the feeling he was nervous. What would he have to be afraid of? He had no one to impress. She held tightly to her pocketbook. Shep opened the front door and ushered her in.

"Gracie," he called. "Sweetheart, I'd like you to come in the living room and meet someone."

Waiting for Gracie to enter, Veezie unsnapped her purse and pulled out the book.

Shep said, "What you got there, Veezie?"

She cupped her hand over her mouth and whispered. "I brung a present for your daughter." When Gracie entered, Veezie blinked; then her eyes widened in shock. She looked past the grown woman to see if a child trailed behind.

Shep put his arm around Veezie's shoulder, drawing her close. "Veezie, honey, I'd like you to meet my daughter, Gracie."

Her eyes widened. "But . . . but I thought—"

Gracie, seeing the book, reached out her hand and grinned. "For me? A picture book. How sweet."

"Uh—" Veezie caught the sarcasm in her voice.

"May I see it?"

Swallowing hard, Veezie handed her the child's story book.

Gracie thumbed through the pages. "Oh, Daddy, you must read me a story from my night-night book when you tuck me in tonight."

His face contorted. "Gracie!"

Veezie's lip trembled. "It's okay, Shep. It's my fault. I should've asked how old she was. Gracie, I would've brung you something more fitting, like perfume or sweet-smelling talcum powder but I didn't . . . I didn't know you was full grown." Her voice trembled. "I feel a mite foolish."

Shep glared at his daughter. "You have no reason to feel foolish, Veezie. You were very thoughtful to bring Gracie a gift. And if she doesn't have the decency to thank you, please allow me to thank you for her, because once again, you've proved to be a very gracious lady."

Gracie shrugged and mumbled. "Sorry, Veezie. Thank you for the book." She tossed it on the sofa, turned and walked toward the dining room. "Supper's ready. We can go sit down, now. It's nothing fancy."

Veezie sucked in through her nose. "Oh, but it smells delicious. I'll bet you're a real good cook. I'm not so good, myself."

Gracie smiled, although it looked artificial. "Oh, I imagiine you're good at a lot of things. I've heard bizarre tales about how you wound up at Nine Gables, but I'm interested in hearing your side of the story. You know how gossip gets started in a small town. I'm sure there's not a word of truth to the nasty rumors."

Veezie fought back the tears welling in her eyes, though it was a losing battle. "Well, Gracie, to tell the truth, mine ain't such a pretty story and I'd hate to put a damper on this nice supper you fixed for us. So, if it ain't being rude, I'll pass and tell you my story later when the time is right." She rubbed her stomach. "I don't feel so good at the moment."

Shep wrapped his arm around her waist. "I've lost my appetite, also. I think Veezie and I will go for a ride."

He escorted her to the car.

###

Veezie was the first to speak. "You got every right to be miffed with me. I ruined everything, didn't I? She hates me. I made such an idiot of myself."

"No, Veezie, I'm not angry with you. I'm upset with myself for putting you in an embarrassing situation. What happened tonight was not your fault. I don't know what got into Gracie. I've never known her to act so rude. She's normally a very sweet, loving girl. That was out of character for her."

He passed by the road leading to Nine Gables.

"Where we goin'?"

"I promised you a dinner, and that's what you're going to get. There's a nice restaurant, called River Junction in Commerce."

She shook her head. "No, Shep. Let's don't go. Take me home. Please? I need to be by myself."

Shep drove her back to Nine Gables and walked her to the porch. "I wish you'd reconsider, but I can't blame you. Gracie managed to ruin the night for both of us."

Veezie wiped her damp cheeks with the back of her hand. "Don't be upset with her, Shep. I think I understand how she feels and she's right. Somebody like me ain't good enough for a man like you."

He pulled her close. "Oh, but that's not true, darling. You're more than good enough. I don't want you to ever change a thing about yourself. I feel as if I've been wandering in a desert for two years, and when I found you, it was like finding a fresh drink of water." He ran his fingers through her hair. "There's a pure, innocence about you that is so rare these days. I love you more than you'll ever know, Veezie Harrington."

"I love you too, Shep." Her voice trembled. "But this is goodbye."

He drew back. "No! No, Veezie."

She pulled a handkerchief from her pocket and blew her nose. "I love you too much to come between you and your daughter."

"She'll get over it, once she gets accustomed to the idea. Don't leave me, Veezie. Please, honey, I need you." He put his hands on either side of her face and leaned down to kiss her.

She pulled away. "You don't need me, Shep. Tonight was a sample of what we'd go through for the rest of our lives if we tried to make it work. It ain't fair to you. I ain't gonna make your life miserable, just so I can be happy." She turned, and without looking back, opened the door and left him standing on the porch.

Veezie heard Beulah puttering around in the kitchen. She walked in and slumped down in a chair. "Beulah, would you make me a 'nanner sandwich?"

"Sho', honey, but I thought you was gwinna have supper with Brother Jackson."

"Nah. That was just a dream I had. I'm wide awake now."

Beulah's dark eyes narrowed. "Is you okay, sugar?"

"Yeah, Beulah. I'm just all tuckered out, but I'll be all right."

"Tuckered out? What you tired of?"

"Tired o' running. All my life I been running. In Goose Hollow, I was in a race, trying to get attention. I ran and I ran. I used whatever means I could, just hoping somebody would notice me. Men did. Then I came here, and I kept on running, trying to get noticed by women of distinction. I wanted to be one of 'em. Well, I learnt real fast that I was the distinct one. They laughed at me. And then I had the crazy notion that a refined man like the Reverend Shepherd Jackson could be happy with an ignorant talking, clumsy walking, know-nothin' hayseed like me. But tonight I saw how wrong I was. So I ain't running no more. From nobody. Folks is gonna have to take me like I am or don't take me at all, Beulah. I'm tired of trying to be somethin' I ain't."

Beulah hugged her. "Well, that's about the most growed-up thing I ever heard anybody say, sugar. And that's perzactly what you ought to do. Be the amazing woman God made you to be and don't try to be nobody else. You is good as gold. And if folks can't see it, they the ones with the problem."

That night, Veezie lay in bed, pondering her new resolution. There was someone else she'd been running from. Adolphus Woodham. He had a sweet wife and three precious children and she didn't want to see them hurt, because of her foolish past. But she was tired. It would be up to Adolphus to do the running from now on.

Chapter Twenty-Five

Sunday morning, Veezie walked into church with a heart aching as if someone had taken the pinking shears and snipped around the edges. It hurt. Hurt bad. But she was thankful God kept her from unraveling. A piece of her heart would always be missing, but it took more love to let him go, than it would take to hold on to him. She wouldn't be responsible for him losing both his daughter and his ministry.

It wasn't her imagination. People glowered when she walked down the aisle and took a seat. She squirmed on the pew when she noticed the raised brows and hands cupped over mouths as people turned and whispered to their neighbors. Had Adolphus talked? She wanted to leave, but she couldn't, for she'd be running. And running was not what she was about. Not anymore. They'd have to take her as she was, or kick her out. Veezie could see the latter happening. She glanced down at her chest and envisioned a huge red letter "S" for sinner. But they didn't know. They couldn't. So why the cold stares?

If only someone would come and sit on the same pew. Why didn't she sit in the back, so she wouldn't be noticed? When she tried to make eye-contact, heads turned away. She picked up her Bible and opened it. Her eyes widened when she glanced down and realized the pages fell open to the book of Ruth. A coincidence? Or was God reminding her to be thankful that for a very short while, she had known love. She tried to blink away the tears. She'd rather have Shep Jackson's love for two weeks than to be loved by a man like Jack Hawk for the rest of her life. Men like Jack didn't know how to give. Only how to take. The minute he found out she was pregnant, he was through with her. Adolphus wasn't mean like Jack. In truth, she pitied him, knowing how he must regret his decision to stop and pick her up on that rainy night.

To keep from being aware of the angry, resentful looks focused in her direction, she cast her eyes downward and read the words from in her Bible.

"So Boaz took Ruth, and she was his wife: and when he went in unto her, the Lord gave her conception, and she bare a son."

She'd dreamed of one day giving Shepherd Jackson a son. Such a ridiculous notion. She should have known better than to think God would allow a woman of her reputation to snag a decent, God-fearing preacher. Heir to a fortune; yet, she'd give it all up, just to have her yesterdays blotted out. Hot, bitter tears dripped on the pages of her Bible.

When a hand rested on her shoulder, she looked up into the

moist eyes of Adolphus' wife, Marcy Woodham. Veezie's heart raced. Did she know? Marcy smiled sweetly and sat down beside her. Their gaze locked and Marcy draped her arms around her and held tightly as Veezie sobbed openly.

What a hypocrite she was, accepting sympathy from the very woman she betrayed. Marcy pulled a handkerchief from her purse and handed it to Veezie. Drying her tears, Veezie whispered, "Where . . . where are your children?"

Marcy smiled. "They'll be in shortly. My husband's keeping them outside until the service starts. It's difficult for the little ones to sit for an hour."

Veezie's instinct was to get up and leave. But she couldn't. She wouldn't. That would be running. Beulah had commended her for making a mature decision, and Beulah's opinion counted more than most folks'. She'd stay seated and face whatever she had to face. She silently prayed, "Lord, I know I have to live with the consequences of my sins, and I'll take my punishment, but I ask you, God, please don't let Marcy be hurt on my account."

When the piano began to play Marcy nudged Veezie and motioned for her to make room for Adolphus and the children. Unable to look their way, Veezie slid down the pew. With her head lowered, she gnawed on her thumbnail as she waited for the preacher to enter.

She thought she was prepared, but when the door opened and she saw Shep's face, her throat ached from the swelling. She needed someone to blame for the way her life turned out, so she blamed Ophelia. If only her mother hadn't swapped her, she would've become a real lady, instead of a little floozy, hanging out at sleazy joints, meeting the wrong kind of men and winding up pregnant. If she'd been raised a lady, Shep Jackson's daughter would've accepted her—and all these good Christian people would consider her to be an asset to their pastor, instead of seeing her as the uncivilized creature that she was.

Shep's gaze locked with hers. She felt his pain. But there was nothing either of them could do about it. This is the way it had to be. He took his text from Numbers 16: 41-42. Veezie had trouble keeping her mind on the sermon. It was something about Moses and his brother Aaron, and a disgruntled congregation. Shep held his hand up, with his finger pointed in the air. "Are you listening, people? The glory of the Lord appeared in spite of the murmuring." Veezie trembled when he shouted, "Repent and behold His glory."

She bit her lip and anticipated seeing God's glory, though she wasn't sure what to look for. But there was one thing she knew for certain: plenty of murmuring had taken place in that room. Something awful must have happened in the community that she hadn't heard about. But that wasn't surprising, since she was never privy to the town gossip.

At the close of the service, Shep asked the pianist to play *Just as I Am*. It was as if the songwriter reached into Veezie's heart and pulled out the words. That's how she wanted folks to accept her— the same way Jesus had—just as she was. Justified!

Veezie didn't understand what caused the influx of people to file down the aisle. Grown men teared up and wrapped their arms around Shep in a bear-like hug. Maybe she missed more of the message than she realized. She heard a man bawling, and turning her head slightly, not wanting to be too obvious, she saw Adolphus with his head buried in his hands. Marcy had her arm draped around his shoulders, and appeared to be praying for her husband.

Seeing a grown man cry, broke Veezie's heart, but it was especially painful, feeling she was the cause for his tears. If only she could let him know he had no need to worry. His dark secret was safe with her. She had no desire to hurt him. What happened that night was her fault. Seemed everyone who tried to befriend her got hurt.

After church, she walked out the door and came face to face with Shep's daughter. Gracie took one look at her, burst into tears and ran toward her father's station wagon.

Chapter Twenty-Six

Sunday afternoon, Shep sat on the front porch drinking sweet iced tea when Adolphus Woodham drove up. He stood and threw up his hand. "What brings you out this way, Adolphus?"

"Preacher, I've got to talk to you. I'm in dire need of Godly counsel."

"Well, pull up a chair and tell me what's on your mind."

Adolphus sat with his head bowed for a good five minutes before he got the words out, but Shep did nothing to try to rush him.

"Shep, I've committed an awful sin." His lip quivered. "I can't sleep, I can't eat. It's affecting my work. I don't know what to do."

"I'm listening."

"Preacher, you know how much I love Marcy, don't you?"

"I think I do. She's a wonderful woman, Adolphus. You have every right to be proud of your family."

"But they have no reason to be proud of me."

"Do you care to explain?"

He heaved a loud sigh. "You know I'm a recovering alcoholic. Quit drinking almost five years ago."

Shep nodded. "I remember."

"Well, if I said I haven't wanted a drink in all that time, I'd be lying. But I made Marcy a promise when we married, that I'd stop drinking, and in five years, I've only broken that promise one time. One time, preacher. That was all. But it will haunt me forever. And that's why I'm here. I've got to get some advice." He paused and chewed on his bottom lip.

"What happened, Adolphus?"

He closed his eyes. "I'd been sober for over three years, when ol' man Smitherman from Smitherman Lumber in Goose Hollow called and said he wanted to talk to me about buying the timber from off my land. At the time, I thought it was a gift from God, because it was near Christmas, and we didn't have any money. Marcy was expecting the twins and we needed a car. I borrowed Dad's car, and I didn't tell Marcy where I was going. I wanted to get the money and surprise her with a vehicle for Christmas. But the old man insisted we meet at a juke, called The Silver Slipper."

"You didn't tell him you were a recovering alcoholic?"

"No. I realize now that I should have. But I was embarrassed to admit I'd been the town drunk before Marcy married me. I needed that job and I was sure he wouldn't hire me if he suspected I might be a drunkard. So I thought I could handle the situation. He was late getting there, so I sat at a table and decided when he came, I'd order one drink to keep him from suspecting. But only one.

While I waited, I saw this young girl in there with some guy pawing her and it made me sick. I remember thinking that a cute girl like her had no business in a place like the Silver Slipper.

Well, then Smitherman came in, and he ordered drinks for both of us. I hoped he'd get down to business to start with, but he dawdled. Then he pointed to the girl at the bar, being shoved around from one drunk to another. He laughed. Seemed entertained by what was going on. It rubbed me wrong, preacher, but I sat there like a nincompoop and watched. I was afraid if I let him know I didn't approve of what he seemed to be enjoying, it would offend him and he'd walk away. I needed the money."

Shep chewed on his bottom lip. Knowing Adolphus as he did, he could only imagine his angst. The man had a heart of gold. Shep recalled when the Garfield family's house burned in late February a few years back, Adolphus sold his plow mule and gave the money to the destitute family. The following spring, with no mule, he had to toil his land with a hoe. But he never complained. Not once. He was like that.

Adolphus blew out a series of short puffs of air and then clasped his lips together so tightly his mouth formed a white line.

It was evident that the events of that night were even more stressful than Shep had imagined from the beginning. Exactly where Adolphus was going with the story, Shep had no idea, but one thing he knew for sure—his friend was sorely distressed.

"Adolphus, perhaps you're being too hard on yourself. How do you know the girl wasn't enjoying the attention?"

His eyes widened. "No, it wasn't like that. She tried to fight them off as they mauled her." Adolphus stopped and pulled at his shirt collar. "I'll admit at first I wanted to think she deserved what she got. After all, no one forced her to go to a juke joint dressed like a chippy. She had on a really low-cut red dress and there was more of her hanging out, than was staying in, if you know what I mean. But still, preacher . . ." He shook his head as his voice trailed off.

"Adolphus, you look pale. Can I get you a glass of iced tea?"

He nodded. "Thanks. My throat does feel parched."

Shep came back out and sat down. "Okay, I didn't mean to interrupt. You said the girl was getting what she deserved?"

"No. I said that's what I *wanted* to think. But Smitherman made jokes and said her family was dirt poor and she wore the same dress everywhere she went. I figured then that's why she was dressed the way she was. Poor kid didn't have anything else to wear. There was a sadness about her that I couldn't shake. I watched her out of the corner of my eye and I wanted to get up, sock the guy that was mauling her, and take her home."

"But you didn't?"

"No. I knew if I got in a brawl, Marcy would find out, and then she'd want to know if I was drinking. I didn't want to be there, but I kept waiting to see how much money Smitherman was going to offer me. When he started to discuss the project, he ordered another round of drinks. I guess I thought I handled the first one, and one more wouldn't hurt. But by the time we'd finished conducting business, I was high as a Georgia Pine. But I still had that young girl on my mind." He looked at Shep and his brow shot up. "Not in the way, you might think, preacher. It was pity I felt for her. Nothing else."

Shep believed him. No couple in Goose Hollow could boast of a stronger marriage. Marcy would no doubt be hurt that Adolphus took a drink, but she'd forgive him. As Adolphus kept rattling off seemingly insignificant details, about some misguided young girl he felt compassion for, Shep's mind wandered. Veezie was right, though he hated to admit it. Their love could never be, because Gracie would always be his daughter and she'd made it quite plain she'd never accept Veezie into her father's life.

Adolphus raised a brow. "Preacher, am I keeping you from something? You seem distracted."

"I'm sorry, Adolphus. I'm listening. You say you got drunk once, a couple of years ago and you haven't taken a drink since? Adolphus, it's not my intent to downplay the situation. You broke a promise and trust is vital for a healthy marriage. But, personally, I wonder if you aren't building this up in your mind to be bigger than it is. Knowing Marcy as I do, I feel confident she'll forgive you for that one indiscretion, especially since it happened so long ago and it hasn't been repeated."

"For that, yes. But it's what happened after I left the juke that could rip our marriage apart."

"I'm listening. Keep talking."

"When I walked out to the car, it was storming. Not just

raining, but a real thunderstorm. I drove slowly, because I realized I'd had too much to drink and it scared me. Not only was I afraid of wrecking Daddy's car on the clay road, but I wanted Marcy to be asleep before I got home. I'd made her a promise not to drink and I broke it. I couldn't face her. And then my car lights shined on someone walking down the road. It was her. The girl. She was soaked to the bone and I stopped and—"

Shep took another swallow of tea. He was getting the picture. Adolphus, of all men, would've been the last one Shep would've suspected of being unfaithful to his wife. Yet, how many times had Shep stood behind the pulpit and said, "Never put your trust in a human being, because man will let you down. Put your trust in Jesus Christ who will never disappoint." Perhaps he should've heeded his own words. "Adolphus, I sense a true repentant heart. Don't feel you need to give me an explanation."

"But I want to tell you, Shep. I need advice. I asked her if she wanted a ride home. Believe what you will, but that's the only reason I stopped. As soon as she stepped in the car, the rain came down so hard, I couldn't see the road, so I pulled over and parked the car and waited for it to let up. We talked a little. Chit-chat at first. While passing time, I made the statement that a young girl like her had no business going to a joint like the Silver Slipper. She teared up and thanked me for being so nice to her. In the midst of the conversation, I told her I was married and I'd promised my wife I wouldn't drink. I told her I was feeling pretty rotten about breaking my promise."

"I remember her saying, 'Your wife is lucky. If I had a husband who loved me like you love her, I wouldn't want nothing else in the whole wide world. I'd be happy.' Then, it sort of grabbed at my heartstrings when she said, 'ain't nobody never loved me like that.' Preacher, I don't mean to make excuses for what happened next, but I won't deny there was a sweetness about her that sort of endeared her to me, in the liquored-up state I was in. I was feeling worthless, and she made me feel worthwhile, building me up the way she did. And that's when she slid over and before I knew what was happening, the girl was all over me like a tic on a dog's ear, kissing me right in the mouth. I didn't even see it coming and that's the truth." He buried his face in his hands and wept.

Shep bit his lip. "How far did it go, Adolphus?"

He looked down at his feet. "Too far."

"Did you even *try* to stop her?" The question had nothing to do with his desire to counsel, but had everything to do with his disappointment that someone he held in such high regard—with a wonderful wife like Marcy—could allow it to happen unless he wanted it to. His own condemning thoughts brought conviction to his heart. He wanted to pull the question back into his mouth, but it was too late.

Adolphus chewed on his knuckle. "I wanted to stop her. I even think I tried to push her away, but then again, I'm not sure if I really pushed or if I tried to convince myself that it's what I needed to do." He heaved a sigh. "No, to be honest, preacher, I don't think

I did, and the guilt has been eating me alive ever since."

Shep stood. He walked over and leaned against the porch rail and stared into the heavens. "Tell me, Adolphus. Have you ever had another encounter with the girl?" Positive he'd get a negative reply, he was prepared to use Jesus' own words when talking to the Samaritan woman. "Go and sin no more," he'd say. But the answer wasn't what he expected.

"Yes."

"Yes?" Shep swallowed hard. "And when was the last time?"

Adolphus dropped his head. "Well, not the same type of encounter, but I ran into her this morning in church. She's moved here."

Shep's pulse raced. *Moved here? In church? This morning?* He turned his back to Adolphus to keep him from seeing the blood drain from his face. *No, it's not her. It couldn't be.* "Adolphus, what's her name?"

He groaned, then in a low voice answered. "Veezie Harrington."

Shep pressed his hand against his stomach, praying he wouldn't throw up.

"Shep, I'm scared to death that Marcy is going to find out. We've had our ups and downs, but most of the downs happened back before we married when I was hitting' the bottle. For the last few years, I dare say any man in this town can brag of having a better marriage. But I don't take the credit. She's a good woman. Oh, preacher, I wouldn't blame her for leaving me, but I don't know what I'd do if I lost my sweet Marcy."

Shep walked over and sat on the porch steps. After a long period of silence, he muttered, "I understand what you're saying, Adolphus. It's an awful feeling to lose the one you love."

Adolphus bit his trembling lip. "Shep, I can't imagine what you've gone through, losing Jenny."

But it wasn't Jenny he referred to. Maybe God had given Gracie the gift of discernment. How could he have been so wrong about Veezie?

Adolphus rubbed his chin. "Preacher, I want you to tell me what to do. Should I confess the truth to Marcy? She has no idea, and if I tell her, she may want to leave me. But if I don't and Veezie lets it slip, Marcy may wonder what else I'm hiding. She'll leave me for sure, if she learns from Veezie and not from me."

Shep glared at a thrasher, scratching in the grass. "I don't know what to tell you, Adolphus."

"Well, what are your thoughts?"

Shep cracked his knuckles. "My thoughts?" His nostrils flared. "Are you serious? You want to know my thoughts? If you'd been at church last Sunday night, Adolphus, you wouldn't have to ask what I'm thinking right now."

Adolphus' brow furrowed. "You sound agitated. You're angry at me for cheating on Marcy, aren't you? Well, think how I feel, preacher. You like her. But I love her. Think how angry you are and multiply it by ten-thousand and you'll only begin to understand how much I loathe what I've done."

Shep shook his head and turned away. "No, Adolphus, you've read me wrong. I can't advise you because I need someone to advise me."

"Shep, I have no idea what you're talking about."

"Well, obviously, you've not heard the latest gossip. The church took a vote last Sunday night to see if I should be asked to leave."

"Surely, you jest. I'm sure it was voted down. Everyone loves you, Shep. We're blessed to have you at Flat Creek Fellowship. Why would anyone even bring up such a vote?"

"Maybe because my station wagon was seen leaving a certain young lady's house at three o'clock in the morning, last Friday night." His eyes narrowed. "Marcy was at church. She didn't tell you?"

Adolphus shook his head. "No, she didn't mention a thing about it. I remember when she came home I asked why she was late, and she said the church had a special called business meeting. When I asked what took place, she shrugged and said, 'Nothing of importance.' So I dropped it and so did she."

"Well, apparently she's the only one who was in attendance that chose to drop it. I must have answered a hundred phone calls this week, and there were only seventy-seven people present Sunday night. So I don't know how you escaped hearing about it."

"I'm not really surprised. Marcy isn't one to participate in gossip, and I'm sure she considered it for what it was. Shep, I don't have to ask you if there was anything improper going on, because I know you. I'm sure if you were at a woman's house until that hour of the morning, you had a very good reason."

Shep heaved a sigh. "Would you still believe it, if I told you the woman's name is Veezie Harrington?"

"Especially if you told me you were with Veezie." Adolphus chuckled. "Preacher, I suppose you chose to use her as the worst example you could think of—and maybe I made her sound like a cheap little floozy, but I blame myself, more than her, for what happened. If you could've seen her that night, the way I saw her. If I'd been cold sober, I could've stopped it and I would have. You know, I honestly think the only reason she initiated it was because she'd been so humiliated earlier. Then when I came along and showed her a little kindness, she thanked me the only way she knew how. I hated myself as soon as I realized what I had done. She was young and obviously naive. I was thirty-six and should've had better sense than to take that first drink."

A sharp pain shot through Shep's chest. Naive. The very word he'd used to describe her. Was she? Really? Or could it be that he and Adolphus were the naïve ones.

"Shep, I'll have to admit, I'm curious. How did such a rumor get started?"

"Maybe because my vehicle really was parked in front of a woman's house until shortly before dawn."

Adolphus' held his tongue in his cheek. "I get it. The widow Barnes. Marcy says it's only a matter of time for the poor woman. I suppose you were sitting up with her, Friday night and one of the town gossips happened to see your car parked there. Am I right?"

Shep shook his head. "Oh, I've already been reprimanded about visiting the widow, but she wasn't the subject of concern last Sunday night."

Adolphus shrugged. "If you'd rather not give her name, I understand. I want to make it clear that I don't care who they accused you of being with, I trust you."

"Maybe you shouldn't." He paused and stared into his friend's face. "Adolphus, I *was* with Veezie."

"What?" His brow formed a vee. "No. I don't believe it. You're just trying to get my reaction. Right? To see if I'll still feel the same about you if you said it was *her*?"

"Do you?"

Adolphus gave a short chuckle. "You and Veezie?" He rolled his eyes. "Now, that's a picture I can't get in my head."

"But it's true. I left Nine Gables at three a.m."

His face paled. "You? Why?" The color quickly came back to his cheeks. "I mean . . . I'm sorry. I don't know what I mean. You caught me by surprise. Whoa!" He rubbed his hand across his face. "I guess becoming a preacher doesn't take away your manhood. But I never would've—"

"Would you still believe me if I told you nothing happened between us?"

Adolphus didn't answer right away. "Is that what you're telling me?"

Shep nodded. He explained what happened the night he fell

asleep at Nine Gables. He also confessed he'd fallen in love with Veezie. But that was before he knew she wasn't the innocent, naïve young thing he thought her to be. Now, he was filled with disgust. "So you see why I can't counsel you, Adolphus? I have some things I need to get straight in my own mind. Seems we both were taken in by her cunning ways. But if I were to give you advice, I'd probably say don't say anything to Marcy until God says it's time to speak."

"But Shep, I've heard you say many times from the pulpit that a healthy marriage is based on trust."

"And I still say it. But words can't be sucked back in, once they're out of your mouth. I'm not in a position to advise you and that's why I beg of you not to say anything until you've had plenty of time to pray about the situation."

His Adam's apple bobbed. "Preacher, I don't mean for this to sound callous, but I can't help wondering. Are you suggesting I keep quiet for the good of my marriage—or could it be that your motive is to protect Veezie?"

Shep bristled. "Protect Veezie? After what you've told me? You know, Adolphus, the Bible warns us to be vigilant, because Satan is as a roaring lion, seeking whom he may devour. And since Jenny died, I've been amazed at the brazen women who've come knocking on my door, and not all of them single; yet, I wasn't fooled by Satan's ploys. I knew he'd do anything to destroy my ministry. But he sneaked this one by me. I didn't see Veezie Harrington for what she was. But never again will I be fooled."

And to answer your question, No sir bobtail, I have no desire to protect that woman."

Chapter Twenty-Seven

Sunday afternoon, Veezie stretched out on the sofa in the drawing room with the same book she'd thrown on the floor in disgust, the first time she tried to read it. Now, she had to know the ending. What happened to poor Hester in the *Scarlet Letter*?

When the doorbell rang, she laid the book beside her and listened. A female. The voice was too low for Veezie to recognize.

Beulah responded, "Yes'm, Miz Veezie is in the drawin' room, and if you is come to bring her some good news, then I reckon she ain't too busy to see you. But if you be up to no good, then you can whip yo' skirt tail around and go back where you come from."

Veezie grinned. Good ol' Beulah. No doubt it was another one of Ophelia's snooty friends. She picked up her book, and settled back down, until she heard footsteps coming down the hall.

Beulah appeared in the doorway. "Miz Veezie, you is got company." When she stepped aside, Veezie swallowed hard, seeing Gracie staring back at her.

"Thank you, Beulah." How should she respond? Hold out her hand? Or would Gracie be offended? Why had she come? Did Shep not tell her they wouldn't be seeing one another again? Perhaps Gracie wanted to ask her not to return to Flat Creek Church.

"Hello, Veezie." Gracie's voice quaked. "Thank you for seeing me." She shifted her gaze to the floor and rubbed her hands together.

Veezie's insides quivered. "Hi, Gracie. Please," she gestured toward the settee, "have a seat." Since Gracie appeared uncomfortable with the task she came to perform, Veezie decided to help her out by speaking first. "I reckon you've come to ask me to stay away from your daddy. But in case he didn't tell you, I ain't gonna see him no more. It's over. So you got no need to worry. And whilst you're here, I apologize again for being such a dope and takin' you that silly little young'un's book."

Gracie covered her face with her hands and sobbed. "I'm so sorry. Please forgive me."

"Me? Forgive you? I don't understand."

She attempted twice to speak, but both times broke down, seemingly unable to get the words out.

Veezie rose from her chair, walked over and sat beside her on the settee. Feeling the need to offer comfort, yet fearful her attempts could be offensive, Veezie resisted the urge to wrap her arms around her distraught guest. Instead, she pulled a handkerchief from her pocket and used it to wipe Gracie's tears.

Gracie lifted her head and stared into Veezie's moistened eyes. "Oh, Veezie, I'm such a dunce."

Veezie shook her head. "You ain't no dunce, Gracie. I'm the real moron. Me and Shep, we come from two different worlds. I've tried to fit into your world by changing how I dress and all, but I'm still the same ignorant girl under all the frills. I reckon Shep couldn't see beneath it all, but you being a woman—I 'spect you saw me for what I was from the first time you laid eyes on me."

"Veezie, I was wrong."

"Nah, you saw the real me. Dressing me up and expecting me to act like a lady is like pouring black paint over a skunk's streak, and expecting him to purr like a kitten, since he don't look like a skunk no more. But underneath all the paint, he's still a stinking ol' skunk. But you came here for naught today, because I love Shep Jackson too much to bring shame to him."

Gracie's eyes widened. "Veezie, I love my daddy, dearly, and more than anything in the world, I want him happy. But I've made him miserable. Please, please, go to him. He needs you. With all that's happened in the church, I'm afraid he may even be considering leaving the ministry, and that would be a terrible mistake. But he's in such pain he isn't thinking straight."

"What do you mean, what's happened in the church?"

Gracie's brow furrowed. "Oh!"

"It don't have nothin' to do with me, does it?" She followed her sentence with a chuckle. "Nah, I reckon not. It couldn't. Nobody in the church knows I'm in love with their preacher.

'Course, I can imagine the tongues that would wag, if they did." She reached over and placed her hand on top of Gracie's. "And that's why I can't let this go on no longer. I won't make a laughing' stock out of him."

"Veezie, I won't lie to you. It does have something to do with you, but that's all the more reason you need to stand with Daddy."

"What are you saying?" Veezie sat with her heart pounding and her mouth gaped open as Gracie shared the events of the Sunday night business meeting.

"Well, that's about the meanest trick I ever heard tell of. And all that happened right there in the church?"

Gracie nodded. "I'm afraid so."

Veezie's chin trembled. "Don't you see, Gracie? No way could I go back in that church, knowing how folks feel about me. I heard a lot of whispering when I walked in this morning, but I hoped it was my imagination." She shrugged. "I always think folks are talking about me, even when they ain't."

"No, Veezie. Only four people in the whole congregation voted for Daddy to leave. The majority stood behind him."

"But don't you get it? They love Shep. They want to believe it was a lie. But deep down, they ain't too sure they weren't no hanky-panky going on. Nope. They ain't none too sure."

"Well, then why don't you march into the church tonight with your head held high, and let them know you have nothing to be ashamed of."

Veezie shook her head. "Me go in there, knowing what they're all thinking? Uh-uh. I couldn't do it."

"Sure you can. I'll be right by your side. We'll walk in church together."

"Oh, ducky, do you mean it? You want *me* to go with you? Sit with you?"

"Why not? We both love Daddy and he loves us. I understand now, why he fell in love with you. You're really sweet. I should've trusted Daddy's judgment, but I jumped to my own conclusions. So what about it? Will you go with me to church tonight?"

Veezie nodded. "I reckon we better take our umbrellas 'cause looking at them clouds, I'd say we're in for a gully-washer."

Heads turned whenever Veezie and Gracie walked into the sanctuary hand-in-hand and took a seat on the second pew. Veezie was glad Gracie chose to sit up front. That way, she didn't have to endure the icy glares from accusing eyes.

Gracie whispered, "I can't wait to see Daddy's face when he walks in. Won't he be surprised to see his two favorite girls sitting together?"

Veezie's lip quivered. She fought back the tears, but for a change, they were tears of happiness.

Gracie glanced at her, smiled and winked. She reached over and grasped Veezie's hand in hers and gave it a little squeeze.

The door opened.

Chapter Twenty-Eight

When Shep stepped up to the pulpit Sunday night, he was well prepared. He'd planned to preach on loving your enemies. Those who despitefully use you. His text would come from the book of James, about unruly tongues and how careless words cause friction.

He'd share with the church that he'd visited with both Eunice and Cora during the past week, and all was forgiven. Surely, his confession would touch hearts and bring healing to a divided congregation. He'd close by suggesting if anyone held a grudge to use the opportunity to approach the person and ask for forgiveness. Shep envisioned a picture of the church coming together in sweet unity.

But all his well-laid plans were for naught when he gazed out among the congregation and saw Veezie and Gracie, sitting side-by-side, both wearing broad smiles. He wanted to shout to his daughter, "Don't be fooled. You were right about her from the beginning. I was the idiot." Poor Gracie. He knew it was her way of wanting to make up for hurting him. The last thing he wanted now was for a little wench like Veezie to be hanging out with his precious daughter. Next time Gracie tried to give him advice, he'd listen.

Shep directed his focus toward the back of the church, to keep from making eye contact with Veezie. "Please stand and sing the first and last stanza of *Trust and Obey*." The words stuck in his craw when he tried to sing, '*When in fellowship sweet, we shall sit at His feet . . .*' Why did he choose that particular song? He knew why. It went along with the sermon he prepared. The sermon that would surely choke him now, if he attempted to preach it.

He bowed his head to pray, but the words came out garbled. He wasn't sure what he said. He leaned forward and clutched the sides of the wooden pulpit. "Please have a seat and turn in your Bibles to the book of—" He pulled a handkerchief from his coat pocket and wiped his forehead. "I'm sorry, folks. I'm feeling faint. Please, excuse me."

Instead of going to the front of the church to stand in the doorway and shake hands with his people, Shep made a quick exit through the side door. The rain gave him a good excuse to scoot to his station wagon and get away before anyone could stop him.

He put the vehicle in gear, backed up and spun out of the church yard. He turned and saw his daughter and Veezie running after the car.

"Daddy? Wait!"

He stepped on the accelerator and sped away. "Oh, Lord, I've been such a dope."

He didn't want to go home. Not yet. He rode down one dirt road and then another in the heavy rainstorm. His destination had become as directionless as his future.

He rounded a curve and hit the brakes when the car went into a spin.

Shep woke up, lying in a strange room with Dr. Flint McCall standing over him. "Where am I?" He looked down to see his right arm in a cast. "What happened?"

"You don't remember?"

His eyes narrowed and he slowly shook his head.

"You ran off the road and wrapped your station wagon around a pine tree. It's a mystery how you managed to crawl out alive, much less walk two miles in your condition."

"Walked? Where am I?" He turned his head and glared at his surroundings.

"The guest room at Nine Gables."

He tried to sit up, but winced and laid his head back on the pillow. "Why did you bring me here? I've got to get out of this place. Take me home, Flint."

"I didn't bring you here. As I said, you walked. You wrecked your car at the curve past Will Redd's store, crawled out of the mangled vehicle and came here."

"That's crazy. I wouldn't have come here on my own. Besides, how could I walk two miles and not know it?"

"George said you were beating on the door and when he opened it, you called out for Veezie, then crumpled on the floor. You were in shock when I arrived."

Shep groaned. "Well, I'm not now. Please, doc, help me out of bed and drive me to my house."

"Shep, you're in no shape to go home."

"Don't be ridiculous. I'm not staying here. He started to pull the sheet back and grimaced. Where are my pants?"

"Hanging in the basement. They were covered with blood. Beulah's washed them for you. Shep, you're banged up pretty bad. Your right arm is broken, you're bruised from head to toe and your kidneys took quite a blow. It's too soon to determine the extent of internal injuries but I've cleaned out a wound on your lower abdomen and stitched you up. It was quite deep, but a straight slash. With proper care, it should mend nicely. George knows how to care for the wound and change the dressings."

"I don't need George. I've got to get out of here."
Beulah walked into the room with a breakfast tray. She chuckled. "You aimin' to go sommers without yo' britches, preacher?" Flint laughed but Shep failed to see the humor.

Flint gathered up his tools and put them in his black bag. "Beulah, he still has some of the morphine in him, but when it wears off, he's likely to be in a lot of pain." He handed her a small bottle of clear liquid. "Give him a dose of paregoric if he gets to hurting too bad. When you go back down, please have George come upstairs to feed him."

Shep winced. "Feed me? I'm capable of feeding myself."

"Ever try eating soupy grits with your left hand, when you can't sit upright in bed? I think after the first spoonful, you'll appreciate a little help." I've given Beulah instructions to give you a bland diet for the next few days. Nothing heavy. Mostly soups and jello.

Shep whispered, "Flint, I'm pleading with you. Don't leave me here."

"Sorry, bud, but I'm doing this for your own good. You should be grateful. Here at Nine Gables, you have someone to take care for you."

"But Gracie can take care of me."

Flint cocked his head to the side. "Do you really want to put your daughter through having to bathe and dress your wounds? Do you, Shep? If that's what you want, I'll take you home. But I think it would be an uncomfortable situation for both you and Gracie. Here at Nine Gables, you have George who is willing to care for you until you can care for yourself. Frankly, I think you should take advantage of his expertise. He's a fine male nurse. He certainly took good care of Gordon Harrington before his death. But you make the call, and I'll abide by your wishes."

Shep stared at the ceiling. "Don't you understand the predicament I'm in here, doc?" His voice quaked. "I'm a minister of the gospel. Can you imagine the gossip that'll be spread when folks find out I'm staying here . . . with Veezie? This is all they'll need to run me out of town on a rail. I'll be ruined."

"Preacher, seems to me you're looking for something to worry about. Why don't you stop fretting and enjoy being pampered?"

"Where . . . where is she?"

"Who? Veezie? Downstairs. She and Gracie are eating breakfast. Shall I call her?"

"No! I don't want her up here."

Before Flint could respond, George walked in the door. "I's come to help you eat, Preacher. But let's pull your pillows up and git you situated 'fore we get started."

"Never mind, George. I can handle it. But when my daughter finishes eating, would you mind telling her I'd like to see her? Alone."

"Yessir. I'll go let her know."

Flint walked out with George. Shep's stomach growled. As soon as Gracie came upstairs, he'd ask her to hand him the bowl of grits. He was perfectly capable of feeding himself.

He heard footsteps on the stairs and recognized his daughter's giggles. He'd tell her she'd been right all along and that he was the one who'd been misled. The veins in his neck pulsated when Gracie and Veezie walked through the door, hand in hand.

His jaw tightened. Unable to look into the face of the conniving little Jezebel he turned his head toward the window. "I'd like to speak to my daughter. Alone."

"Sure, Shep." Veezie's voice cracked. "I understand." She slipped out the door.

"Daddy! I know you didn't mean to sound so gruff, but I think you may have hurt her feelings. What is it you want to say to me and then I'll go down and tell her you'd like to see her."

"But I don't want to see her, Gracie. And I don't want you seeing her, either."

She rolled her eyes and a slight smile crossed her lips. "Oh, I get it. Because of the way I acted Saturday night. Well, that's all settled. I was wrong. Veezie and I had a long talk yesterday. She's very sweet. No wonder you fell in love with her, Daddy. If you hadn't left in such a hurry last night, we would've told you that we both want the same thing—for you to be happy."

"Well, if you want me to be happy, stay away from her, Gracie. She's not the kind of girl I want you hanging out with. She's cheap."

Gracie glared at her father. "Did I hear you correctly? Where's my sweet father, who never judges anyone? The man lying in this bed looks like him, but he certainly doesn't sound like him." She took his hand in hers. "Daddy, I believe what I'm hearing is the medication speaking. Please try to get some rest. I'm going home, and I'll come back later—hopefully, when you're at yourself." She walked out the door.

At himself? For the first time since meeting Veezie Harrington, he was finally "at himself." His imagination worked overtime. Had Veezie bragged over town that she'd hoodwinked the preacher? No doubt he was the only person in Flat Creek who didn't know about the girl's loose morals. He supposed the whole town was laughing behind his back. Well, he was fooled once. But never again would a woman—any woman make a dope out of him. He supposed Satan was having a grand time, rejoicing over such a victory.

After Gracie left, Shep tried to reach the bowl of grits. He hit the corner of the tray and it fell to the floor, splattering everywhere. Disgusted, he yelled for George.

George cleaned up the mess, then brought another bowl of grits and spoon fed the preacher.

Shep wiped his mouth with a napkin. "Did my daughter go home?"

"Yessir. Her and Miz Veezie, they both done left."

He took a swallow of coffee. "Together?"

"Yessir. Miz Veezie, she's gonna be staying with Miz Gracie 'til you is able to go home. It was Beulah's idea. She said it was best not to give folks cause to gossip." George picked up the empty bowl, but before walking out, he turned and smiled. "You is got you a fine young lady, preacher."

He huffed. "Veezie is not my young lady."

George scratched his head. "Nahsir. I didn't figure she was. I was a talking about Miz Gracie."

Shep's face burned.

Chapter Twenty-Nine

After Veezie and Gracie finished breakfast, Veezie stood over the sink and pumped water into the dishpan.

Gracie sat at the kitchen table reading the morning paper. Her eyes muddled with tears. "Liar, liar," she whispered, as she read the nasty editorial in the Flat Creek Ledger.

WHEN ANGELS FALL, by Garth Graham

It's not exactly news when mortal man falls into perdition because of the wiles of an alluring woman. Take Adam. Or Samson. Or David. But ask the people of Flat Creek Fellowship Church about their pastor, The Reverend Shepherd Jackson, and they'll quickly tell you the man is a saint. Above reproach.

Therefore, it becomes big news when an immortal, sinless man such as the Reverend Jackson displays a lustful eye. Many will be shocked to learn the Reverend's angelic wings have been clipped by a woman of ill repute. Could it be the man is part human, after all? His station wagon was seen at the home of a local woman until three o'clock in the morning, Saturday last. Think he was there to lead her into the paths of righteousness? You decide.

The woman in question is none other than Miss Veezie Harrington, the former popular play-toy of drunks who frequented the Silver Slipper in neighboring Goose Hollow. Ah, but that was before she inherited the Harrington estate, met the handsome preacher and quickly got religion. It appears Miss Harrington's licentious tastes have improved—from pepper-hot sinners to salty saints.

The higher the man, the harder the fall. There was Adam. And Samson. And David. And now, the almighty Shepherd Jackson. So goes another fallen angel.

Veezie dried her hands. "What's wrong?"

Gracie balled her fist and shuddered. "That . . . that new editor at the Ledger. He's printed a bunch of lies in an attempt to discredit Daddy's ministry."

She reached for the paper, but Gracie shook her head.

"No, Veezie. Don't read it. It's nothing but a bunch of nasty lies. That horrid editor is nothing but a mud-slinging scoundrel. Trust me, no one will believe a word of it."

"Are you sayin' my name's in there?"

She groaned. "I don't suppose I can keep it from you. The man is despicable. I've a mind to call and cancel our subscription."

Veezie's eyes burned as she read. She folded the paper and sat quietly sipping her coffee. She knew what she needed to do. But what she needed to do wasn't what she wanted to do. The night she invited Jesus into her heart, Beulah told her it meant she was a new creature. Old things were passed away. Yesterday was gone. Said God forgot all about her confessed sins. So why couldn't everyone else forget? She buried her face in her hands and sobbed. "Gracie, what he said—"

"Stop it, Veezie. You don't need to defend yourself to me. I'd love you, even if everything he said were true. It's a disgusting article, but the rogue is simply trying to shock people in order to sell more copies. Just remember—those who matter won't believe it, and those who believe it—well, they don't matter."

Veezie was glad Gracie stopped her. Why should she blurt out the truth? Gracie had already said it didn't matter whether it was true or not. Keeping her mouth shut wasn't the same as lying. Was it?

The phone rang and Gracie jumped up to answer.

Seeing a look of anguish on her face, caused Veezie's heart to beat faster. She swallowed hard. "What . . . what's wrong?"

"That was Doc McCall. They transferred Daddy to the hospital."

"Oh, Gracie—"

Gracie placed her hand on Veezie's arm. "No, it's nothing to worry about. The doctor says he's no worse, but Daddy insisted on leaving Nine Gables. I'm sure he didn't want to put you out of your home. Why don't you go on to the hospital and make sure he's got everything he needs? I'll be there later."

Veezie shook her head. "I can't go. Not now. Don't you see, Gracie? Me and Shep ain't never gonna have no life together. He won't never feel the same about me after reading them awful things in the paper. Besides, he acted kind of peculiar last night. Like he was mad with me about something."

"I'll admit Daddy sounded irritable, but he was in pain and medicated. He loves you, Veezie. I know he does. You go on up to the hospital and tell him I'll be there shortly."

"You going somewhere?"

"Yes. I have an important errand to run. It shouldn't take long for what I have to do."

Flint McCall stood over Shep's hospital bed and shook his head. "You aren't being rational, Shep. Your body has been through a shock. No need to make any drastic decisions until you're feeling well again. It's not unusual for depression to set in after the body goes through a healing process."

"Doc, you seem to think I don't know what I'm doing. Trust me, I've thought this out very carefully, and there's no doubt that it's the right decision. I'm handing in my resignation as soon as I'm able to get back into the pulpit."

"But why, Shep?"

Shepherd picked up a folded newspaper lying on his bed. "Apparently, you haven't read the morning paper."

"Nope. I came to work at four o'clock this morning. Why? What's in it?"

"Read today's editorial, and I think you'll understand."

Flint took the paper. As his eyes flitted back and forth across the lines, his expression changed. "Good grief." He stroked his chin. "Poor Veezie."

Shepherd jerked his neck around and dropped his jaw. "Poor Veezie? What about me? She duped me into thinking she was something she wasn't, and now my ministry is ruined."

"You know, preacher, you're the last person in the world I would've thought would've blamed someone else for his actions."

"Hey, the only thing I've done that I'm ashamed of, is that I believed her to be something she wasn't. So why are you taking her side?"

"I'm not taking sides. But I know how much she wants people to respect her, and now for that editor to stir up something like this . . . well, I think it was a low blow. I can't help feeling sorry for her. It rubs me wrong for people who don't really know Veezie to judge her."

"So are you saying she's not guilty of the charges?"

"What about you, preacher? You guilty of the charges levied against you?"

"That editor can say what he will about me—I've done nothing to be ashamed of. But I see you don't want to answer my question."

"If you're asking me if she hung out at the Silver Slipper when she lived in Goose Hollow, the answer is yes. And did a bunch of no-account town drunks try to make her think they were crazy about her? You bet. I've pulled her out of jukes more times than I can count, but she was starved for attention and she went to the only place she knew of to get noticed. But she's changed, Shep. She's not that same girl and I credit Beulah for that."

"Well, too little too late, for me. You know, it's funny, but . . ." Shep gritted his teeth. "I actually thought I was in love with her." He shrugged. "Go ahead. Laugh."

"I'm not laughing. She's in love with you, too, and that's why it hurts me to see you turn on her this way."

"Shame me all you want, doc, but if I ever do decide to marry another woman, I won't be looking for damaged goods."

"So you're saying you don't believe in forgiveness?"

Shepherd shot back. "Maybe you should take up preaching, doc. Seems you're better at it than I am and I happen to know a church that will soon need a pastor."

Flint shook his head in disbelief. "Maybe I was wrong. Perhaps turning in your resignation isn't such a bad idea, after all." He turned and stalked out the door.

Chapter Thirty

Gracie parked in front of the Flat Creek Ledger building, grabbed her pocketbook and stormed into the glass-front office. An elderly lady with her gray hair pulled into a bun, stood behind the counter. Looking down her nose at Gracie, she said, "May I help you, young lady?"

"Yes ma'am. I'm here to see the new editor . . . I believe his name is Mr. Graham?"

"Mr. Graham is on the phone at the moment, but if you'll have a seat, I'll let him know you're here. Who shall I say is calling?"

"Tell him it's an irate reader. The name doesn't matter. He doesn't know me—but he will before I leave here."

The woman pushed a button on her phone. "Mr. Graham, a young lady is here to see you." There was a long pause. "She refused to give her name. Said to tell you she's an irate reader."

Gracie bristled, when the door to his office swung open and she heard him laugh. He walked out with his hand extended. "Miss Irate, I presume?"

She swallowed. He was much younger than she'd imagined. Twenty-four or maybe twenty-five, but not a day older. He ran his hand through his chestnut-colored hair. Gracie focused on eyes so brown they appeared black and lit up when he smiled. Remembering why she'd come, she stiffened. "My name is Grace Jackson. Ring a bell?"

His eyes squinted. "Let me think. We met in a Pub in Birmingham. Right?"

Was he trying to be cute? "I've never been to a Pub in my life, and furthermore, I think you know we've never met. But you should recognize the name."

With his tongue stuck in his cheek, the pompous smirk simply fanned the flames of the fiery rage in Gracie's heart. Never had she encountered such a self-centered jerk.

"I hate guessing games. Could you help me, please?"

"I happen to be the daughter of the man you trashed in your newspaper."

"Well, that does narrow it down to less than a couple of dozen. Was it in today's—" He stopped and slapped his hand against his forehead. "Jackson! The preacher's daughter?"

"That's right."

"Well, come on into my office, Miss Jackson. It's a right nice place for yelling and I have a feeling that's your intent." He held the door open.

Gracie walked inside and took a seat across from his desk. He sat down in a high-back leather office chair and swiveled around with the expression of a child playing on a merry-go-round. "Now, Miss Jackson, would you like something to throw at me?" He shoved an ash tray in front of her. "I find most women prefer ash trays, since they're easier to fling than, say, a rolodex, which tends to fall apart before it reaches me."

Her jaw tightened. "Your facetious attitude doesn't amuse me. I came here to tell you that I—" Heat rose from her neck to her cheeks. What did she come here to tell him? "Uh, I want to say that . . . that you should've checked your facts before writing that repulsive article about my father and my dear friend. It was all a disgusting pack of lies."

He leaned back in his chair and clasped his hands together back of his head. "Well, if I erred, it won't be the first time. It happened once before, back in the sixth grade. If you'll kindly point out my mistake, I'll be happy to make a retraction. I love retractions. Fills more space in the paper, you know."

His flippant attitude was revolting. Gracie had never met a more despicable creature. "Point out your errors? Where should I begin? You took a tad of truth and carefully wound a ball of lies around it until the facts became buried beneath the mound of sordid falsehoods."

"My apologies, Miss. But before I can make a retraction, I must know which part of the article is fact, and which part is fiction."

"Well, I would've expected you to know that before you printed such a ludicrous story, but apparently, you didn't bother to check the facts."

"But that's where you're wrong. However, you seem to be having trouble pointing out the errors, so perhaps I can help you. Permit me to search for the truth. He picked up a paper from his desk and put his finger on the article. Is your father's name Shepherd Jackson?"

She twisted in her chair. "Yes. I told you that, already."

He seemed to be taking notes. "Just want to make sure I have all the facts, straight, Miss Jackson." He cocked his head and with his lip slightly curled, he said, "May I call you Grace?"

"No. Miss Jackson is fine."

He shrugged a shoulder. "Okay, Miss Jackson. So we've determined that you're Shepherd Jackson's daughter. And is your father pastor of Flat Creek Fellowship Church?"

"That would be the *Reverend* Shepherd Jackson, and you know he's the pastor."

"Ah, but madam, I don't wish to presume anything. I must ask you to confirm. And is it true that the church had a special called meeting last week for the purpose of voting whether or not to fire your father . . . " With a closed mouth, he billowed his cheeks, then released a puff of air. "Uh, pardon me, but this is most embarrassing. Yet, I see no way around it, if we're to unravel that ball of yarn you spoke of."

"Stop hedging."

"Is that what I was doing?" His brow raised. "Oh well, I suppose I was. But tell me, Miss Jackson, is it true that the church meeting was called to discuss an allegation that your father's station wagon was seen at the home of twenty-two-year old Miss Veezie Harrington?"

"Well, yes, but—"

"But are you saying the allegation was false?"

"No, but—"

"I think we're making headway. We should arrive at the truth shortly, and after all, that's what we both want. One more question: Did he admit to being there until the wee hours of the morning."

Tears welled in her eyes. "But it isn't what you think?" If only he'd wipe that grin off his face. He unnerved her.

"Miss Jackson, do you have a license to practice fortune-telling?"

Her brow furrowed. "What a silly question."

"Silly? Not silly at all. You're attempting to tell me what I think. I assume you must be a seer of sorts."

"I wish you'd stop confusing me. I came here to tell you that I demand you print a public apology for the pack of lies you wrote."

"But we haven't come to the lies, yet, so how can I print an apology if I don't know what I'm apologizing for? Now, where were we? Oh, yes, I remember." He bit the inside of his cheek, as if attempting to chew away a malicious smirk.

When his gaze locked with Gracie's, she quickly averted her eyes.

"We were about to get to the part about the Harrington dame."

"I resent your referring to Veezie as a dame. She's a very

sweet young woman. Too good for the likes of someone like you, that's for sure." She crinkled her brow when he jotted something down on a yellow pad.

"What are you writing?"

"I'm making a note to myself. Would you care to read it?" He shoved the lined pad in front of her.

She read: "Never refer to a female who frequents juke joints for the purpose of committing hanky-panky with married men as a dame. The correct term for such a character would be 'lady.'"

Gracie shoved it back and shuddered. "You are impossible. I should've known it would be useless to expect you to listen to reason."

"But you're wrong, Miss Jackson. I want nothing more than to get to the truth." He dropped his head and chuckled. "Well, now, I suppose if you want to call my hand on that one, you'd have a right—I do want to get to the truth, but I lied. That's not all I want. I'd like very much to take you to dinner tonight. What do you say?"

Gracie's jaw dropped. "I wouldn't go out with you if you were the last man on earth." She grabbed her pocketbook and left in a huff. She cried all the way to the hospital. She'd wanted to assure Veezie and her father that there'd be a retraction forthcoming. And to tell them that everyone in Flat Creek would soon recognize the editor for what he was—a man without a conscience who made a practice of twisting the truth to suit his needs. But she'd failed in her attempt to discredit the irksome Garth Graham.

She shouldn't have jumped up so quickly. Perhaps that's what he was counting on. Of course. When he realized he was about to be cornered, he resorted to flirting with her, knowing she'd react exactly the way she'd done. Leave. Well, he hadn't heard the last from her.

Chapter Thirty-One

"That's her." If the heavy-set nurse meant for it to be a whisper, she needed more practice. Veezie flinched, seeing four eyes glaring in her direction.

The two nurses grinned broadly. "You here to see Preacher Jackson?"

Veezie nodded.

"Well, he's been given something for pain, so don't be surprised if he falls asleep on you."

Was the pun intended? Veezie winced hearing snickers as she turned. Her knees wobbled as she walked up to Shep's bed. How would he take the news of her leaving town? Naturally, he'd try to talk her out of it, but she'd have to make him understand that she had no choice. God had called him to preach and as long as she stayed in Flat Creek, the gossip would never end. Tears muddled in her eyes. He looked so distraught. It broke her heart. She sucked in a lungful of air and reminded herself that she had to be strong. It was necessary that she not break down. "How you feeling?"

His eyes darkened. "What are you doing here?"

Stunned, she tried to swallow the lump in her throat. She reflected on Gracie's words: *'Those who matter won't believe it, and those who believe it don't matter.'* Well, Gracie was wrong. Shep obviously believed every word of it. And he mattered. He mattered very much. Beulah was a wise woman, but she too was wrong when she said Veezie's yesterdays were all gone. As long as Veezie remained in South Alabama, she'd never be able to outrun the yesterdays. He hated her—and for just reason.

Shep closed his eyes. "Haven't you caused enough trouble?"

Her gaze fell on the newspaper in the trash basket by his bed. *Today's paper?* Her pulse raced. Of course, it would be today's. Yesterday's trash would've been emptied. A chill ran up her spine. Yesterday's trash? Her life would never be emptied of yesterday's trash. It would follow her around until the day she died.

Shep was right. She'd caused enough trouble. She turned and ran out of the room and didn't stop running until she reached her car in the parking lot.

She wasn't ready to go home. Beulah would sense something was wrong and Veezie didn't feel like explaining. She rode by the Silver Slipper. The bright orange neon light on the second "S" had apparently burned out, making it read, "Silver lipper." She choked at the memory of the many nights she sat in the smoke-filled room, swallowing costly lies from Silver Lips Jack Hawk. A couple of miles down the road, she rounded a curve and relived the rainy night Adolphus stopped his car to pick her up. Yesterday's trash.

That's all she was. All she'd ever be.

She pulled up in front of the empty cabin in Goose Hollow, where she grew up. Everything looked the same. The door to the outhouse still hung on by a single hinge. She got out and walked over to the well, and drew a pail of water. Cupping her hands into the water, she splashed it over her swollen eyes.

She ambled up the rickety steps and fell when her foot caught on a loose board on the porch. Knowing no one for miles around could hear her, she lay sprawled out on the porch, face down and screamed, "Oh, God, I want to come home. I want my brothers back . . . Jim and sweet Lucas, and my baby sister, Callie. They loved me in spite of who I was or what I did. I understand that now. If only—"

"Veezie?"

Recognizing the voice, but ashamed to look up, she lay still, trying to garner the nerve to speak. Finally, she garbled, "What are you doing here, Brother Charlie?"

"Maybe I should ask you the same thing, child. Come on inside and lets you and I have a little talk."

"I don't want to talk. I just want . . . oh preacher, I don't know what I want. I'm so mixed up."

"Get up, child, and let's go inside."

Veezie reached up and took hold of his hand.

Everything in the front room looked the same as the day she left—the day the Harrington Will was read. The only thing missing was the picture of Mae West that she ripped from a movie magazine and taped to the wall above her cot. Not surprising that Harper would've taken it down when she lived there.

She sat down on the faded sofa. Coarse straw poked out of the torn cushion. The linoleum rug on the floor was worn. Surrounded by the familiar, shabby as it was, it felt good to be "home."

The elderly preacher sat quietly with his hands folded in his lap, as the words spilled from her lips like water flowing from a well-primed pump. She told him about her conversion experience and how Beulah explained that old things were passed away and all things were become new. "Preacher, maybe that's true for some folks, but not for somebody like me. As long as the only things folks can see is the old me, then what chance will I ever have to lead a decent life? I might as well live up to their expectations."

"Is that what you want to do, Veezie?"

She dropped her head. "No. I don't expect you to believe it, no more than anyone else will, but truth is, I have no hankering to go back to my old ways. If only I could wipe my slate clean, so everyone could forget the kind of girl I was back then."

Brother Charlie looked into her eyes and smiled. "Veezie, you need to see yourself as God sees you. Your slate *has* been wiped clean and I'm so proud of you."

She shrugged. "Well, I thank you for saying it, preacher, and I don't doubt that God wiped it all away. And I don't doubt that you and Beulah believe I'm different than I was—but don't you see? A decent man like Shep Jackson wouldn't want to put his foot on a used floor mat where other men have wiped their nasty boots, if you know what I mean."

"I think you underestimate the Reverend Jackson." The preacher glanced down at his watch. "I have an errand to run. Why don't you go back to Nine Gables and trust God to take care of the situation that troubles you. He will, you know."

"Maybe I'll do that. But you never told me why you happened to be here."

"We had a storm last night with some strong winds. I stopped by to check out the roof."

"That was right nice of you, preacher. I'm sure Harper appreciates you looking after the place. I wonder if she'll ever try to sell it. I doubt she could get much for it, though, with the shape it's in. Not much to it. Don't reckon it'd mean nothing to nobody but me. Funny, how I hated this place growing up, and yet today when I was feeling down and out, it's the one place I came looking for. Isn't that strange, preacher?"

"Veezie, I suppose all of us have our own little harbor where we choose to go when the storms of life are raging. I think this must be yours."

She reflected on what he said and thought about Harper growing up at Nine Gables. Did Harper consider Nine Gables to be a safe harbor for her? At least the cabin was unoccupied and Veezie could slip over there any time she wished. Did Harper ever feel sad and need to go to her safe place? Veezie shrugged. Why should Harper ever feel sad or lonely? She had Flint and he loved her.

Several days ago, Veezie received a letter in the mail from Panama City, Florida. She didn't given it much thought at the time. But suddenly, she knew what she needed to do.

After Brother Charlie left, Veezie drove to Nine Gables to pack a few things.

Beulah wrung her hands. "But why, child? Where you going?"

"It's somethin' I have to do, Beulah. It won't be forever. I may be back in a couple of days—but I shouldn't be gone longer than a week."

"Just tell me where you're goin', sugar."

"I can't tell nobody. Not yet. Don't worry, Beulah. I think what I'm about to do will be the right thing for all of us."

"All of us? Sweetpea, sometimes you don't make a lick o' sense."

Shep was standing beside his bed with his slacks on and pulling his shirt off the hanger when his daughter walked through the door.

"And where do you think you're going?"

He looked up. "Gracie, I'm . . . I'm—" He rocked back on his feet.

"Daddy!" She grabbed him by the elbow and led him back to the bed. "You're not going anywhere until Flint says you're ready. What possessed you to think you were ready to go home?"

He pulled his legs up on the bed and lay back on the pillow. "I thought I could do it. I need to get away from here. From prying eyes."

"Prying eyes?"

"Yes. Sweetheart, I might as well tell you. I'd like you to hear it from me before reading it in the paper."

Shep went into full detail about the awful article in the morning paper, and his daughter listened intently without responding. "I guess your ol' man was going through some stupid sort of pandemonium, common to middle-aged men. You tried to warn me, but I wouldn't listen. I suppose unconsciously, I was trying to hold on to my youth by flirting around with a woman young enough to be my daughter. Now, I'm the laughing stock of this hospital. I see it on the faces of every nurse that walks into the room. I want to go home and bar the door." He broke down and sobbed. "If only your mother were here. Why did God have to take her from me? I need her so."

Gracie leaned over the bed. Embracing her father, she wept with him. "I miss her too, Daddy. But she'd want life to go on for both of us. Locking yourself up is not an option Mama would choose for you." She stood upright at the sound of a knock on the door. "Come on in."

He clinched his jaw. Veezie, no doubt. "Gracie! I wish you would not have invited—"

Brother Charlie Yancey stuck his head in the door.

Shep's jaw dropped.

"Reverend Jackson, I pastor a church in Goose Hollow. Would it trouble you too much if I came in for a short visit?"

"I know who you are, preacher. I heard you speak at the

Associational Conference a couple of years ago. Please. Do come in."

Gracie acknowledged the preacher's presence with a handshake and smile, made an excuse to leave and slipped out the door.

Since Shep was seeking confirmation that he'd be doing the right thing by giving up his church, he considered Brother Charlie's visit to be a God-send. A mature man of faith wouldn't have to think twice before agreeing it was the only thing he could do, under the circumstances.

He was no longer fit to lead a flock and everyone in town would know it by sundown.

Chapter Thirty-Two

Veezie drove to Panama City, Florida and walked into White Sands Realty. The secretary, a rather prune-faced looking woman with a long nose and large glasses pulled a folder from a file drawer and appeared to be studying the contents.

Feeling like an intruder, Veezie stood patiently waiting to be acknowledged. She twisted a handkerchief in her hands and hoped she could remember everything Beulah taught her about how to converse like a lady.

The woman turned and glared over the top of her spectacles. "May I help you, miss?"

"Thank you. I'm Veezie Harrington and I have an appointment with Mr. Robert Jaggers."

"Yes, Miss Harrington. Mr. Jaggers is expecting you." She escorted Veezie into a huge, plush office.

A pudgy man with a pencil-thin mustache greeted her. "Ah, Miss Harrington. I'm so glad to see you. Thank you, for coming. Please, have a seat. I trust you've given the offer due consideration and are here to negotiate."

"Well, I was surprised to get your letter, saying someone wants to buy Nine Gables. Who?"

"You ever heard of Johnny Mack Brown?"

Veezie gulped. "Land sakes, you ain't—" She grimaced and let out a puff of air before beginning again. "You aren't talking about the cowboy are you?"

He smiled. "That's the one."

"Well, I used to go to the picture show whenever I'd get a spare dime—which wasn't very often, but I saw him in Billy the Kid. You ever seen that show?" There seemed to be something wrong with the sentence, though the thought of selling Nine Gables to Johnny Mack Brown left her too excited to care.

The attorney smiled. "I don't believe that I have."

"Well, what made a famous movie star pick Nine Gables?"

"Mr. Brown is from Alabama."

"No lie? From Flat Creek?"

"No, he grew up in a town not far from here. A place called Dothan."

"I've never been there, but I've heard of it. So why would he want to live in Flat Creek?"

"He's looking for a large estate not too far from the beach, yet with a large acreage where he can raise horses. He happened to ride by Nine Gables and fell in love with it. He's willing to make it worth your while to sell. This is an opportunity of a lifetime, but if I were you, I wouldn't take too long to make up my mind. The offer may not stand long. He's eager to buy."

"Just how much is he willing to pay me?"

The realtor smiled and pushed a clamp board in front of her. He pointed to line number fourteen. Veezie gasped. "That much?"

He leaned back in his chair and chuckled. "Yep. That much. So what do you say?"

Veezie fumbled with the keys she held in her hand. "How long before I have to move out?"

"He's giving you forty-five days. I think that should be ample time to find another suitable place to live, with all the houses on the market."

"Where do I sign?"

He chuckled. "I didn't think it would take you long to make up your mind. Can't say as I blame you." He pointed to the line at the bottom of the page.

Her heart raced as she dipped the fountain pen in a bottle of ink and wrote her name. Was she doing the right thing? She didn't need the money. But then again, she wasn't doing it for the money.

There was nothing in Alabama to compete with the beauty of Nine Gables—a fine mansion sitting on twelve-thousand acres of gorgeous pasture land in Flat Creek. Handsome palomino ponies could be seen from the dining room window, galloping gracefully along the edge of the white picket fence, surrounding the property. A picture of perfection. But twenty-two years earlier, inside that beautiful house a wicked scheme was born.

In a strange sort of way, Veezie was like Nine Gables. Fresh paint covered the outside, but the inside was a harbor for dirty little secrets.

Brother Charlie propped his cane at the foot of the hospital bed, and pulled up a chair. "Shep." He paused. "May I call you Shep? I believe that's what your friends call you and I hope you'll think of me as a friend."

"Of course, Reverend."

Brother Charlie crinkled his nose. "Please, leave the Reverend handle for the city preachers. Plain ol' Charlie will do fine, or Brother Charlie, if that's more comfortable for you. I was sorry to hear about your accident." He paused. "Shep, I've been—" Pausing again, he seemed to be searching for words. "Well, what I'm trying to say is—"

Shep shot his hand in the air. "Oh, I think I get it. You didn't come because I had an accident, did you? You're here because of the gossip." Heat rose to his face. "Did the parishioners from my church call on you to reprimand me for hanging out with a woman of ill repute? Well, that's just dandy. You can go back and tell them they have nothing to worry about. My resignation is forthcoming."

Brother Charlie stood and reached for his cane. "Well, son, I see my presence here isn't welcomed, so I won't trouble you further."

If the old fellow had come to make him feel like a heel, he couldn't have done a better job, although Shep knew it wasn't the intent. What had happened to him? He'd never had a problem with his temper until lately. Now, it seemed everything irked him. "I'm sorry, Brother Charlie. I shouldn't have blown up like that, but if you've heard what's going on in my life, then you understand my frustration." When Brother Charlie didn't respond, Shep lifted his brow. "Do you know?"

"I think I do. I believe David said it well, in Psalms fifty-one, the third verse when he lamented, 'My sin is ever before me.'"

Shep nodded. "That's it. You hit the nail on the head, preacher. I don't have a moment that it's not at the forefront of my mind. It's driving me crazy. I guess it's an age-old story—the preacher and the prostitute. Satan must be laughing out loud. I've always believed myself to be a good judge of character, but Veezie Harrington pulled a fast one on me. She had me going. I can't get over how I let a little hussy take me for a fool." Shep hadn't intended to say so much, and the word 'hussy' jumped out, but there was no denying it felt good to vent. And now, surely, the old man would understand his angst.

Brother Charlie's eyes darkened. "Slow down, friend. Surely, I'm missing something. Are you saying Veezie is the sin you referred to, as being ever before you?"

Shep's brow furrowed. "You seem surprised. Wasn't she a member of your church in Goose Hollow? Don't tell me she fooled you, too. Don't you know what she is?"

The old man scratched his bald head. "I know Veezie. I know her quite well. And I'm aware of the slanderous attack on her character in the morning paper."

"Wait a minute . . . *her* character? What about *my* character? Maybe you should sit back down while I fill you in on little Miss Veezie Harrington, because apparently you don't know her as well as you think you do."

Brother Charlie accepted the invitation and plopped down in the chair. He rubbed the back of his neck. "Shep, it seems to me you've been misguided by your pride. The sin that is ever before you is not that you fell in love with Veezie . . ." He paused. "You did fall in love with her, didn't you?"

Uncomfortable at being reprimanded, he shifted his gaze, unable to look the preacher in the eyes. "Of course I did. If I hadn't been in love with her, I wouldn't be in the mess I'm in, now. But how was I to know she had such a tainted past?"

"Shep, your sin is not that you fell in love with a young woman who has a past. We all have a past, or there would've been no need for the cross. Your sin, as I see it, is in not standing up for the one you love when the world wants to tear her down. That's pride, my son. Instead of standing by her, you've joined the pack of wolves who wish to devour her. God has forgiven her for her wrong-doings. Why can't you do the same?"

Shep rolled his eyes. What was wrong with all these people? First Flint, then Gracie, and now the elderly preacher. Didn't they understand the havoc Veezie had wrecked on his life? Because of her, he'd never be the same.

Brother Charlie stood and picked up his cane. "Well, I think I've said more than I came to say. But before I leave, I'd like to have a word of prayer."

The words to the humble prayer pricked Shep to the core. The icy hostility that had formed in his heart began to melt away like a wax candle in the noonday sun. How did he allow such bitterness to enter into his life? It seemed to have crept in, bit by bit until the anger and resentment consumed him. He didn't like who he'd become.

At the sound of 'amen,' Shep blinked back the tears. "Oh, Brother Charlie. Please forgive my rudeness. I don't seem to know what I'm saying, anymore. My life is in such a mess, and I'm lashing out at everyone, even those I love best. I can't even seem to pray anymore, without making excuses for why I do the wretched things I do. Pray that God will deliver me from my own stubbornness."

The old man smiled and reached out his hand. "Sounds like a repentant heart, to me."

Shep heard the cane plunking against the tile floors as the preacher slowly made his way out of the hospital.

Chapter Thirty-Three

After spending over a week in the hospital, Shep was home.

Gracie helped him into bed, set several good books within his reach, and poured him a glass of freshly squeezed orange juice. "Daddy, can I get you anything else?"

"No sweetheart, you've taken care of everything. I'll probably read for a while and then take a nap."

She walked out on the porch, just as Arnie rode up on his bicycle and tossed her the morning paper. Gracie had known since grammar school that Arnie was sweet on her and she hated to hurt his feelings. She could never become interested in him, though she sometimes wished that she could. He seemed crazy about her, which made it awkward being in his presence.

"Morning Gracie."

"Good morning, Arnie." When he seemed to want to hang around, she said, "If you're here to collect for the paper, tell me how much Daddy owes you, and I'll go get the money."

"Nah, he's done paid up for the month."

"That's good. Well, thank you, Arnie. I'll see you around."

He nodded, and sat back down on his bike. "Gracie . . . uh, I want you to know that I don't care what that newspaper fellow says about Brother Jackson. Your daddy is a good man and I reckon he's got a reason for doing what he's done." He frowned. "Well, I don't suppose you know what I'm talking about, since you haven't read today's paper."

Gracie sat in the swing and quickly opened up to the editorial page. The skin around her eyes tightened.

SIN IN THE CAMP, By Garth Graham

This editor makes no pretense of knowing the Bible, since I happen to hold to the notion that my time is better spent researching facts and not folklore. But I seem to recall my sweet Grandmother, a lady steeped in Holy legends, relating a Bible story to me about how one man's "sin" brought destruction upon the whole camp.

If that's the way the Almighty God works, then the members of Flat Creek Fellowship Church best take cover before the fire and brimstone rains down heavily upon their religious heads. According to a reliable source, there's sin in the camp.

Recently, I broke a story about Reverend Shepherd Jackson's fall from grace. Kerplam! Even with such a loud thud, the good folks at Flat Creek Fellowship Church chose to turn a deaf ear. Many were appalled. Not appalled that their pastor was fooling around with an attractive harlot, but revolted that the Ledger had the gall to print the truth.

Shortly after the article went to press, this office was visited by a lovely young woman, whom I'll refer to as Miss Gee Whiz. One would have to admire the way she passionately defended Miss Veezie Harrington's virtue, and lambasted this editor for printing what she deemed to be a pack of lies.

Her strong objection to her friend being referred to as an "woman of ill repute" was not quickly dismissed. Yet, how else could one describe a voluptuous-looking female who from her youth frequented such places as the Silver Slipper for the purpose of—well, Gee Whiz, you fill in the blank.

The goal of this newspaper is to present the truth, regardless of how ugly or uncomfortable it may make some feel. Therefore, after Miss Gee Whiz accused this editor of not being truthful, I set out to get the facts—all the facts. What I discovered will pluck the feathers right out of the Reverend Shepherd Jackson's clipped wings and leave him earth-bound forever. His flock may have failed to hear the fall, but perhaps they'll hear the chilling echo, which resounds loud and clear.

When Miss Gee Whiz learns the woman she defended so vigorously gave birth to an illegitimate child, will she still feel disgusted that her friend was referred to as an attractive harlot? Perhaps she will. Perhaps this newspaper owes all the harlots of the world an apology for the comparison.

Gracie wadded the paper into a small ball, walked around to

the back of the house and threw it in a barrel, used for burning trash. She sat down on a picnic bench, buried her face in her hands and sobbed. She didn't want to believe it. But what if the editor was right? It was hard to believe that he would've proceeded to write something so shocking, unless he was able to prove it. She couldn't imagine what the news would do to her father.

She walked back in the house and called Nine Gables. Beulah answered the phone.

"Beulah, this is Gracie." Her voice cracked. "Could I please speak to Veezie?"

"But Miss Gracie, didn't she tell you, neither?"

"Tell me what?"

"That she was going away."

Gracie's jaw fell. "No. I didn't know. Where did she go?"

"That's just it. She wouldn't say. I was hoping she told you. Somebody needs to know where she is. Sometimes when Miss Veezie gets all down and out, she's prone to spells. I'm worried slap crazy. If you hear from her, will you let me know?"

"Sure, Beulah. But don't worry. I'm sure wherever she is, she's okay."

"I hope you right, sugar. I sho' do."

Gracie hung up the phone. Had the editor called Veezie to confirm the story? Is that why she left without telling Beulah where she was going? Gracie's emotions see-sawed. She didn't know whether to be angry or to feel sorry for her. Maybe if her father wasn't caught in the middle, she could better sort her feelings. She bowed her head and prayed, "God, please help me see this situation as you see it."

Chapter Thirty-Four

Veezie hoped she was doing the right thing. Yet, if it was right, why did it feel so wrong?

This was her first trip to the beach and she'd do her best to enjoy it. She was glad the realtor had invited her to stay in one of his vacant cottages. Maybe she'd buy one of the A-frame houses along the strip. What would Beulah and George think of living on the beach? They were getting too old to care for a place as large as Nine Gables and there was no way she'd leave them behind.

The previous three mornings, she awoke with the smell of salty air filling her lungs and the soothing sound of ocean waves gently lapping at the shore. Yet, this morning was different. Before opening her eyes, Veezie heard waves lapping furiously, as the ocean raged its fury against the sand dunes—her only protection from the invading tempest. Chills crossed her spine. She had the distinct feeling that the clouds looming above were a warning of an approaching storm in her personal life. She tried to shrug it off but the eerie feeling made her wonder if selling Nine Gables was the right decision. The thought of never seeing Shep Jackson again hammered at her heart like the waves pounding against the beach.

A promise to Gracie, that when the time was right, she'd share the story of how a hick like her wound up at Nine Gables, crossed her mind. She supposed now was as good a time as any to set the record straight, since there were at least a dozen different versions circulating around Flat Creek. But none quite as strange as the truth. With pen in hand, she carefully wrote the salutation:

"Dear Ducky—"

She paused, then smiled at the pet name. It seemed appropriate. She and Gracie got off on a wrong start, but now she couldn't ask for a better friend. She missed her already.

When someone beat on the front door, Veezie grabbed her robe and opened the door.

"Mr. Jaggers!"

The realtor held one hand to his head, to keep the fierce winds from blowing his hat away. "May I come in?"

Rain whipped in and stung Veezie's face. She quickly stepped aside and ushered him in. "My goodness, fellow, what are you doing out on a day like this?"

He appeared to hedge, as if he'd come bearing bad news. But that was impossible. Veezie knew how eager he was to make the sale and how pleased he was when she signed the necessary papers. He'd even offered her the use of the cabin, rent free, for the next two weeks.

He took off his hat and apologized for dripping on the

linoleum floor. Peculiar, since it was his floor and not hers. "Miss . . . Miss—"

"Harrington." Veezie thought it strange that he couldn't seem to remember her name. "Is there something I can do for you, Mr. Jaggers?" The thought came to her that perhaps he had second thoughts about allowing her to stay in the cabin. If that was the case, she'd set his mind at ease. Sure, she'd enjoyed it, but soon she'd buy one of her own, so it wouldn't be devastating if he told her he had a renter who needed use of the house."

"Yes. Harrington." He nodded.

She almost laughed out loud. He sounded as if he were confirming that she'd given the right answer. No doubt he had a lot on his mind, for he seemed quite distracted. Veezie thought she'd help him. "Mr. Jaggers, do you have more papers for me to sign?"

He glanced away. "No, I came by to tell you that you should contact your attorney for further instructions."

But of course. She should've known there'd be other legal documents for her to take care of. "No problem. I'll wait for the storm to pass and then head on back to Flat Creek to attend to the details." She reached up on the bureau for the key and handed to him. "I'll lock up when I leave. I've enjoyed my stay and hope to see you again real soon. Thanks for letting me stay in your cottage."

By noon, the rains ceased and she took one last stroll down the sandy beach before packing up and driving back to Flat Creek.

###

Veezie walked up to the door of the attorney's office and read, Paul Aycock, Jr., Esquire.

When the secretary led her into his office, she took one look and shook her head. "Either I'm in the wrong place or you are. I know Mr. Paul Aycock, and you ain't . . . you aren't him."

He stood and held out his hand. "I'm his son. Folks call me Bud. My father retired several months ago. May I help you?"

"Maybe you can, maybe you can't. That's what I come to find out. My name is Veezie Harrington."

He gestured toward the chair. "Have a seat Miss Harrington. Mr. Jaggers called and told me you'd be coming today."

Mr. Aycock seemed to listen intently as she poured out her story—how she was born to Ophelia Harrington, who then hired a midwife to switch her with the newborn of an unsuspecting couple.

"I'm familiar with this case, ma'am."

"Then why did you let me sit there and spill my guts?" She bit her lip, quite sure that a refined lady would never use such a crude word as 'guts.'

"My apologies, but I was waiting for you to explain why you decided to sell Nine Gables."

She bristled. Why should she have to explain to a complete stranger that she wanted to sell? What purpose would it serve to explain that she was in love with Shep Jackson, and for her to remain in Flat Creek could be devastating to his ministry? No, she owed the man no explanation. "What difference does it make why I'm doing it?"

Before he could answer her question, the door opened. The young attorney seemed relieved. "Come on in, Dad. Maybe you can handle this better than I. After all, you were the Harrington's attorney when the Will was executed."

Veezie's brow furrowed. "I feel like I'm getting the runaround. What's going on?"

The elderly attorney gave his black vest a yank over his protruding belly and took a seat. He ran his hand over his bald head. "Well, Miss . . . "

"Harrington," Veezie said, disgusted that he seemed to be hedging.

"I'm sorry." He glanced at his son. "How much have you told her?"

The younger man lifted a shoulder. "Nothing."

"Well, I don't suppose there's an easy way to say this, ma'am, but the truth is, you can't sell Nine Gables."

She stiffened. "And who said?"

"The law, I'm afraid. You see, Nine Gables doesn't belong to you."

"Of course, it does. You were the one who read the Will. You know it's mine. And I can do whatever I will with what's mine."

The lawyer popped his neck. "According to Ophelia Harrington's will, Nine Gables and all assets were willed to her biological daughter."

"That's right. And I'm her."

"That's what we first believed, because Ophelia had directed a midwife to switch her baby with the O'Steen's baby." He pulled out a handkerchief and wiped the sweat from his upper lip. "Well, it's come to the court's attention that the switch never took place."

"No. That's not true."

"I'm afraid it is. You see, the midwife has made a confession. She faked the switch. Ophelia died, thinking that Harper was the O'Steen baby, when in fact, Harper is the baby Ophelia gave birth to."

Veezie jumped from her chair and pounded her fist on the oak desk. "I don't believe you. Are you saying you're taking the word of some midwife? What makes you think she's telling the truth?"

"Because there were two witnesses who were there when Harper was born, and cared for her for two days before the alleged switch. They were privy to the deception and both have given sworn statements."

"Well, maybe they're in cahoots with the midwife. What's in it for them?"

"Nothing. That's just it. They have no reason to lie."

"Did Harper have something to do with this? Is she trying to take it all away from me?"

"To the contrary. She was notified that she was the rightful heir, even before she and Flint married. But she wanted you to continue believing it belonged to you. I guess none of us considered the possibility that you might decide to sell. But when the realtor came to us with a contract . . . well, there was nothing we could do except to let you know that you have no legal right."

"Who are these two people you claim were witnesses?"

Paul's face was contained. After a long pause, he said, "The Harrington servants."

Veezie found it hard to speak. "You mean. . . George and Beulah?"

"That's correct."

Her shoulders slumped. "Well, if they said it, I reckon it's the truth. They wouldn't lie." Her head was in a spin. "I suppose I need to call the realtor, but I've already signed a paper. Am I in trouble?"

Paul shook his head. "No, you're fine."

Her first thought was to pack her things and go back to the shanty in Goose Hollow, but she quickly dismissed the thought. The people there knew her too well. She didn't know how she'd do it or where she'd go, but she had to get far enough away that her reputation couldn't catch up with her. But it wasn't her reputation that troubled her as much as how her presence could affect Shep's ministry. For his sake, she had to leave and give the people in the surrounding communities time to forget.

Feeling numb, she stood. "If that's all, I reckon I'll go. Mr. Aycock would you please tell Harper that Johnny Mack Brown wants to buy Nine Gables? She'd be crazy not to sell it to him."

He lifted his shoulders. "You'd think! However, the realtor approached her as soon as he discovered the title was not in your name, and she turned him down. Veezie, Harper indicated that she'd prefer to leave things as they are; but even if she wanted to sell, according to a stipulation in the Will, Nine Gables goes to the heir and can never be sold. She wants you, Beulah and George to continue making that your home."

"That's mighty nice of her, but I got plans and I'll need your help."

"Excuse me?"

"I was thinking I might buy me one of those beach houses. Not a great big one, but with just enough room for me, Beulah and George." She swallowed hard. "Well, I don't know if they will want to go with me, now. Maybe they'll want to stay with Harper." She bit her lip to control the trembling. "Mr. Aycock, could you let me borrow enough money to get a fresh start in a different town? Don't need much. Just enough to get by until I get a job. Then I'll pay you back." She thrust her hand over her heart. "I promise. But I got to get away from here."

"Veezie, a trust remains in your name, and another has been set up for Jim, Lucas and Callie. You'll continue receiving a monthly sum. That hasn't changed."

"But that ain't right. It ain't mine." She grimaced. *It isn't right. It isn't mine.* Veezie had tried hard to talk like a lady, and as long as she had time to think about the words before they came rolling off her tongue, she did much better. But there were times like these, when the wrong words spewed up to the top, like pouring salty peanuts into an RC Cola.

"But it is yours. Please understand that Harper has a right to designate how she wants the money from the estate to be disbursed, and frankly, I think she's made some wise decisions. Gordon Harrington was a very wealthy man. Though I had to do some convincing, I've made sure that Flint and Harper will be able to live comfortably, also."

"Well, tell Harper I'm grateful, but she and Flint can move in as soon as I can get a few things together and get out."

"But don't you understand what I'm saying? They have no intention of moving to Nine Gables. One would think that would be the logical decision, but I've known Harper all her life—and her decisions are often based more on compassion than logic. And she's made it quite clear that although she isn't allowed to sell it, she wants nothing to do with Nine Gables. She seems quite happy living in the modest little house on Chinaberry Street." His eyes squinted into tiny slits. "You look troubled. I'd think you'd feel quite relieved. You don't have to leave Nine Gables, and your lifestyle doesn't have to change, since you'll continue to receive a monthly check, just as in the past."

"I understand."

"So what's the problem?"

"It's just . . . well, I had my heart set on moving to the Gulf. But I'll have to save up three monthly checks to have enough money to put down on a beach cottage."

He smiled. "I'm sure that's about right. But that gives you time to think about the situation before you make a decision. You may change your mind in three months. Come back then, and we'll talk."

Her brow furrowed. "So you're saying I can't borrow ahead?"

"That's right, Veezie. I'm sorry, but you've been given some shocking news, today. I feel it's in your best interest that you not make any snap decisions that could adversely affect your future."

If only he knew. By not allowing her to have the money, she had no future. And neither would Shep Jackson, as long as she was forced to remain in Flat Creek.

She stood. "If that's all, I reckon I'll go."

Paul and his son stood. Paul reached out his hand. "Harper has had some nice things to say about you, Miss O'Steen, and I now understand why. You are very pleasant to work with. I wish you well in all your endeavors, and hope you'll feel free to call on Bud anytime you have a question."

Miss O'Steen? He called me Miss O'Steen. Her heart fell. She hated the name—hated the way people in Goose Hollow had referred to her as "that O'Steen girl." But like a horrible nightmare, the description had come back to haunt her. Was there no escape?

Veezie could give up Nine Gables and the lifestyle she'd been afforded, but to give up the Harrington name was almost too painful to bear.

Chapter Thirty-Five

Hot tears burned in Gracie's eyes as she prepared her father's supper. She couldn't get her mind off the horrid accusation in the newspaper. How could the editor be so bold unless—

No, it couldn't be true.

Her daddy yelled from his bedroom. "Gracie, are you burning something in the kitchen?"

She gasped and grabbed a pot holder. Smoke billowed from the oven. "It's okay, Daddy. I have everything under control." Under control? Nothing was under control. How did life get so complicated?

Gracie whimpered. Even Mr. Williford's hogs would turn up their snouts at her supper. Wiping away the tears, she reached in the ice box and pulled out a small package wrapped in brown paper. Disgusted, she unwrapped the bologna, cut off a couple of slices of the meat, a hunk of hoop cheese and smeared some homemade mayonnaise on two pieces of light bread.

"Sorry, Daddy, but I burned the chicken." Her voice cracked.

"Do you mind having a sandwich for supper?"

"Hey, what's wrong, sweetheart? You aren't crying over burning a chicken, are you? I happen to love bologna sandwiches." His gaze locked with hers. "But this is not about a burned chicken, is it? What's wrong, Princess?"

She shrugged. "Nothing, really. I'm just feeling a little weepy. I guess it's a girl thing."

"Oh!" He seemed to understand, although he had no way of knowing the pain that was in her heart. Pain that he too would be experiencing, as soon as he learned of the awful allegations. She wanted to protect her father from the gossip, but in a small town like Flat Creek, by noon it was already all over town. It would only be a matter of time before some well-meaning church member would be calling to discuss the latest news.

He crawled off the bed and flinched with each painful step as he made his way to the table. Taking a bite of the sandwich, he winked and smiled. "Mmm . . . hits the spot. As good as your mother used to make for me. Thanks, honey. "

As Gracie cleaned the kitchen, she pondered her options. Should she go back to the office of the Flat Creek Ledger and give the galoot a piece of her mind? But what if it were true? What if Veezie really had given birth to an illegitimate baby?

Shep hobbled back to his room to go over the sermon notes he planned to deliver on Sunday. Gracie had begged him to give himself another couple of weeks before returning to the pulpit, but her pleading did no more good than if she'd been standing on her head, whistling Dixie. Her father was a stubborn man.

She put away the last dish, dried her hands and had no sooner sat down with a tall glass of sweet iced tea, when the phone rang.

"Miss Jackson? This is Garth. Garth Graham."

Surely, she misunderstood. "Who?"

"Garth Graham, I'm the editor of the—"

Her pulse raced. "Yes, I know who you are." She purposely tried to make the tone of her voice reveal the level of contempt she held for the man.

"I can tell you're angry with me, and I don't blame you." He paused.

If he was waiting for a denial, he'd have a long wait. "Is that all? You called to say you don't blame me for being angry? Well, trust me, your opinion means about as much to me as bitterweed does to a milk cow. Turns my stomach."

"I understand. But I really would like to sit down and talk with you. Would that be possible?"

"Are you serious? After what you've said about my father, you expect me to want to hear anything you have to say?" Though she didn't want to admit it, her curiosity was up. She groveled. "Where do you propose we meet?"

"I was thinking I'd go to your house, if that's agreeable."

Gracie determined not to let down her guard, lest her name appear in the Sunday gossip section. "After the awful things you said about my father, you now have the nerve to march yourself up to his door? Have you no shame?"

"Please, Gra—Miss Jackson. Ten minutes. That's all I ask. Just hear me out. Is it okay if I come on over?"

"Now?"

"Is this not a convenient time for you?"

It was convenient enough for her, but at the moment her thoughts were on her father. He'd been so busy preparing his Sunday sermon that he didn't even ask about the newspaper. But someone was bound to tell him. Gracie couldn't imagine that no one had called to discuss the article before now. How would he feel, knowing the editor who lambasted in print everything he held sacred, now had the gall to ask if he might come calling? Surely, her daddy would be furious, and of course, he'd have every right to be.

He said, "What if I drop by in about an hour? Say, eight o'clock?"

Gracie wanted to have the pleasure of telling him 'no,' and she wasn't quite sure why she couldn't. "Make it nine."

"Nine o'clock it is. Thank you."

At least her daddy would be asleep by then and she wouldn't be forced to answer questions, which could be too painful for him to hear.

When car lights flashed through the window at exactly nine o'clock, she eased open the screen door, hoping the squeak wouldn't awaken her father. Gently closing it back, she waited on the porch for Mr. Graham to get out of the car.

Gracie didn't remember him being so muscular. The day she

met him in the office of The Ledger, he had on a sports coat and dress trousers. Tonight, he had on dungarees, a white tee shirt and cowboy boots. His broad shoulders seemed to accent his small waist and huge biceps bulged from beneath the rolled up sleeves.

He looked at her and smiled. "Thank you for seeing me." He walked up the steps and stood beside her, looking down. She didn't remember him being quite so tall. In fact, it seemed she was seeing him for the very first time. Gracie stiffened. The nerve of him referring to her as Miss Gee Whiz. He must've thought he was being cute, but anyone who read the article would consider it very unprofessional to use common slang in a newspaper article.

His smile faded. "You did agree for me to come, didn't you? Are you not going to invite me in?"

She shook her head. "I didn't exactly invite you. I simply agreed for you to come, after you were so insistent. But my father is asleep and needs his rest, so whatever you came to say can be said on the porch."

"That's fine. Do you have any objections to us sitting down or must I stand?"

Gracie shrugged. "Sit if you like." She walked over and sat in the glider, expecting him to take a seat in the chair. Instead, he walked over and plopped down beside her. She bristled. If he was trying to irritate her, he was doing a swell job, but she wouldn't give him the satisfaction of knowing he succeeded. "Now that you're here, do you mind sharing with me the purpose of your visit?"

He rubbed his chin and stared into the night sky. "Gracie . . . uh, may I please call you Gracie?"

She rolled her eyes. "Call me anything you wish. I don't recall you asking anyone else if they mind the names you chose to call them. Is this a new habit you've picked up?"

"Well, I don't expect you to believe it, but actually it's an old habit I wish to break. And that's why I wanted to come talk to you and to say I'm sorry. Gracie, two hours after the newspapers left for distribution Friday morning, I regretted that article. I knew I'd made an idiot of myself."

Her jaw dropped. "And you call that an apology?"

"Actually, I do. But I didn't expect you to understand."

"Oh, I understand perfectly. You're saying you're sorry that you're an idiot. Frankly, I don't care that you're an idiot. But I do care that you have such low regard for people's feelings that you'd make up lies to sell a few papers."

Seeing the forlorn look on his face reminded her of a whipped puppy. She almost wanted to pat him on the shoulder and tell him all was forgiven. But she wouldn't, because it wasn't. How could she ever forgive him for ruining the lives of those she loved? "If that's all you have to say, I guess you can go."

His gaze locked with hers. "But I came to tell you why I wanted to recall the papers."

"I think you've already explained. It was because you were insane when you wrote it."

"Go ahead. Crucify me. I deserve it."

Gracie bristled that he'd compare his wounded pride with something as horrific as a crucifixion. "It's not up to me to mete out your punishment. I think you're probably your own worst enemy."

That seemed to draw a slight smile. "Truer words have never been spoken, m'lady."

"Okay, I'm curious. Can you explain to me why you would make up such a filthy lie and accuse a sweet girl like Veezie of giving birth out-of-wedlock? Even though it isn't true, there will always be people in this town who'll wonder. The stigma will follow her the remainder of her life. She'll never be able to erase the image from their minds."

He glanced away, but not before she saw moisture glistening in his eyes. When he didn't respond, Gracie tugged on his shirt sleeve. "Garth?"

He still didn't turn to face her.

"Garth, it was a lie, wasn't it?" Still no answer. "I have to know. Please, tell me. Did Veezie have a baby? It wasn't . . . it couldn't have been my—" She couldn't get the words out. Not until this moment had she considered that he might have been telling the truth about both Veezie and her father. The thought nauseated her. She burst into tears.

Garth gently put his arm over the glider and drew her close. "Please, don't cry. No, the baby isn't your father's."

Unable to look at him, she said, "But there was a baby?"

"No, Gracie. There was no baby."

She slowly lifted her head and looking into his eyes she said, "I don't believe you."

Dimples dug into his cheeks. "You didn't believe me when I said there was a baby and now you don't believe me when I'm telling you there wasn't. Why don't you believe me?"

"Because you said the baby wasn't my father's. That tells me that she did have a baby."

"No it doesn't. It simply put the supposition there. And that's all I had. Supposition. I lied about having facts, because I had none."

"Then what possessed you to write the article?"

"What possessed me?" He ran his fingers through his hair. "Bitterness."

"I don't understand. What's Veezie ever done to you to cause you to be bitter?"

He stood, ambled over and leaned against a porch post. "It had nothing to do with Veezie."

"Then it was a personal vendetta against my father?"

"No, not your father. But it's what he stands for. For thirteen years I've been angry with God. And I've made it a point to try to destroy the faith of all believers. So when I heard about the chaos at the church business meeting the night your dad was accused of staying late at Nine Gables, I immediately jumped on it. Then, to my disappointment, it quickly died down. So I had to dig deeper. I went to Goose Hollow to try and get some trash on Veezie. I talked to every low-life I could find, but all I could get was that she was from a poor family, and had no one to really care where she went or what she did. No one seemed to want to give me the goods I was looking for. I asked about the people who raised her, and was told they were buried in the church cemetery. So I thought if I got names off the headstones, I could look up court records. I wasn't sure what I was looking for, but I wanted anything I could get my hands on that would help cast suspicion on your dad. That's when I found the grave."

Gracie sighed. "Maybe we should sit back down. What grave?"

"The baby's."

She clinched her eyes shut. "Then it was true? Veezie gave birth?"

"I don't know. The tiny plot is next to Sally O'Steen."

Gracie sucked in a lungful of air and let out a long, slow breath. "Then maybe Mrs. O'Steen died after giving birth."

"No, the baby's birthdate is May 07, 1937—Mrs. O'Steen died November, 1934. However, if the baby was Veezie's, I assume she was pregnant when she moved here. Gracie, I never believed the baby was the Reverend Jackson's, although with so much hatred inside me, I wanted people to think the worse."

Gracie couldn't take it all in. "Then you have nothing at all on which to base your assumptions. You were just hoping the baby was Veezie's?"

He nodded. "Yep. It wasn't her that I was after. It was an attempt to link a preacher of the gospel with a woman of ill repute."

"Then what caused you to have a change of heart, all of a sudden?"

His lip quivered. "I've wondered that myself. Call it posthumous prayers."

"I don't get it."

"That's not something I wish to explain, yet. I only came here tonight to apologize for the cruel things I said in the paper."

"I'm not the one you owe the apology to."

"I intend to apologize to your father and Veezie, but I wrote that second article after you came and pleaded in their behalf. You were right and I was wrong. I needed to let you know that your words didn't fall on deaf ears. I've spent hours thinking about what you said that day in my office and I want to thank you. Others have tried to set me back on the right path for years, but it took you to reach me."

"This has been a lot to take in. I don't really know how to respond."

"There's no response needed on your part, though I long to hear you say I'm forgiven. Gracie, please believe me when I say I'm sorry for all the trouble I've caused."

"I do forgive you, Garth." She swallowed the gasp that rose from the pit of her stomach. *Did I just say I forgave him? Am I crazy? He's thoughtless and cruel.*

He drove away and she wondered what had taken place. Did he really mean it? Was he truly sorry, or was it a smooth line he conjured up, in an attempt to win her affection? There was something about the way he looked at her that made her suspect he was drawn to her—in the same way she sensed a magnetic emotional pull toward him. A voice inside prodded her to forgive, though she couldn't forget a single word in the disparaging articles. Would she feel the same tug in her heart if he looked like Arnie? Or would she still want to run hide every time Arnie came in sight if he looked like Garth Graham? The notion drew a smile, though she felt almost wicked for the fleeting thought. Was she really so small-minded that physical appearance clouded her senses?

Gracie lay in bed unable to erase the conversation from her head. What would her father say if he knew she'd entertained thoughts of a romantic liaison with the man responsible for trying to ruin his ministry? Admitting it was almost more than she could stomach. How could she? It had nothing to do with his jaw-dropping good looks. Instead, it was the sorrowful look in his eyes when he made the pathetic attempt at an apology, which caused her to lose her head.

Who was she trying to kid? It wasn't compassion that caused her heart to race at the very thought of him, nor compassion that branded his image on her brain as if seared with a hot iron. It wasn't compassion that made her feel such misery and utter loneliness when his car drove out of sight. But it wasn't love, either. Couldn't be. The only thing she knew about Garth Graham were things to detest. He was an obnoxious, self-centered, arrogant snob.

And she was crazy about him. She choked back the tears.

She recalled her daddy once explaining how to deal with unwanted thoughts, when he said a person can't help a bird flying over his head but he doesn't have to let it nest in his hair.

Shoo bird.

Chapter Thirty-Six

Veezie twisted her hands together. The lines on Gracie's face confirmed this was not a casual visit. "Gracie, spill it. What's wrong?"

She covered her eyes. "Oh, Veezie. Obviously, you didn't read yesterday's paper or you wouldn't have to ask."

Her muscles tightened. "That editor again?"

Gracie nodded.

"What did he say this time?"

Gracie fiddled with the ring on her finger. "Veezie, he said . . . well, he said you gave birth to an illegitimate baby." She quickly added, "But I want you to know I didn't believe a word of it. I simply thought I should give you a heads-up, before someone approached you about the subject—and I'm sure they will."

Veezie sat silent. *No more running.* Her gaze locked with Gracie's.

Gracie's eyes squinted as she reached for Veezie's hand. "Then it's true?"

She nodded. "I wonder—how did he find out?"

Gracie didn't have the heart to tell Veezie she entertained the louse on her porch the night before, in the moonlight. "Veezie, I don't think he knows for sure. And who's going to believe him?"

"You're sweet, Ducky. But the real question is 'Who *won't* believe it?' Well, no sense in leaving folks wondering. I'll go to the gallows."

"Gallows? What are you talking about?"

She shrugged. "Ever read *The Scarlet Letter*?"

Gracie nodded and burst into tears. One look at Veezie's face and her hand shot to her mouth. "Where . . . where's your baby? Did you put it up for adoption?"

She shook her head. "My little girl, she died." Giant tears fell down her cheeks. "Flint and Beulah said she was beautiful, but I didn't even see her."

"Oh, you poor, poor darling." Gracie flung her arms around Veezie's neck. "I can't imagine the pain you've suffered. I'm so very sorry."

"Sorry? You don't hate me?"

"Hate you? Why should I hate you?"

"Maybe for allowing your daddy to fall in love with me? It was wrong of me not to tell him 'bout the baby. Oh, but Gracie, I knew if he ever found out what I'd done, he wouldn't have nothin' to do with me. I reckon it was dumb of me to think I could hide it. It was bound to come out sooner or later."

"Oh, Veezie, you're so wrong. If you think my daddy would

look down on you for something you did prior to becoming a believer, you don't know him very well. Whatever you've done in the past, is passed. Daddy would tell you, 'old things passed away and all things became new, the day you trusted Jesus as your Savior."

"I know that's how God feels about me, Gracie, but I ain't—" She bit her lip and started over. "I'm not sure that's how Shep feels."

"Oh, but it is. I've heard him preach on the subject of forgiveness, too many times. He believes it, all right."

Veezie chewed her bottom lip. "But don't you see, Gracie? Even if Shep could find it in his heart to forgive me, the good Christian folks at Flat Creek Fellowship would hold it against him for having anything to do with me. So I'm leaving."

"No, Veezie. You can't. Daddy will make them understand. Please, don't run away from this."

Run away? Strange, Gracie should've used those words. That's exactly what she was doing—still running. She smiled. "Thank you."

"For what?"

"For helping me understand. I can't run."

Gracie reached over and gave her a hug. "I'm glad." She stood. "I wish I could stay longer, but I need to get back home and fix Daddy's lunch."

"How's he doing?"

Gracie smiled. "Why don't you come over and see for

yourself?"

Veezie shrugged. "Is he well enough to preach tomorrow or will someone else be preaching?"

"Oh, I'm not sure he should, but he's planning to be there."

"Then I'll see you both at church tomorrow."

Veezie thought about what she had to do and though it wouldn't be pleasant, she'd do it. For Shep's sake.

Sunday morning, Veezie trudged into the dining room wearing a pitifully drab-looking dress, fashioned from a chicken-feed sack. She plopped down at the table.

Beulah walked in and scowled. "Honey chile, where in the world did you find that outfit? Is it done Halloween and I don't know it?"

"Nope. Look at me, Beulah." She turned around slowly. "This is who I am. My mama made this dress. She tried to dye it blue, but the coarse threads wouldn't take the dye and it turned out to be this faded gray."

"You josting me?" Beulah's belly jiggled when she laughed. "Miz Ophelia wouldn't know which end of the needle to poke into a piece o' material. Maybe it's wrong to speak ill of the dead, but I declare that woman didn't never make nothing in her life but trouble for the folks around her."

"Not Ophelia. My real mama. Sally. It was stuck up in the top of the closet at Goose Hollow, and I brought it back with me when I drove by there the other day. I thought it'd be a reminder of what

I once was and how far I've come. But instead, it's a reminder of who I still am."

Beulah's jaw dropped. "Oh, m'goodness. You know, don'tcha?" She buried her face in her hands. "Oh, honey, bless yo' little ol' heart. I hope me and George didn't do the wrong thing. I been dreading this day a coming. If we had it to do over again . . . well, I don't reckon I know what we'd do. Miz Ophelia was an evil woman and me and George couldn't stand the thought of Miz Harper being shut out in the cold, when we knowed all along that she was Miz Ophelia's flesh and blood. And that's why we went to the midwife and begged her to tell the truth—that she faked the switch. But we got attached to you right off and then we got scared we'd done wrong by telling. The thought of you going back where you come from made us plumb sick. Then we learnt Miz Harper was getting married and was happy, so we figured everything worked out for the best. Sugar, how did you—"

Veezie gave a dismissive shrug. "Excuse me, Beulah while I say the blessing. I'm kind of hungry this morning."

Beulah's eyes glistened. "Yeah, honey. You go ahead and pray." She walked out of the room, but Veezie could hear the sobs coming from the kitchen.

When Beulah returned with a pot of coffee, Veezie spoke first. "Beulah, you and George did the right thing. And you said if you had it to do over again, you didn't know what you'd do. Well, I know. You'd do the same thing, because to hide the truth would be dishonest and there's not a dishonest bone in your body, or in

George's. I wouldn't even want you to hide the truth on my account. So don't ever feel you did the wrong thing, because you didn't."

Beulah sniffed. "I don't reckon I could love you more if you come outta my own innards. I ain't never birthed a baby before, but I feel almost like you belong to me. Naturally, I love Miz Harper, too, but in a different way. I never felt like she needed me as much as you needed me when you came to us."

"I did need you, Beulah. I still need you."

Beulah wiped her eyes with the tail of her apron. "I reckon we needed each other. But honey, I now need you to do somethin' for me."

"What?"

"Burn that ugly ol' rag you wearing. You a lady, now. You even sounding like one. Don't even sound like the same little gal who come here last fall, talking like white trash." She let out a little chuckle. "You was a mess, you was. But I reckon when you hang with hogs, you likely to find yourself wallowing in a sty. And them bunch o' drunks down at that juke-joint ain't nothing but a bunch of pigs."

"If I'm different, I have you to thank, Beulah. You taught me a lot about how to walk and talk and how to dress like a lady."

"Well, I can't read and I can't cipher, but I can look at letters and tell they ain't numbers, so I reckon that shows I ain't stupid. I know the difference when I see 'em. And I can tell the difference in the way a lady talks and the kinda talking white trash does." She chuckled. "And sugar, I sho' thank ya for allowing me to take the credit, but I'm afeered I didn't have nothing to do with learning you how to talk proper. To tell the truth, I ain't got it down pat yet, myself."

Veezie smiled. "But you taught me not to say ain't and t'weren't."

"Aw, sugar, that t'weren't nothin'." They both laughed. "But now that you've been associating with the likes of Miz Gracie, I done and seen a big change in the way you talk. Yes'm, you sound as much like a lady as Miz Harper ever did. So ol' Beulah wants you to hold yo' head up, pull them shoulders back the way I taught you to do and show everybody what a fine lady you is. I'm real proud of you, sugar."

Veezie shrugged. There was no need to hurt Beulah by telling her ahead of time what everyone else in town already knew . . . or to tell her what was going to happen at church today. Though Beulah was bound to find out, Veezie couldn't bear to be the one to tell her. No one had ever been proud of her before.

"But honey, that ol' garment you is got on ain't fit to wear to a hog-killing. I want you to get yo'self back up them stairs and put on something befitting the lady you is."

"No, Beulah." She chewed on her thumbnail and muttered, "This is what Hester wore, and if it was good enough for her, it's good enough for me."

"Why, sugar, what you talking about? Miz Harper ain't never wore nothin' that homely."

"I didn't say Harper. I said Hester. I don't mean to say she wore this same dress. But she had on a coarse gray frock, and I think it might've looked a whole lot like this one."

"Well, I don't know a gal named Hester but there ain't no sense in you going around dressed like po' white trash, when you got gobs of pretty clothes." Beulah cocked her head. "Veezie, baby, what's worrying ya? You look all down in the dumps, like you going to a funeral."

She lifted a shoulder. "Might say that I am."

Beulah's brow raised. "Zat so? Well why didn't you say so sooner? Who died, sugar?"

"Love died, Beulah. Don't you see? My love for Shep was doomed from the beginning. And after I say what I have to say today, it'll be time to bury those feelings and face the truth. It's over."

Beulah plopped her hands on her hips. "You talking foolishness, and I ain't gonna have it. Now, whatever you got on your mind, you best forget. Get back up them stairs and put you on something frilly. What about that dress with all them little pink flowers on it?"

Veezie shook her head. "No, Beulah. This is what I'm wearing. It's befitting the occasion."

"Well, sometimes I don't understand you, girl. But when you make up your mind, I done learned there ain't no changing it, so I'll go find you a hat. Maybe the pretty little black and white straw will spruce it up a bit."

"Don't need no hat, today." She pushed her plate out of the way. "Excuse me, Beulah, but I'm not very hungry this morning."

Chapter Thirty-Seven

Veezie arrived at church early and took a seat on the front pew, afraid if she sat in the middle where she could watch the people as they came in, she might lose her nerve. She could do this. She had to—for Shep's sake—regardless of what people might say about her. After reading *The Scarlet Letter*, Hester Prynne had become her heroine. If Hester was willing to die for the Reverend Dimmesdale, surely Veezie could face the humiliation she must bear, in order to save the Reverend Shep Jackson's reputation.

Sticks and stones may break my bones but words . . . It was a cute little ditty, but not a word of truth in it. She'd much rather be beaten with sticks and stones than to relive the names she'd been called in the past. The horrid names she thought no one in Flat Creek would ever associate with her. But she could never outrun her past. Why try? She rubbed her hands together. *No more running*.

By sitting up front, she wouldn't have to look at anyone until the time came. Maybe it was the tears clouding her eyes—or her mind playing tricks—but her focus became distorted. She gasped and blinked twice before being convinced she was not seeing a scaffold, but only wood molding, which surrounded the baptismal pool. She pulled a linen handkerchief from her pocket and blotted the perspiration from her forehead.

Behind her, she could hear people arriving and the sound of muffled voices. She didn't have to wonder what they were saying. Though she couldn't make out sentences, words such as "heathen, loose woman, and Jezebel," rang loud and clear in her ears. Her tear-filled eyes burned when the door facing her opened and Shep walked in. She dropped her gaze. Instinct made her want to run out the door and never look back. But there was something stronger than instinct urging her not to run. She loved him too much to leave him all alone to answer the charges. Unable to stop the flow of tears, she tried to be inconspicuous when she reached up to blot her eyes. *Poor Hester. How she must have loved the Reverend Dimmesdale.*

The attendance board, hanging to the left of the baptismal pool, listed one-hundred-fifty-two people attending Sunday School at the earlier hour. Veezie plainly remembered the first day she visited the church only weeks ago, when the count was ninety-eight. She didn't have to wonder why there would be an increase of fifty-four people in attendance today. Apparently, every Flat Creek resident had read the wicked article in the Ledger and didn't want to miss out on getting the latest gossip first hand.

The choir stood and led the congregation in singing and though she didn't look anyone in the eyes, Veezie could feel the stares. They sang "What can wash away my sin, nothing but the blood of Jesus."

She glanced down when someone tugged on the tail of her dress. Though her lips quivered, she managed a smile, seeing a little tow-head boy, no older than six, with two front teeth missing. "My mama says you're nothing but a—" An arm reached around, seemingly out of nowhere, grabbed him by the elbow and jerked him away. Veezie began to shake.

Shep stood to preach. He said a few words about how good it was to be back in the pulpit after having been out for a while and thanked those who filled in while he was recuperating. "My text today comes from the book of James. It's a sermon I prepared and planned to preach the Sunday night of my accident. But if those of you who were in attendance will remember, I changed my mind after arriving here. Instead of preaching the sermon God laid on my heart, I was wallowing in self-pity and chose to dismiss the church. I was wrong. It's a sermon we all need. It was relevant then, but even more so today."

Buster Watts raised his hand.

"Yes, Buster, is there something you need to say before I read from God's word?"

"As a matter of fact, there is preacher. I'm aware of what James says about the tongue, and I for one feel you made the right decision that night by not trying to preach something you don't practice yourself."

Veezie's pulse raced as she heard a chorus of "Amens", and then a loud male voice shouted, "Sit down Watts. You don't speak for all of us. Preach it, Shep."

Buster walked up to the platform among both jeers and cheers.

Veezie put her hands over her ears and clinched her eyes shut. She wanted to stand up and shout, "Do with me what you will, but leave him be. He's not guilty of anything but loving me and by now he's repented even of that grave sin." But though the words screamed out within her heart, she couldn't bring them to her lips.

Shep held up both hands and quieted the crowd. Veezie shuddered. It seemed the deacon would only be stopped by physical force and though she wasn't the one to do it, she almost wished she could.

Shep stepped aside and Buster Watts took his place. With both hands planted firmly on the oak pulpit, the big burly man turned and glared in his pastor's eyes. Then, with a pointed finger, he said, "Excuse me, preacher for the interruption, for I'm sure you've prepared an eloquent speech for us poor wayward sinners this morning." He looked out among the people with a smirk on his face. "Frankly, I don't like being up here anymore than you want me up here, but there's a matter that needs to be brought before the church, and as chairman of the deacons, I feel it my place to attend to this urgent issue. The sooner we deal with it, the sooner we can put it behind us."

Curtis Dobbs stood. "Buster, if I remember correctly, you

stood in that same place a couple of weeks ago and announced you were turning in your resignation as chairman of the deacons." There was a stir among the crowd.

"So I did. But a vote was never taken. Therefore at this time, I am still acting chairman."

The murmuring grew louder, and once more, Shep stood with lifted palms, urging the crowd to settle down. "Brother Watts, I'm sorry, but you're out of order. This is not a business meeting. I'm afraid I'll have to ask you to please be seated. If you have a problem that needs to be addressed, I'll be most happy to meet with you after the service. Then, if it needs to be brought before the church, we'll tackle it at the appointed time. But the Sunday morning worship service is neither the time nor place."

The deacon's jaw jutted forward. "No, preacher, it seems you're the one who is out of order. It pains me to say it, but your dirty laundry has been hung out to dry in front of the whole town. You've harmed the good name of this church, shamed us and made us a laughing stock."

Veezie shut her eyes and envisioned Shep standing helpless, beside Hester Prynne's evil husband, Roger Chillingworth. She blinked again. Roger Chillingworth? Or was it Jack Hawk, the father of her little Diamond?

Diamond. She'd never thought of the irony until now, but both she and Hester gave birth to true gems. Hester had her little Pearl, and Veezie gave birth to a precious little Diamond. Her insides quivered. If not for her, Shep would not be going through such ridicule. She deserved all the shame heaped upon her. The editor had called her a harlot and she couldn't deny the charge. There was not only Jack, but Adolphus. *Poor Adolphus.*

She slowly turned her head to the left and shivered at the sight of him sitting beside his lovely, unsuspecting wife and three precious children. Strange she should feel such sympathy for the man. If only he hadn't stopped that night. No doubt he'd had the same thought countless times.

The deacon's ranting pulled her attention back to the front.

"We should've ousted this wanton hypocrite—a wolf in sheep's clothing who dares to call himself God's servant—at our last Business Meeting. But I understand many of you found it hard to believe a man could stand before you, Sunday after Sunday and preach about the wiles of the devil, while hiding his own disgusting, immoral lifestyle the other six days a week. I'm as appalled as many of you, to learn that the man we put our trust in is nothing more than an infidel."

The room was so charged with tension, Veezie suspected if one more hot head stood to voice his opinion, the air would surely ignite. She rubbed the perspiration gathering around her collar.

When Arnie Phelps asked for the floor, Buster refused the request and motioned for him to have a seat. Buster then gestured toward the editor from the Ledger and with a big grin pasted on his face, said, "As tough as it is to swallow, we should be thankful that the competent Mr. Garth Graham saw fit to bring this to our attention. People, we've been deceived long enough. Though it pains me that it's come to this, we have a responsibility to God as well as to ourselves to do the right thing."

He motioned to someone in the front of the church, though Veezie didn't turn around to look.

"Since these new allegations have come to light, the ushers will pass out slips of paper to give our members another chance to vote. And before you cast your vote, I beg of you to ask the question, 'Is this the sort of role model we want for our children?' I'm sure you'll agree there's only one answer."

Two men started down the aisle, with paper and pencils.

Gracie ran to the front and stood facing the congregation. Tears flowed down her cheeks. "Why the secret vote, people? Why not stand up and be counted? But before you vote, I'd like to request we have an orderly discussion, where everyone has an opportunity to ask questions. Others besides Arnie may have something they wish to say."

Heads nodded in agreement. Buster Watts smirked. "Fine. Makes no difference to me. I've left no question as to where I stand and I feel that my brothers and sisters in this church are as disheartened by the actions of these two sinners as I am. So, young lady, we'll grant your wish. It was for your sake only, that I suggested a secret vote. I thought it would go easier on you if you didn't have to see your friends stand in opposition to your father."

Shep walked over, wrapped his arm around his daughter's shoulder and tried to lead her back to her pew. She shook her head. "No, Daddy. I'm not through."

Buster motioned to the ushers. "Have a seat men. We'll do it Miss Jackson's way, but it's customary when such a vote is taken that the guilty . . . uh . . . that is to say, the accused, be absent. I'll agree to a show of hands, but only if the preacher leaves the room."

Shep turned and without a word spoken walked down the aisle and out the double doors at the front of the church.

The deacon gestured toward Gracie. "If there's nothing more, Miss Jackson, you can take your seat."

She fiddled with a ring on her finger. "I'm not through."

Buster shuffled his feet and made a point to look at his watch. "Well make it snappy. This has been drawn out far too long. We don't need to drag it out much further." He shrugged. "But go ahead, sugar, and say what you have to say and let's get on with it."

Gracie flinched at hearing the horrid man refer to her with such an affectionate term. She gazed out among the congregation. "Frankly, I'm shocked as I look out among you and recall the times when many of you were in need. And my daddy was there for you. Not because it was required of him or that he'd get anything in return, but because of his love for you. His people. I've always been fascinated at the stories in the Old Testament where God named babies before they were born . . . like Jacob and Esau. Names had a special meaning. And I can't help but believe my grandmother must have heard from God when she named my father, Shepherd. For he's truly been a Shepherd to the sheep that

God entrusted to him. And I've seen his anguish when one of the sheep has gone astray. He'll stop at nothing until that one is redeemed back into the fold." Her voice cracked. "Well, I guess that's all I have to say."

A woman with four children sitting on the pew beside her stood. "Well, I have something to say. I'm ashamed I sat silent this long. I don't know if he's guilty or not, but don't we owe him the courtesy to explain? He's always been here for us, and now because of hearsay, we want to lynch him? It's not right. Last year my girls were embarrassed to go to school, because they didn't have anything decent to wear. I was too proud to tell anyone our situation, so I don't know how Brother Shep could've known. But it wasn't long after he lost his wife, and he came to the house and brought me Miss Jenny's Singer sewing machine. It was practically new and he could've sold it. Yet, he gave it away. Not only that, but he brought a stack of pretty print flour sacks he'd collected. I'm sure several of you donated yours without knowing why he wanted them. Must have been at least twenty yards of beautiful cotton material in those sacks." She glanced around the auditorium. "When my girls started school, they were the best dressed girls in their classes. And I for one—"

Deacon Watts' lip curled in a wry smile. "Thank you, but I think you've made your point, Maggie. Now, if there's no other discussion."

A young man raised his hand. "When Rebecca and I bought twenty acres on the other side of the creek and moved here, we didn't know a soul. But Brother Shep showed up one day, grabbed a shovel and helped me dig my well. I'll always be grateful to him for that."

The deacon ran his hands through his hair. "I don't think any of us here doubt that Shepherd Jackson has done a few good deeds, but isn't that what we paid him to do?"

A tall man, wearing faded overalls and worn brogans, stepped out and made his way down the aisle. When a shank of dark, greasy hair fell between his eyes, he blew upward, but his grim expression never changed. His hollow eyes caused prickles to rise on Veezie's arms. Whispers could be heard as questioning gazes followed him. She didn't know who he was, but there was a feeling of electricity in the room.

He walked right up to the deacon and standing almost nose to nose, said, "Hold on, Buster. I've got something I need to get off my chest."

The deacon shifted on his feet. "Have a seat, Walker. We've taken your name off this church roll and therefore you have no right to speak."

"Well, I intend to have my say, and afterward, if you think you're man enough to throw me out, you can try." He turned to face the crowd. "As most of you know, I spent the last eighteen months in prison for selling moonshine. I broke the law and I deserved what I got. I won't point them all out, but will suffice it to say that three of my best customers are members of this church. One of them turned me in." His chest rose as he heaved. "Buster, you got rid of me, but I'll be John Brown if I'll stand by and let you railroad this preacher the way you railroaded me. He don't deserve it. Not a week went by while I was in the hoosegow that I didn't get a visit from Brother Jackson. Where were you *Deacon* Watts, when I was in prison?"

Buster reached in his back pocket and pulled out a handkerchief. He wiped his brow. "This has gone far enough. We're wasting time listening to the disgruntled ravings of a former convict. I say we vote."

Arnie stood. "Not yet, Mr. Dobbs." His mother yanked at his pants leg. "No, hon."

He looked at his mother and smiled. "I'm not ashamed, Mama. I was, but no more. Now, I'd be ashamed if I didn't tell. The truth is, folks, when my daddy left, he left us with bills to pay and nothing to pay them with. There were days when we had nothing in the house to eat. I reckon I was about eight or nine years old. Then one day, the preacher showed up with two fishing poles and invited me to go fishing with him. We caught a fine mess and he showed me how to clean 'em. Mrs. Jenny brought a tub of lard and a five-pound bag of corn meal over and gave it to Mama." He grinned. "That night we had a fish fry that I won't ever forget." He pursed his lips and whistled. "Now, that was good eating." His comment drew smiles. "And the preacher didn't stop there. He bought me a bicycle and got me a job delivering newspapers. I didn't make much, but it was enough to get us by until I got the job at the Jitney Jungle delivering groceries. I've managed to keep my route and I'm now Assistant Manager of the store. We're doing fine. Every Thursday afternoon when the store is closed, I go fishing."

An elderly gentleman sitting back of Arnie, patted him on the shoulder. "And this young fellow has become quite the angler. Caught ol' Grumpy, the catfish many of us had been trying to land for years. Caught him with a piece of soap."

Deacon Watts threw up his hands. "This is what I was afraid of. Everyone seems to want to hear themselves talk. Discussion is closed. Now, Miss Jackson, I'll allow you the last word to speak in defense of your father, and then we'll take a vote."

Gracie shook her head. "What purpose would it serve? You've all already made up your mind how you want to vote."

Veezie wanted to wrap her arms around Gracie and beg forgiveness for causing her father such grief. She buried her face in her hands. If only she could relive her past, there was so much she'd do differently.

The deacon had a sly grin. "Fine. We'll now take a vote."

From the far side of the room, a dapper-looking young man in his mid-twenties, with chestnut hair and eyes of coal stepped out in the aisle. "Not so fast!" he yelled.

Chapter Thirty-Eight

Veezie supposed it was the man's rugged good looks that brought forth giggles from the four teenage girls sitting near the door. The steel taps on his cowboy boots clicked against the oak floor as he strolled to the front of the church and stood beside Gracie. Wearing dungarees and a plaid shirt, he stood out in the crowd, since most of the men—even the farmers in overalls—put on white dress shirts and ties to come to church.

Buster rolled his eyes. "I don't recognize you, young man. Are you a member here? If not, perhaps whatever you have to say can wait."

"Pardon me, sir, but I believe I deserve a chance to speak, since I'm the one who stirred this hornet's nest in the first place."

Confidence appeared to ooze from every cell in his body. With a bold voice and posture as straight as that of an army officer, he said, "My name is Garth Graham."

Buster's mouth split into a craggy smile and he thrust forth his hand and gave a hearty shake. "Mr. Graham? But of course. As chairman of the deacons, allow me to welcome you and to thank you personally for visiting with us this morning. And in case you didn't get the name, I'm Wallace P. Watts. That's spelled with two ells and two tees. I go by 'Buster,' but you can use my legal name in your write-up. I'm the only Watts in the community and folks around here all know me."

Veezie expected to see Mr. Watts slobbering on himself, the way he gushed. She fiddled with her earbob and glanced around the room in an attempt to read the varying range of facial expressions. Contempt? Sympathy? Fear? Pity? It was difficult to tell. One thing for sure, there was no indication of boredom.

The young editor raised his brow. "May I have the floor?"

Buster Watts almost bowed at his feet. "But of course. Naturally, we want the truth, so don't feel the need to spare us. I follow your editorials religiously. If not for your boldness to print the facts, no telling how many young men in our community could've been dragged into this woman's den of iniquity. But you nailed her. Yes sir, you're an asset to this community. Quite the investigative reporter."

Garth glared at Buster and nodded. "I nailed her all right. Just as the Roman soldiers nailed Jesus to the cross for something He wasn't guilty of."

Veezie flinched. What was he saying?

Buster's mouth gaped open. "I think I know what you meant to say, Mr. Graham, but to keep down misunderstanding, let's make it clear. The analogy lacks merit, for there's a major difference. She *is* guilty."

Garth's brow shot up. "Oh yeah? Of what?"

Buster flared back. "What *is* this? You're the one who plainly said in your article—"

"That I was presenting the facts? That a reliable source presented information that she gave birth to a baby?" He shook his head. "I lied. I received no confirmation to the story I printed."

Once more, the church buzzed.

Buster flung his shoulders back. "I don't believe you."

"Why is it deacon, that when I falsely accused the woman of something, you chose to believe me. But now that I'm telling you that it wasn't true, you call me a liar?" He looked out among the congregation. "Why don't you go home, people? A real circus will be coming to town in a couple of months. Wait and go to that one, where donkey's walk on four legs instead of two."

Cora Watts gave a loud gasp and fanned her face.

The young man showed no signs of yielding the floor. He held his head back, and the light caught the tears streaming down his cheeks. With the voice of an orator he quoted scripture from the book of Matthew.

"Then shall the King say unto them on his right hand, Come, ye blessed of my Father, inherit the kingdom prepared for you from the foundation of the world."

Veezie immediately recognized the passage, but it was if she were listening with fresh ears.

"For I was an hungred, and ye gave me meat: I was thirsty, and ye gave me drink: I was a stranger, and ye took me in: Naked, and ye clothed me: I was sick, and ye visited me: I was in prison, and ye came unto me. Then shall the righteous answer him, saying, Lord, when saw we thee an hungred, and fed thee? or thirsty, and gave thee drink? When saw we thee a stranger, and took thee in? or naked, and clothed thee? Or when saw we thee sick, or in prison, and came unto thee? And the King shall answer and say unto them, Verily I say unto you, Inasmuch as ye have done it unto one of the least of these my brethren, ye have done it unto me."

Deacon Watts stood with his mouth turned down and his jowls hanging low. His nostrils flared when he spoke. "Thank you, Mr. Graham. Frankly, I fail to see the relevance of your recitation, other than your need to impress us with your sharp memorization skills. Now, please take a seat or excuse yourself, while the members of this church attend to urgent business that is no concern of yours."

"Begging your pardon, sir, but this very much concerns me. And as far as the relevance of the scripture I quoted, I fail to understand how you could've missed it. I came here tonight to get a story. And I got one. As I listened to one by one stand and tell how the pastor of this church had met their needs, I was reminded of the passage my grandmother encouraged me to learn when I was ten years old." His face lit up with a smile. "She gave me a whole dollar for memorizing it." He pressed his trembling lips together.

"I never knew my father—and my mother dumped me off at my granny's when I was only five years old." His Adam's apple bobbed. "Oh, how I loved that woman. But she died on my twelfth birthday, and I was sent to live with an aunt who resented me for interrupting her life. I became bitter at God for taking my Granny and I've been working diligently for the past twelve years to discredit His name. But something happened to me as I sat on that back pew this morning. I can't help but believe my Granny's prayers got through to God, after all."

He choked up. "I'm so sorry, Miss Veezie Harrington for the horrid things I said. May you, Brother Jackson, this church and God forgive me."

Curtis Dobbs stood. "Buster, can we go home now? Cora's got a roast in the oven."

Buster smirked. "Well, this is far from being finished. We've yet to take a vote. I urge you not to let the tear-jerking speech of a man who makes his living making up stories, influence your decision, people."

Veezie's knuckles were white from holding on to the pew in front of her, but she had to turn loose. She stood, turned around and faced the congregation. The room became so still, one could've heard the flutter of a butterfly's wings. "May I have permission to speak?"

Garth held up a flat palm. "No. You don't owe them an explanation."

Buster's eyes widened. His voice boomed. "Well, I'll be . . .

so that's it. The writing was on the wall, and I was too blind to see it. There's only one way this editor would've known about this harlot's past. No wonder he wrote such an angry article, wanting us to know about the sins of our pastor. Ah, he's fallen prey to one of the seven deadly sins listed in the Bible. Jealousy! But seems now he's had a change of heart." With a sarcastic chuckle, he said, "Makes a body wonder what's in it for him."

Buster left the podium and paced back and forth in front of the congregation. "Don't you people see? She's standing there with the father of her illegitimate child. I wondered what brought him to Flat Creek. Now, we know. He followed her here, then became furious when he discovered a preacher was moving in on his girl." His upper lip curled. "Seems the lovers have made up."

Veezie screamed out, "No, it isn't true." She gazed into Garth's eyes. "Tell them."

He shrugged. "You honestly think they'll believe anything we have to say?" When she made a move to step into the aisle, Garth reached out and took her by the arm. "Don't give Mr. Watts the satisfaction."

Gracie said, "Let her go, Garth. She deserves a chance to redeem herself."

He turned loose, but not before whispering. "You're already redeemed. You don't have to do this."

Ignoring his plea, Veezie faced the crowd and took the time to look each individual in the eyes. Clearing her throat, she said, "I've sat back and listened to all that's been said, but it's time for me to speak the truth."

The deacon yelled. "We aren't interested in anything you have to say, woman. You should be run out of town on a rail. Sit down, you Jezebel."

Gracie jumped up and put her hands over her ears. Sobbing, she screamed, "Stop it. Please, stop it."

Garth motioned to Gracie with a head jerk. "Let's get out of here."

Gracie nodded and they left the sanctuary.

Marcy Woodham stood. "Mr. Watts, you don't speak for me. I for one would like to hear what Veezie has to say. But first, I wonder if I could ask a couple of the teenagers if they'd mind escorting the children outside and playing games with them until this business meeting is over. There's already been more said than any child should've been subjected to."

Two girls, apparently eager for an excuse to leave, quickly volunteered, and all the children followed. A teenager came and took the baby from Marcy's arms and the twins followed the others out the door.

Adolphus pulled on Marcy's skirt and whispered. "Sit down, darling. Don't cross Buster."

She gazed down at her husband and smiled. "Sorry, Adolphus." She walked over and put her arm around Veezie. "I'll stand with you, my sweet friend. But let's you and I go up to the platform."

Sweet friend? "Oh, Marcy, no—" Her voice broke .

Chapter Thirty-Nine

Veezie's knees wobbled when Marcy took her by the hand and led her up the steps.

Adolphus Woodham jumped up and ran out. When he slammed the double doors at the back of the church, the windows rattled.

Deacon Watts stomped off the platform on the left side, as the women approached the steps to the right of the podium. He threw his hands in the air and in a raised voice, said, "Though I fail to understand why Mr. Graham needed to interfere when this is the first time he's ever set foot in this church, he was right about one thing. This has turned into a circus—a three-ring circus." He plopped down on the front pew, shaking his head.

Marcy gripped Veezie's hand. "You have the floor. Whatever God would have you to say, speak it with boldness."

Veezie hung her head, unable to face her accusers. "Folks, what Mr. Watts said about me and Mr. Graham ain't true, because today is the first time I ever laid eyes on him. But all that stuff he wrote about me in the newspaper—well, it *is* true." She paused and waited for the whispers to die down. "If I understand what a harlot is, I reckon I am one." She could hear the gasps. "I did hang out at juke joints, like he wrote about."

Her knees locked when the double doors opened and Shep walked in, followed by Adolphus, who held a brown burlap bag in his hands. People turned and whispered. Shep's steps were long and deliberate as he made his way toward the front of the auditorium, glancing neither to his left or his right. He strode down the aisle with his broad shoulders held back, his square jaw set.

As the congregation murmured, Adolphus started from the back pew and passed the burlap bag, quietly urging each person to reach inside and pull out a piece of gravel. No one seemed to understand, yet with their eyes riveted on their pastor, one by one they reached in, pulled out a small rock, glanced at their neighbor, and shrugged before refocusing their attention to the front.

Shep stepped up to the podium. Veezie's gaze locked with his. She couldn't speak. Wouldn't have, even if she could. The muscles in her right eye twitched. Could she go through with the plan? Then she remembered brave Hester. She couldn't back down. *No more running.*

Shep nudged Marcy and edged up between the two women. He leaned over and whispered in Veezie's ear. "Don't let these people intimidate you. Remember, 'If God be for us, who can be against us?'"

She bit her lip to control the trembling. With a lump the size of a goose egg in her throat, she turned her back to the congregation, pulled something from her pocket and hung it around her neck.

When she whirled back around, people gasped, seeing a giant red "S", fashioned from felt, hanging around her neck. Searching each face in the congregation with her eyes, she patted the large letter and proclaimed in a clear, strong voice, "In case some of you don't know what this stands for, it stands for sinner."

Cora Watts shrieked. "Get her out of here. The woman has no shame."

But Buster made no effort to move. His broad grin indicated he enjoyed the surprise confession.

Veezie took the time to look into a bevy of widened eyes on startled faces. "And . . . and although Mr. Graham didn't have the facts to prove his story, his guess was right. I did give birth to a baby girl and I've never been married. So I'm standing here to confess to you that I'm a sinner. And although God's forgot about it, I don't expect you folks to ever forget. I won't hold that against you, since I can't forget it either. I reckon it's asking too much to ask you to forgive me. But it's not asking too much to plead with you to forgive Shep for falling in love with me. He didn't know about my past."

She paused at the touch of Shep's hand on her upper arm. Then, looking into the eyes of her accusers, she straightened her spine and held her head high. "I didn't want him to know, because he's the first man who's ever looked at me like I was a lady. I reckon that's one reason I fell in love with him from the start. I prayed he wouldn't learn the truth about me, because I wanted him to love me as much as I love him. I couldn't bear to see in his eyes, what I saw in the eyes of the men at the Silver Slipper."

Shep's hand gently squeezed her elbow.

"So I beg of you . . . do with me what you will, but don't punish an innocent man for my mistakes. Your pastor has never been anything but a gentleman in my presence."

"She wouldn't know a gentleman from a plow horse," Buster yelled from his pew. His wife, Cora stood, and shouted, "Well, I Suwannee, if these two infidels don't deserve one another."

Lud Snodgrass, the milkman, jumped up. "I know some of you are confused by all of this, but don't let this woman's babbling or your fondness for Shep Jackson cloud your thinking. People, I saw what I saw. This is not a popularity contest, so regardless of how much you like Shepherd Jackson, ask yourself—Is this the kind of man I want standing before me in the pulpit? My answer is 'no'."

Harlon Griffin shouted from his pew. "Lud's right. She's done admitted to having a young'un, and she's a member of this church. I didn't want to believe Cora and Eunice when they told us our preacher was a womanizer, so I voted at the last meeting for him to stay. I was wrong. I say we vote to kick him and his woman out."

All over the church, people with anger-filled eyes stood and chanted, "Time to vote, time to vote."

Adolphus, a soft-spoken man of few words, yelled, "Wait. You're making a big mistake."

Buster ran his hands through his hair. "Oh, my lands, what next? What are you up to, Adolphus? You've never said two words in church. Why now, for crying out loud?"

Adolphus stomped to the front, facing Buster. "Did you pull gravel from the bag, Buster?"

Brows furrowed. Buster held his fist in the air and smirked. "Yeah, but whatever you've got in mind can wait. I for one, am ready to vote and get home."

"Then let's do it, Buster." Adolphus ran up the steps and stood on the platform in front of Shep, Veezie and Marcy. He reared his shoulders back and planted his fists firmly on his hips. "Get ready to cast your vote. All of you, hold your stone high in the air."

With confusion etched on every face, the members looked at one another. Slowly, all around the sanctuary, clinched fists were raised.

"Thank you. I urge each one of you to cast your vote with the piece of gravel you hold in your hand. Who among you is without sin? Let him cast the first stone."

A few people seemed to think it was a joke and snickered. Lud snarled. "Are you serious?"

"Very serious. Throw it, Lud, and hurl it at me, because I'm chiefest among the sinners. I've carried guilt in my heart for something I did years ago. God's forgiven me, but if you can't find it in your heart to forgive, then hurl your stones, people."

Hands went back down.

He shouted, "Well? What are you waiting for? Don't sit there holding a grudge in your heart and the stone in your hand. Get rid of both at the same time. Throw it! You know you want to."

Veezie, spotting anger burning on selected faces, stepped in front of Adolphus. "No, Adolphus. No. It's me, they want. If not for me, none of us would be standing here." She squeezed her eyes shut and stiffened, expecting the first rock to be tossed from close range, straight from Buster's hands.

Shep quickly shielded her with his body. "Not her. Hit me. Go ahead. Throw your stones and cast your vote. You've judged us already."

Buster grumbled. "Can we cut out the dramatics? I say we—"

It was then Veezie heard a familiar voice. She opened her eyes to see Brother Charlie, her former pastor. She supposed he had plenty of time after preaching at Goose Hollow to get to Flat Creek, since it was now nearing two-o'clock in the afternoon.

The old man stood in the aisle, leaning on his cane. "Adolphus has the right idea. If you've lived a sinless life, then you have the right to judge all those standing before you. Hurl your stones at the rotten sinners and cross their names off your rolls." He paused until the noise died back down. "However, if you've ever sinned against a Holy God and have had to seek forgiveness, then cast your vote of forgiveness by tossing your stone into the collection plates sitting on the table at the front."

Curtis Dobbs led the way, with his wife Eunice close behind. Then Arnie followed and soon, one by one the people left their seats and soon both collection plates were running over with gravel and people quietly filed out of the church.

Buster pocketed his stone and left the building.

Shep recalled the ire he felt the day Brother Charlie visited him after the accident. The old man's words were not appreciated at the time, but looking back, it was the turning point that put him back on track. *Shep, your sin is not that you fell in love with a young woman who has a past. We all have a past, or there would've been no need for the cross. Your sin, as I see it, is in not standing up for the one you love when the world wants to tear her down. That's pride, my son.* Pride goeth before a fall, and Shepherd Jackson wasn't ready to go down.

So maybe Veezie wasn't the lily-white maiden he'd assumed her to be. But as many sermons as he'd preached on the grace of God, it was the message delivered by Adolphus that spoke to his heart. *Who is without sin?* He was wrong to hold in remembrance a sin that had already been cleansed by the blood of Jesus.

Chapter Forty

Shep pulled a small knife from his pocket, reached over and snipped the string around Veezie's neck. The red felt letter fell to the floor.

"There, that's better," he said. "You were wearing the wrong letter. God has drawn the letter *F* in blood and branded it on your heart. It can't be cut off, washed off or wished off. It's permanent."

Her lip trembled. "I think I understand." She hung her head. "F for Fornicator?"

Shep's brow furrowed. "No! Forgiven!"

Adolphus choked back the tears as he drew his wife close. "Marcy, I love you so much."

She smiled. "I know."

"I've sinned against God and against you."

"I know."

His face turned red and he looked at Shep.

Shep shook his head. "Adolphus, Marcy understands that you're asking her forgiveness. Why open old wounds and risk making new ones? I'm not sure you should—"

Adolphus appeared bewildered, as if he had to get the heavy weight from off his back.

Marcy cupped her hands around her husband's wet cheeks. "Honey, there's no need to confess anything. Didn't you hear what I said? I know. I've known for nineteen months."

Low sobs came out in short spurts. "No. No, Marcy." His lip trembled. "Baby, you can't possibly know. But why . . . why would you say nineteen months?"

"Because that's how long you've been forgiven. I forgave both you and Veezie, even before I ever met her."

"But how?" He looked at Shep.

Shep shook his head.

She threw her arms around her husband's neck. "Dear, does it matter how I found out?"

He reached in his pocket and pulled out a piece of gravel and placed it in her hand. "Here, you have every right."

"Adolphus, sweetheart, I don't need a stone. God's forgiven you and so have I. Isn't that enough?"

"Oh, Marcy, it's more than I deserve."

Veezie covered her mouth with her hand. "Oh, Marcy, it wasn't his—"

Shep stopped her. "Veezie, what's that hanging around your neck?"

She glanced down. With a brow raised, she answered. "Forgiveness?"

"Exactly. If God chooses to forget, why shouldn't we?"

Marcy smiled. "Forget what? I can't remember what we were talking about. I guess it's time to go home. The church is empty."

The back door to the church flung open and Gracie and Garth walked in together, holding hands.

Shep's jaw jutted forward. "What's the meaning of this?"

Garth, shifted on his feet and appeared nervous. "Brother Jackson, first I'd like to beg your forgiveness for the stupid articles. I now see the error of my ways and I wouldn't blame you if you hate me for being such a nincompoop." He bit his lip. "But I hope you'll find it in your heart to forgive me, because there's something I need to ask you." Garth rocked back and forth on his heels while ringing his hands.

"Well? Get on with it, young man."

He licked his lips and nodded. "Sir, I know there's six years difference in mine and Gracie's ages, but I wondered . . . well, I'd like to ask you if . . . uh, sir, I know you have every right to want to run me out of Flat Creek, but I'd like to say I was wrong. Dead wrong." He wiped the sweat from his brow. "Sir would you have objections to me courting your daughter? I think . . . well, I know it's sudden and you may not understand what I'm about to say, but we think we may be in love."

Gracie looked into Shep's eyes and pleaded. "Please, Daddy? We've had a long talk and he's wonderful. You'll like him when you get to know him. I know you will. He's apologized for the nasty articles. He wrote out of his pain, but the bitterness he's held since losing his grandmother is gone. He's truly sorry. Honest, he is."

Shep saw a sparkle in his daughter's eyes that he remembered seeing in her mother's. He'd tried to keep his little girl from growing up, but the Gracie standing before him was no longer a child in pigtails. She was a woman. A beautiful, intelligent woman and it seemed to happen in spite of his trying to hold on to her.

"Well, Daddy?"

Shep's eyes squinted into little slits. "Young man, let me ask you a question."

"Sure, sir."

"I'm appalled that you'd bring up the age issue. What does age have to do with love?"

Garth grimaced. Then noting the broad smile on the preacher's face, he let out a sigh and chuckled. "Nothing sir. Nothing at all."

"I didn't think so. Then why are you two still standing here? Gracie needs to get home to put dinner on the table, and I expect you to be in the kitchen helping her by the time I arrive."

"Yes sir. We're on our way, sir."

Gracie hugged her father. "Thank you, Daddy."

"Sweetheart, I'll make a deal with you."

"A deal?"

"I'll give you permission to date this young man, if you'll give me permission to ask Veezie to marry me."

"You mean you haven't asked her already?"

"No, but time's wasting." He fell on his knees and took Veezie's hand between his own. "Veezie Harrington—"

Her lip quivered. "O'Steen. My name is Veezie O'Steen."

A smile stretched across his face. "Your last name doesn't matter, for I'm hoping you'll allow me to change it to Jackson. Veezie, my beautiful angel, will you become my wife and promise to love and cherish me 'til death do us part?"

Veezie sighed. "Land sakes. Me, a preacher's wife! Now, don't that beat all?"

Epilogue

Dear Gracie,

Shep and I rode down to Panama City yesterday to celebrate our third anniversary. My, how the time has flown. (Perhaps I should say, 'has flew by,' to make your father happy.) He teases and says he longs to hear me say 'ain't and tweren't,' the way I did when he first fell in love with me. He facetiously claims that I turned into a proper lady without his approval. He's such a funny man. He declares it was my unpretentious ways that first drew him to me. Sometimes I pour on the vernacular, just to see him smile.

We're staying at the Panama City Hotel and you should see this place. We had supper in a swanky seafood restaurant tonight. It was my first time to eat oyster stew, but it won't be my last. We took a moonlight stroll along the beach last night and you should've seen all the people gathered in and around a little white building, they call The Hangout. As far as I can determine, it was a good name for it. Though some were dancing to music from a jukebox, it looked as if most were just hanging out.

I suppose Garth wrote you about the prestigious award he recently received. The Ledger was voted best paper in the south. I was real proud for him. (I had to look up "prestigious" in the dictionary to make sure I knew how to spell it, but I got it right my first try.)You remember Mrs. Rachel Crawford from church, don't you? Well, she lets me sit in on her English class at the State Teacher's College. She's been a great help.

I know it seems early to start thinking about Christmas, but Marcy Woodham is writing the script for the Children's Christmas Pageant this year and she's asked me to play the piano. I've been practicing every day.

Gracie, Shep and I explained to Harper that we plan to move back into the church Pastorium the first of next month. I can't bear to stay at Nine Gables, now that Beulah is gone. I miss her so much. I'm sorry you weren't able to come home for the funeral. We gave her a big send-off with a chariot and six big fine white horses, just like she requested.

George has gone to live with his brother in Michigan.

Shep was glad when I suggested we move. He's never been comfortable at Nine Gables. Says all the rooms make him feel like he's living in a museum and not in a home. The church has been steadily growing. We now average two-hundred in Sunday School.

I thought Harper and Flint might decide to move into Nine Gables, once we moved out, but they don't want to live there, either. Harper has too many sad memories linked to Nine Gables and Flint feels he needs to remain in Goose Hollow, to be near his patients. Funny, how I used to think all it took to make a lady was a fine house to live in and lots of money to toss around. Now, I know better.

Gracie, Harper came up with an idea for your graduation

present that I think you'll like. She knows of your dream to operate an orphanage. She wants to offer Nine Gables as a place to house the children. The deed will remain in her name, but she wants you to treat it as your own. I hope the idea excites you as much as it does me and your father. We like the idea of having you close by.

Well, sweet Gracie, I've saved the best news for last. You are about to become a big sister. Isn't that swell? We've agreed if it's a boy, Shep will name him, but if it's a girl, I'll name her. Shep has picked the name Jonathan Obed. I like it. Has a dignified ring to it, don't you think?

If it's a girl, I want to name her Jennifer Emerald and call her Jenny, after your mother. I know she was a real lady and I feel my daughter would be honored to have her name.

Last Wednesday, Shep and I carried a bouquet of gardenias and placed on little Diamond's grave. I look forward to the day when we'll meet face-to-face. What a glorious day that will be.

Well, goodbye, ducky. Your dad and I plan to take a boat ride to Shell Island in the morning. Another first for me, and I'm excited. What a wonderful life is mine, filled with nothing but great big, beautiful tomorrows—and as Beulah would say, "There ain't gonna be no more yesterdays."

Sending all our love,

Veezie and Daddy

ABOUT THE AUTHOR

Kay Chandler is a multi-award-winning author of Southern Fiction with a speaking ministry called LIFE ROCKS. An enthusiastic motivator, she shares personal experiences, seasoned with humor, to illustrate that life rocks when God's in the center. If you'd like to have Kay visit your church, civic group, or book club, she can be reached by email at kay@liferocksministry.com. Her Facebook account is Kay McCall Chandler. Kay and her husband, Bill, have retired and moved back to their little hometown in lower Alabama.

If you've enjoyed UNWED, a favorable review is always appreciated.